Sarah's Life of Lady Lovers

by Monty Mawes

Sarah's Life of Lady Lovers

Monty Mawes

Table of Contents

Table of Contents

Introduction

Sitting nervously in the back of her father's top-of-the-range BMW. She was apprehensive about her future, scared, and sat on her own because her parents were way too busy to accompany her, Sarah B Briany is nearing her destination which is. The Regal School for Young Ladies. The school is situated in Sutton in Surrey and is for the education of young ladies from the age of sixteen to eighteen. The Regal is a private finishing school for parents that seem to think that their little darlings need to learn that little bit extra about life, that little bit extra that our parents maybe didn't tell us but should have.

Sarah is a beautiful blonde sixteen-year-old with the gangly body of a young lady leaving adolescence, but it's her eyes, they are the light brown of freshly ground coffee and if she was honest she was glad to get away from the young lads at her last school as she was teased dreadfully about her small breasts and thin body, deep down she hoped that she wouldn't be treated in the same way at the Regal.

The car turns into the gravel driveway, slowly winding its way between two rows of Alder trees, through the branches she can see the red brick of the old building, which will be her home for the next two years. Now that she is near the Regal she can feel her pulse begin to race. Her driver Leigh drops Sarah off with her cases, he passes her a brown envelope and without a word, leaves her to it. She stands there and looks at the ancient-looking, red-brick building which is situated in a large country estate. All around her other young ladies are arriving, some in limousines smiling, others alone and by taxi.

In the upper windows of the school, ghost-like faces of older students stare down at them, knowing what lay ahead, a teenager appears beside her and took her hand. She turns and the girl is smiling "My name is Ria, shall we go in together?" Sarah smiles "yes, I would like that" the pair almost skip into the school, following directions they end up in a large hall filled with large antique tables, chairs and on long tables at the side of the huge room stood cups, saucers and plates laden with biscuits and fairy cakes.

Mr Dawson the headmaster stood on the stage then clapped his hands together to get everyone's attention and smiled broadly as he welcomed the young ladies to the Regal, he suggested that they made friends as this would help them in not only their initial settling down period but also in future life. All the young ladies were informed that a registry would begin in one hour in the main library. Once they are registered each lady would then go to the conference room and be seated, and when her name is read out, she was to stand and acknowledge all the other ladies. Finally, they were informed that some of the rooms are two bed and other rooms four bed, if you have formed a friendship and think you would like to share a two-bedroom, there are a limited number of the said rooms, the list is by the registry table, I suggest that you register your names at once.

Ria, a girl about the same height and build as Sarah, just as pretty with eyes that are a sparkling light blue, and to die for, tugs excitedly at the hand that she is still holding, and says, "please share with me Sarah, we will get on so well, please" Sarah smiled broadly "oh yes, we must share, let's put our names down quickly", they wrote their names down and hugged each other "we will be such good friends Sarah, I just know it "said Ria, smiling warmly at her new friend.

With the registering of names completed and their room number allocated, the new friends excitedly head for their new dorm, they enter the room, stand hand in hand, and survey the 18-century oak-paneled room, there are two beds, two desks with plenty of electrical sockets on the walls. The en-suite is in a light blue and just perfect, with beds chosen, they help each other with their luggage, and stow their belongings in the spaces provided. Together they sit and chat excitedly, getting to know each other, finding out their likes and dislikes and they both agree that they do not like boys. Sarah opened the envelope that Leigh had given her, to discover it was full of money.

Sitting down for the first meal together at the Regal, they get to sample the authority of the headmaster, with a room full of chattering young ladies, he stands and claps his hands, the room is instantly quiet. Mr Dawson begins talking, "Ladies, I want you to enjoy your meal today and you will be allowed to chatter amongst yourselves, as you are all new ladies this will be allowed today only. As from breakfast tomorrow the dining room will hold all of our ladies, and teaching staff, and we will expect any conversation to be kept to a minimum. Good manners will be observed at all times.

Now as you see we have some final year ladies standing at the rear of the room, each of our older ladies will take four of you new ladies on a tour of the Regal, you will then be informed of the rules and the way that you will be expected to behave at all times. The ladies that are your guides will also act as your mentors and will be there to help you at all times. Finally welcome to the Regal ladies, I hope that you enjoy your time with us, and don't forget my door is always open".

With the tour completed and heads full of do's and don'ts the pair settle down for their first night sharing a room together, they are sat on Ria's bed holding hands trying to work out some rules for the room, with that done they then move onto talking about their family lives and they were not surprised to find that there is not much difference in their home lives, they always seem to be in the way, their parents were always busy and even the smallest thing seemed to be too much trouble.

Chapter 1

Life at the regal began with a shock at six am the next morning, when a loud bell sounded, telling them that it was time for them to get out of bed and start the day, having both showered and dressed in new uniforms, they stand, look at each other, both then slowly turn in a complete circle to be inspected by the other, assured that all was well, life at the Regal was about to begin.

The pair were inseparable all through their first year at the Regal, and because of their ever-deepening friendship, both of them blossomed in body as well as in learning, their grades were first class, with both ladies achieving A stars in every subject taken.

Shopping on Saturdays down in Sutton high road was always a treat, one they looked forward to, lunch at Mc Donald's was a special treat that they enjoyed immensely, as the sixteen-year-olds-year-olds were always arm in arm, some of the local lads teased them and called them lessies and lezbo's things like that, but they just giggled and ran off.

Chapter 2

Things changed slightly one Sunday evening in the month of June of their second year, they had had a particularly brilliant weekend together, shopping as usual on Saturday, they had played hockey on Sunday representing the Regal and won, [with Ria scoring the winning goal], with their homework done Sarah stood ironing their uniforms, while Ria lay on her bed watching. Sarah was slightly shocked when Ria suddenly stood up and pulled Sarah into her arms and hugged her, they stood looking at one another when Ria kissed her friend on the cheek and said "I love you Sarah" then went and lay back on her bed. Sarah was confused as any young lady in this situation would be, Sarah's mind told her one thing but her body was telling her another, Sarah had just had her first confused sexual stirrings, and she wasn't sure what to make of them.

Nothing was ever said about the event, and it was never repeated [to say never would be telling a lie] as they continued to score straight A's and as their bodies began to change, their friendship deepened even further, and Sarah began to become confused by some of Ria's actions, she would walk around almost naked at times, and she would intentionally lean over Sarah's shoulder, just to look at what she was reading, making sure that she rubbed her firm naked breasts against her, all sorts of things like that, but what confused Sarah the most was the fact that she was beginning to enjoy it, she began to get feelings between her legs that she could not explain, for a late developer at almost seventeen years old, "surely I should be thinking of boys and not Ria in that way".

They as best friends were on their Christmas break with their parents but they still spoke every day on skype, on Christmas eve, as deepening friends they had been talking all night about their family's plans for the big day, and what they each hoped to receive gift wise, things that they had been doing that day, any and all such rubbish as best friends do, it was as they were saying goodnight, just before Ria went off line again she said "I love you Sarah" and kissed the skype camera, and then she was gone. Sarah just sat and looked at the blank screen, she was even more confused now, because in her own strange way, she thought that she loved Ria.

Christmas day was a blur for Sarah as her mind was all over the place, the Christmas dinner, the gifts and time with her grandparents, all this passed her by with her thoughts towards Ria, Sarah decided that she wouldn't log on, this would be the first day in over two years that she would not speak to her best friend. Sarah needed time to think, her phone buzzed in her pocket but she ignored it, knowing very well who it was. Three more times her phone buzzed before it rang, Sarah excused herself and went to her room and answered her phone, "hello?" "Please log on Sarah, I need to talk to you, PLEASE" begged Ria, Sarah promised that she would and she did.

They just sat and looked at each other for a while, it was Ria that spoke first " I'm sorry Sarah,

I shouldn't have said what I did, but I have feelings for you that are beyond friendship, I can't help it, I realised a while ago that I loved you more than a friend should, but I don't know what other way to let you know, I mean, Christ Sarah, I have dropped enough hints over the last year, I even thought about walking around naked to see if that would do anything, crawling into your bed in the middle of the night, all of these thoughts have gone through my mind, there I've said it now, so if you want to change rooms, then I will understand and I won't hold it against you" they sat and looked at each other, it was Ria that looked away first and logged off.

Sarah sat there looking at the blank screen for over an hour, she just didn't know what to do about the situation, should she simply give in to her feelings, or should she fight them and change rooms, but the problem with that is if she did ask to change rooms, then how would she explain the reason why, without causing Ria problems, a tear ran down her cheek and dropped from her chin, in the next instance she was sobbing her heart out, why does life have to be so difficult.

Chapter 3

Sarah and Ria as roommates didn't speak for three days and with only two days until they had to return to the Regal, Sarah sent a message to Ria asking her to log on, within seconds Ria was online, and Sarah looked at her best friend with her head bowed, she could see that Ria was crying and this broke her heart " please don't cry Ria, surely we can sit and talk when we get back to the Regal, please" Ria lifted her head slowly and looked at Sarah, with tears streaming down her face, in a husky voice, she whispered, " do you hate me ?" Sarah smiled into the camera and said "How could I hate you Ria, you know that I love you but in the same way as you say that you love me, that I don't know" Ria smiled "does that mean that we are still roommates, still friends?" "I could not be enemies with you Ria, we will be friends forever" the girls agreed happily to see each other back at the Regal the following Sunday.

Ria sat on her bed wringing her hands in her lap, when Sarah walked into their room, looking up Ria gave a nervous smile, to which Sarah pulled her to her and hugged her, Ria whispered "I'm sorry Sarah for putting you in such a position, it's just me being silly, please ignore me" Sarah held her best friend's face in her hands and said, "let's carry on as we are and see how we get on, shall we?" Ria nodded her head and hugged Sarah again, kissing her neck as she released her. For the first time in a year, Ria went into the bathroom to get changed for bed, normally she would undress in full view of Sarah, her roommate had been flaunting her body as she now realised, but the strange thing was that Sarah missed seeing Ria undress, missed seeing her firm breasts, erect nipples and lithe young body.

Sarah sat on her bed looking at her best friend who was lying in bed facing away from her, she could see that Ria was almost shaking, Sarah bit her bottom lip, and made her decision, she was very damp between her legs and her heart was beating fast as she removed her clothes, all the way down to her damp pants, she then slid into bed behind Ria and gently wrapped herself around her best friends trembling body, Sarah placed her arm around her best friends waist and Ria folds her fingers in hers, they were trembling as they hold each other, both of them unsure what to do next, Sarah freed her hand from Ria's and placed it onto her breast, with this Ria turned her head and they kiss for the very first time, as they kiss, Sarah moved her hand from her lover's breast that she was fondling through her thin nightdress and slid her hand under Ria's nightdress, her hand trembles as she neared her best friends naked breast, that first touch made Ria gasp out loud.

Ria pulled herself away from Sarah and sat up, she then removed her nightdress, and when she lay back down she faced her soon-to-be first lover, they nervously eased into a first full-on kiss as their naked breasts squeezed against each other, it was Sarah that pushed her tongue against the lips of her lover, which was received with a deep moan, both sets of hands rubbed up and down each other's backs occasionally straying to the top of each other's damp pants. Again it was down to Sarah who pushed her hand down inside her lovers wet pants, squeezing her bum cheek, digging her fingernails into the firm flesh making her lover moan even more, Ria returned the favour and within seconds both of them were pushing their mounds at one another, not really sure why, but it felt like the right thing to be doing, Sarah reached under Ria's bottom and just far enough to get the tip of her finger inside Ria's virgin sex, but that was more than enough to take Ria over the edge to her first ever orgasm, she gave a silent scream and clung onto her, trembling, moaning and thrusting her mound at Sarah.

Once again it was Sarah that took control, she slid out of the bed and removed Ria's pants and then her own, leaning over the goose-bumped naked body Sarah began to rub her nervous hands all over the firm virgin flesh, Ria lay there squirming with her eyes closed, her hips slowly rising and falling, Sarah lowered her mouth to the right breast and sucking the hard nipple deep into her mouth, slowly rolling the nipple between her teeth, Ria lifted her hand and rubbed her fingers through Sarah's hair, applying just enough pressure to the back of her head to pull her harder against her firm breast. Sarah slid her hand down the firm young body to her thick pubic hair, after rubbing her finger through the thick curls, Ria automatically opened her legs.

Sarah eased her finger down to the swollen sex lips of her lover, Ria opens her legs even wider and raised her hips up high in anticipation, she held her breath as Sarah's finger's searched for her lover's opening when her trembling finger slipped inside Ria's hot sex, Ria let out a long held breath, Sarah worked the finger in and out of the hot wet slit for a few seconds before adding a second finger, with a bit of practice she soon discovered what her lover liked the best and Sarah was soon rewarded when her fingers were soaked with Ria's virgin cum, Ria was thrusting her hips up and down, she has her eyes closed and was lost as her second orgasm made its erotic journey through her virgin body. The young woman had to place her hand over her own mouth to stifle an escaping scream, as her dream had just come true.

Seeing how much pleasure she has given Ria, Sarah kept her fingers moving in and out of her best friend's sex, only now she had turned her hand, the fingers reached deeper and moved faster, which brought yet another body-shaking climax; when Ria calmed down, she reached down she eased her lover's wet fingers from her fanny, Sarah held them up and looked at them, covered in thick pale cum. Sarah smiled at her achievement; but was unsure as to what to do with the sticky fingers, so she climbed down from the bed, found a tissue and wiped them clean

Whilst she is stood wiping her fingers Ria stepped up behind her and places her hands on Sarah's breasts, first fondling them, then rolling the nipples between her fingers and thumbs, all the time rubbing her mound into Sarah's bottom, Sarah closed her eyes and pushed back at her new lover, both of them were moaning now as they moved their bodies together, both getting more and more adventurous, Sara more so in anticipation of pleasures to come. Ria ran her shaking hand down the firm body to the small patch of smooth pubic hair, she ran the tip of her middle finger over her lover's clit and along the swollen fanny lips, pressing harder each time until her finger slipped between the crinkly lips.

Sarah heard herself moaning because she has tingling between her legs like never before, her leg seemed to part on their own as Ria explored deeper, and the movement of her finger was getting more and more urgent; because she wanted desperately to please, Sarah leaned back against Ria, reached up and placed her hands behind her lover's head, she closed her eyes, abandoning herself totally to the other woman, her young nipples straining more than ever before. When Ria entered a second finger into her lover's fanny, Sarah felt her legs begin to go weak as her first proper orgasm shook her to the core, the feeling was like no other feeling that she had ever experienced before.

Sarah began to slowly calm down, she turned to face her first lover, the lovers kissed deeply, urgently, their tongues doing the dance of love.

Caressing each other's bodies, they could feel each-others hard nipples pressing into their own breasts, mounds moving against one another, it was as if a silent signal passed between them, because they turned slightly sideways, thus allowing the other access to their most intimate place. As they insert fingers into each other, their actions become more urgent as they sink to their knees in joint earth-shattering orgasm. As new lovers glow in their first sexual experience, they hold each other, gently running finger tips all over the other's body, sending shivers through every nerve ending in their lover's bodies.

They wake in their own beds and just lie there and stare at each other, love and wanting in their eyes, eventually Ria reached out and wiggled her fingers at Sarah, as Sarah reached out and they could just about touch, with touching finger tips, Sarah stretched just a little bit further and they lock fingers, Sarah tried to pull Ria to her, she resists at first but when Sarah pulls the bed clothes back to reveal her still naked body, all resistances leaves Ria, she climbs from her bed and slipped in beside her young lover, as it was a school morning their lovemaking was very urgent; very passionate, both sated for the moment they share a shower and prepare for the day ahead.

Chapter 4

It was mid-morning on Saturday and Ria had been in the bathroom for an age, when she appeared she has a wicked grin on her face, Sarah watched her and asked "What?", Ria continued to smile," you will have to wait until later won't you, I have another surprise for you but we will have to wait until after the evening meal" They went back to their room at lunch time but despite all of Sarah's pleading, Ria still refused to tell her anything.

Now changed into normal clothes at the end of the school day, Sarah was desperate to find out what Ria was hiding from her. Ria picked up her computer and placed it on her lap, she logged on and tapped the bed by her side, signaling for Sarah to sit by her, she looks at Sarah " do you remember at Christmas when we sort of fell out [Sarah nodded eagerly] well I began to doubt myself sexually and so I began to do a bit of research, on the net, [she pressed a few buttons] and this is what I found, but first promise me that you will watch it all before you pass comment" Sarah nodded again and urged "hurry up then", Ria pressed a button and strange tinny sounding music began playing,, two girls of a similar age to themselves appeared on the screen, one sat on a bed and one lay across the bed reading a magazine, and began to kick her legs.

Her already short skirt becomes much shorter, until her firm bum cheeks come into view, the girl sat on the bed looked down at her friend's bottom and licked her lips seductively, she reached out and strokes the exposed flesh and runs a fingertip along the red pants, following the line of her hidden slit, the girls have a conversation in some foreign language, the girl that is laid down turned over which allowed the other girl to rub her right hand between her legs, with her left hand she lifted up to the other girl's breast, the girl responds by pulling her top up and exposed her breasts.

The girl fondles the breasts of her friend and eased her other hand inside the other girls pants, on the screen you can see the fingers of her hand moving up and down her slit, laying down she parts her thin legs and begins to squirm, the other girl stands and removes her friends pants. Very seductively indeed, she then removes the rest of her clothing leaving her naked on the bed. The first thing you notice is that her sex is naked, shaven clean.

The girl that was sitting on the bed kneels down and parts the other girl legs with her hands, she then places her mouth to her sex and using her mouth and tongue slowly brings the other girl to orgasm, [Ria glances at her lover to see excitement in her eyes]. She then stands and removes her own clothes. When the camera returns back to her friend, strapped to her waist is a long black rubber cock some six inches long, the other girl bends over the bed with her legs splayed, only to be mounted by her cock wielding friend, [Sarah and Ria sit with open mouths as they watch proceedings, the women on the screen change positions time and time again, when the receiver finally reaches her climax, the girl wearing the cock encourages her friend to suck that black cock, once the girl has the rubber cock in her mouth, the cock wielding girl starts to fuck the other girl's mouth.

Ria closed the lid of the computer and looked at Sarah who sits with a broad smile on her face, she placed her hands on her hips, "We have got to get one of those, and soon" Ria holds Sarah's hands and said "What did you think of the rest of it?" Sarah looked closely at her lover "would you do it, I mean, like with your mouth?" she asked, Ria nodded her head and said "yes, definitely " Ria jumped down from the bed, standing in front of her friend she undid her jogging bottoms and pushed them down to the floor, she then placed her hands on the top of her pants and said excitedly, "ready?" Sarah nodded with anticipation, Ria pushes her pants down to expose her shaved fanny, Sarah placed her hands over her mouth and gasped out loud.

Ria sits on the edge of the bed and opened her legs wide, she smiled at her lover and playfully said "Come on then" and she reached down and parted

her fanny lips, just the same as they had done on the
screen, Sarah repeated what she had witnessed on
the screen, and enjoyed every minute, even when
Ria came on her tongue, Sarah joined her and came
herself.

Sarah stood up and stripped naked and stood
with her legs wide open " shave me first, then make
me cum with your mouth" she demanded, Ria went
in to the bathroom and fetched a towel, a razor and
some soap, she was about to start shaving when her
lover said "start the film again" Ria did as she was
told, while she shaved her friends fanny, Sarah
watched the two women on the film doing all sorts
of things to each other, as she watched the film
Sarah subconsciously began to move her hips back
and forth, she jumped when without warning, Ria
placed her mouth to her sex and used her tongue
expertly, Sarah closed her eyes and held Ria's head
in place while she used her tongue, to bring her to
orgasm.

Ria stood up and the young women held each other

as they watched the screen fascinated; when the actresses placed themselves into the position where both had their mouths to eachothers fannies, at the same time, Sarah said excitedly "Can we try that?" Ria didn't hesitate, she took her lover's hand and they went to the bed, she laid Sarah down and positioned herself on top, it was a bit hit and miss at first but with a bit of adjustment both women received their required rewards, which was a strong climax, Ria came first, when she was done she made sure that Sarah achieved the same result.

Still naked they watched more and more films and gleaned more and more ideas, they decided that as it was nearly the end of their time at the Regal they would go into town at the earliest opportunity and visit a local adult shop, as they desperately wanted a strap on cock. The best friends had sort of talked about their time after they finally finished school, they had plans to stay together as lovers, but nothing had been confirmed yet.

Chapter 5

They stood across the road from; The Pleased Miss adult shop; trying to build up the courage to go inside, they finally find the courage and enter, a tall black-haired woman in her mid-twenties welcomed them with a smile "just shout if you need anything" she said as she looked Ria up and down. The girls were standing looking at the strap-on cocks; when the assistant moved up behind them and stood by the side of Ria, the assistant smiled at Ria who smiled back, she placed her hand flat on Ria's back and slowly rubbed it up and down.

The assistant tried to advise them as she continued to stroke her, she dropped her hand to Ria's tight bottom, and when she didn't object the assistant pushed her fingers under Ria's bottom towards her fanny, taking the thin material with her, again Ria did not object so the assistant lift's Ria's skirt, she then eased her fingers underneath her bum towards her fanny, she reached under and rubbed her fingers along her slit, Ria eased her leg apart to try and help, the assistant tried her utmost to get her finger into the side of her pants but they were simply to tight, when Ria looks at the older women, the older woman mouths the words " take them off" Ria then asks if there is a toilet, having been told where the toilet was, Ria goes and excitedly removes her pants.

Moving back to stand behind Sarah and by the side of the assistant, she spreads her legs and waits, within seconds the older woman's fingers are on her naked ass, they make their urgent way between her legs and slip deep inside Ria's wet fanny, Ria leans forward slightly which pushes her pelvis backward, the assistant knows what she is doing as Ria quickly climaxes, the assistant removes her fingers and looks at Ria as she places them in her mouth and sucks them clean.

Three more times she puts the fingers back inside Ria's fanny, and each time she licked them clean, the assistant moved back behind the counter and writes something down on a piece of paper, she walked back over to Ria and pressed the paper into her hand, Ria squirrels the paper away into her pocket, the pair leave the shop, Ria holds the door open for Sarah who says that they will think about it and come back, as Sarah leaves Ria turns to the assistant and mouths the word " thanks" and smiled, the assistant puts her finger to her ear and mouths the words " phone me" Ria taps her pocket and smiles. As Ria walks down the street she feels extra special as she is sopping wet down below and she has the phone number of an older woman who will hopefully teach her everything that they need to know.

Two days later Ria announces that she has to attend a family dinner, she will be meeting them in town, and that she will be dropped off before the gates closed at eleven pm, Sarah hoped that she has a good time and says that it is a good job that all of the lessons have finished as it was finishers fortnight.

Ria gets of the bus and walked nervously to the Pleased Miss shop, as soon as she entered, the same assistant smiled and walked up to her "Hi, I was so glad you rang, come in and take your coat off, would you like a coffee?" Ria removed her coat and sat on the stool behind the counter, feeling a little bit nervous now, not quite so confident, "my names Shelly what's yours?" asked Shelly, "Ria" she answered, Shelly brought her coffee and placed it on the counter in front of her, she immediately placed her hand on Ria's back "did you tell your friend that you were coming to see me, [Ria shook her head] we don't want her getting jealous do we? Don't take offense but can I ask how old you are?"

"I don't take offense I'm seventeen, that's ok isn't it?" asked Ria Shelly kissed her just below the ear " just perfect" as she took the young hand In hers and took her out the back, as soon as they were out of sight Shelly pushed her against the wall and placed her lips against the trembling teenager's lips and pushed her hand up Ria's top to her naked breast, bringing a moan from Ria, not wanting to show her innocence she pushed her hand up Shelly's top and found her hand was too small for the size of the older woman's tits, Shelly said " let me lock the door and then we can get comfy" Ria stood stock still, terrified, wishing that Sarah was here to save her, wishing that she had never come.

Shelly locked the door and walked back through the shop past Ria, taking her hand as she went, " I have a bed out the back for when I take stock to people's homes for a demonstration, we will be fine out here" the older woman led the teenager into a room at the back, in the center of the room stood a large metal bed, on a dressing table standing by the side lay all sorts of sex toys, all around the room were shelves full of boxes that contained who knows what, but now she was really nervous.

Shelly walked up behind her and folded her arms around her waist, she held her there nibbling her ear and swaying her gently, when she felt Ria relax slightly, she released her and pulled her top up and over her head, exposing her firm young breasts, next she undid Ria's skirt and took it off, she put her fingers into the top of the skimpy pants and pushed them down, holding them there until Ria stepped out of them, now naked she felt very vulnerable indeed.

Nervously Ria moved to the bed and sat down with her arms across her breasts, Shelly stood in front of her and stripped herself naked, she also had a shaved sex. She lifted Ria's hand and placed it between her open legs, "play with me, stroke me first," she requested, as Ria did this, the older woman reached out and took the young breasts in her hands and fondled them, she eased the young woman back onto the bed and spread her legs, Shelly went down to her knees and buried her face into the sex of the beautiful young woman, this was when Ria began to relax a little, this was just like the film she had watched, Ria had her first orgasm, she lifted her head and looked down at Shelly who was smiling back at her with her eyes.

Ria began to relax as the older woman did things with her tongue and lips that she didn't think were possible, after the next climax Shelly stood up and looked down at the youngster, "now I'm going to teach you how to do all of those things to me and that is what she did She sat on the side of the bed and held the student's hand and explained about womanly love, she pointed to the toys " we will get to those later when Rose gets here" Ria looked up at the older woman" who is Rose?" she asked " Rose is my partner, we live together, we like to help young girls like you, give you a start in lesbian life, now let's see what you have learned and the older woman lay back on the bed and let the young woman pleasure her and Shelly had to admit she was a fast learner.

They were lying in each other's arms when they heard a key in the door, a woman aged about thirty with red hair that was cut short, she was tall and thin with small breasts, she bent and kissed her partner and then kissed Ria " hi" she smiled and began to remove her clothes, standing naked she had a grape size clump of pubic hair, she looked at the pair lay on the bed " you two look well happy [she turned to the sex toys]who wants fucking?" they watched as she expertly strapped a thick black rubber cock on, she picked up a bottle of lube and squirted some on to its length and rubbed it all around, she then turned to the bed and took hold of Ria's legs and pulled her to the edge of the bed, " do you want me to do this little one?" Ria smiled and nodded even though she was scared to death, Rose lifted Ria's legs and opened them wide" oh, just what I like a nice tight virgin fanny, don't worry dear I will be gentle, just relax, Shelly held the cock at Ria's entrance before she could say anything Rose pushed the cock forward and into Ria, she went to scream but Shelly placed her hand over Ria's mouth " shush dear, it's over now, just enjoy it".

Shelly fondled and kissed her young breasts and watched as Rose rode her slowly, she began to relax a little bit as she neared her first cock climax, sensing this Shelly bent over Ria and moved her hands to the point where rubber met skin and eased her mound back and licking her fingers she

searched out her young clit and rubbed fingers
sideways across the tiny white button as fast as she
could, which helped Ria through her orgasm, the
two older women gave her pleasure beyond belief,
they kept swapping from each other to Ria, when
they made love to each other, Shelly showed Ria
how to find the hidden G spot, she demonstrated on
Rose, they let Ria practice on both of them. After
they would let Ria watch closely, as they made love
to each other and Ria couldn't wait to show Sarah
what she had learned, she would have to say that
she had learned everything from a book, as she dare
not tell her the truth.

Chapter 6

Sarah crept into bed next to her lover and folded herself into her when she touched her breasts Ria shrunk away from her, Sarah pulled her over, she was shocked when she looked at Ria's body, Ria had love bites under her tender breasts, "what the fuck have you been doing Ri, I can't believe it, look at your body, it's covered in bites" Sarah jumped up and ran into the bathroom and locked the door. Ria tried to explain through the bathroom door, "I did it for us Sarah, I thought if I learned I could teach you, c'mon Sarah, please open the door" she could hear Sarah crying, she then realised what she had done, what she had thrown away. Sarah waited until she heard Ria leave, before she left the bathroom, as she came out of the bathroom she reached for her phone and called her father and asked him to send Leigh the driver, as she wanted to return home early.

All that remained in the room of Sarah was a pink box that was tied with a pink bow, in the box was a key to the flat that her father had put a deposit on in Brighton, a flat for them to live in.

Having collected Sarah it was when Leigh drove into the drive of her home, Sarah couldn't believe her eyes, there was a sold sign outside the house and in the drive stood a big blue container, Sarah ran into the house looking for her mother, she found her upstairs" what the hell is happening Mother", her mother turned to her and tried to hug her "hello darling, we were going to tell you, you see your father has been offered a business deal in Toronto, and him and I are going, we leave in two days' time, sorry darling" she said " so I am not going then" asked Sarah with her hands on her hips " well, no dear, we thought you were planning to live in Brighton, so we thought that well, you had made your mind up" Sarah went to her bedroom to find it completely packed away, with all the boxes marked * CHARITY* she stormed down to the garage and found her father " hello darling, I could hear that you were back, this is not how it looks, we are not abandoning you, we would have written to you in the future and invited you down" he said "and where would you have written to dad, eh?. "I, em, well the new flat in Brighton, look I even have the check made out to pay for the whole thing" Sarah grabbed the check and walked towards the car, a motor bike courier pulled up by her side and gave her a letter and a board to sign, when she looked at the letter it was for her, from Ria.

Sarah left her family home without a word, sat in the car she opened the letter, it read:

My Darling Sarah,

Please forgive me, I got myself into something with an older woman, it was only a one off, you may not believe this but I did do it for us, I thought I could learn things that we could share. I know the evidence may not look like that, but I promise you it is true, I love you Sarah, you know that, I know that I have no right to ask but please forgive me. Please write to me.

Love
Ria

P. s. What was the key for?

Sarah's reply>

  Ria.

   *It was you that made me feel guilty
enough to enter the relationship with you in the first
place, you knew that I was confused. But once the
relationship began, I quickly fell in love with you,
deeply in love, so much so that the key you asked
me about, well that key is to a flat that my father
had put a deposit on for me in Brighton, that flat
would have been our home together, forever and
ever. But you ruined all that, you have broken my
heart and I will never speak to you again for as
long as I live. You will never know what you have
lost. I hope it was all worth it.*

      Sarah.

Sarah was dropped at the station and she caught a train to Brighton, she would stay at the flat for a short while until she could make her mind up on what to do next.

Chapter 7

A few days later while walking down the front in Brighton she caught sight of Ria and dodged into a shop to avoid her, it was while hiding that she saw a sign that made her smile, and that smile gave her a new direction. The sign read "Sea the world, join the Royal navy" and that is what she did, she signed on that week. Sarah banked the check from her father and gave up the flat in Brighton. Within a month she was on a train heading for her training camp in Farnborough, she was housed in a two man room with a nervous girl named Stacy Jordon from York, she was a pretty enough girl but she became beautiful when she pinned her hair back ready to go into her navy beret, on their first night together she asked me if I would go and stand by the shower door while she had a shower and in the dorm that we shared, she asked me not to look at her while she dressed, the shower could well have been shared by three people it just turned out that Stacy was very shy, and had waited until midnight before taking a shower.

So Sarah sat her down on her bed and held her hands, she persuaded her that she need not be shy with her, Sarah even offered to walk around naked if that would help, she made some progress a week later when she shared the shower with her, there were just the two of them, she turned to Stacy and said, "Stacy, turn and look at me", it took her several minutes to get the shy woman to find the courage look at her naked body, when she saw her naked fanny she gasped and covered her eyes, Sarah went to her and held a towel around her, as she dried her back she turned and rested her head against Sarah's shoulder " thank you for being so patient with me".

Back in their room, Stacy sat shyly on her bed with her towel wrapped around her, Sarah walked into the room and stood looking at her "can I sit with you Stacy?" she shrugged, so Sarah locked the door and sat by her side, Stacy never moved. Sarah said "look Stacy I want to help you but I can only help you if you will let me, so talk to me and tell me what the problem is?" she began to cry, great big tears ran down her cheeks, "it was my stepdad,

he was doing things to my stepsister and threatened
me that as soon as I was big enough he was going
to do the same things to me, well I hid away, I
never let him see any part of me and when I began
to, well, develop I would walk around hunched over
so that he couldn't see my breasts.

Well, I have been the same ever since, you are
the only person to ever see my breasts, apart from
the doctor, and she was a woman" Sarah removed
her towel and sat there naked "look at me Stacy,
look at my naked body" Stacy stole a glance at her
nakedness " take a good look, look at my body,
look all over" when she didn't move Sarah tried
again " I can't help you, if you won't let me, now
turn your head and look at my naked body" this
time she turned her head and looked, Sarah held her
head and knelt in front of her, she parted her legs so
that Stacy could see everything, her eyes traveled
over Sarah's naked body from top to bottom, when
she let go of her head, her head stayed where it was,
with her eyes searching Sarah's body.

Sarah lifted her arms and put them slowly behind Stacy, she gripped the towel that Stacy had around her. Sarah said" Stacy is my body beautiful [she nodded] well your body is just as beautiful as mine, can I remove your towel and look?" a look of fear came into her eyes "please" she asked Stacy, Stacy gave the slightest of nods and Sarah slowly lifted the towel from around her, she immediately covered her breasts, Stacy sat there naked shaking like a leaf, Sarah reached forward and took her wrists and slowly pulled them a part all she did was hunch her shoulders Sarah took Stacy's hands and put them onto her breasts, Stacy stared at her hands as they held another woman's breasts " show me your breasts Stacy, I want to see them, now" she looked up into Sarah's face and slowly straightened her shoulders bringing her tits into view, Sarah moved her hands towards her friends breasts Stacy watched the hands all the way until they touched her breasts.

Within a few minutes Stacy sat with her arms wide open and her tits in open view, Sarah pulled her arms down and said "that will be enough for one day, we will try again tomorrow, do you agree Stacy?" the shy woman looked into her eyes " I think I could do some more today if you wanted to" said Stacy, Sarah got off the bed and stood there naked, all she did was hold her hand out to Stacy, Stacy stared at the hand and slowly reached out and took it, they clasped hands and Sarah gently persuaded her from the bed, she stood naked in front of another person for the very first time ever, after a few seconds Stacy smiled and threw herself into my arms " thank you, oh thank you Sarah" and Stacy walked around the room as if the weight of the world had been lifted from her young shoulders.

Sarah was lying in bed thinking about the day and Stacy. She jumped when Stacy said. "Can I ask you a question Sarah?" she sat up "you can ask me anything Stacy?" " why do you shave your privates?" she asked me "it is called a fanny Stacy, call it a fanny" she spoke under her breath " ok, why do you shave your fanny?" she asked "well there are a few reasons, first with all this training we will have to do, we will get all hot and sweaty, shaving will help, second periods, a lot easier with no hair, thirdly sex, no hair is definitely better, trust me" after a long silence, Stacy asked "will you shave me tomorrow?" Sarah smiled "Yes, of course I will".

Chapter 8

The pair had had a busy day, spending hours on the parade ground marching, they lay on their beds knackered "Thanks for last night, Sarah you have changed my life and I will never forget what you did" Sarah looked across to her "you're welcome".

In the shower later Stacy showed a lot more confidence regarding her body, when Sarah stood and stared at her she did a little twirl, they dried themselves and walked back to their room, Sarah had taken her razor out and waved it at Stacy "well" the woman smiled and nodded, Sarah locked the door and spread a towel out on the floor, she told Stacy to stand on the towel and to open her legs, she did as she was told but she still had her towel wrapped around her, Sarah went down to her knees and looked up at her, "take your towel off Stacy" she blushed and reached up and opened the towel, she looked around the room before taking it off all together, Sarah set about removing Stacy's pubic hair " do you want it all gone or do you want me to leave a little bit?" she looked down at herself" you do as you think best" she said, so Sarah carried on. She removed all that she could from this angle and said " you will have to lie on the bed for me to do the rest" Stacy looked at all the curly hair on the towel " I didn't think there would be so much" Sarah laid a towel out on the bed and told her to lie down on it, when Stacy was lay down Sarah went to open her legs but Stacy resisted "I'm not sure I can" Sarah looked up into her eye "trust me Stacy" and she relented and let Sarah open her legs, she tried to do a close shave but the angle wasn't quite right so she stood up and looked down at Stacy "please lift your feet up onto the bed [she did as she was told] now let your knees flop open [reluctantly she did this as well, but she covered her eyes with her hands] Stacy, look at me, Stacy I won't carry on until you look at me [she removed her hands and looked at her] just look at yourself, the position you are in [she lifted her head and looked, and instantly blushed] I don't want to be to crude but if you ever do have sex, you may have to open your legs like this for that person".

Stacy was bright red at the thought, Sarah carried on and finished the shave, but as she was just about to finish the shave she noticed that Stacy was getting really turned on, she was covered in tiny goose bumps, her nipples were rock hard and she had love juice seeping from her fanny lips, she finished the shave and stood up and looked down at her, she was really very flushed and highly aroused, Sarah leaned over her and whispered " do you want me to make you cum?" she stared back "I don't know, will it hurt?" Sarah went to her locker and took a vibrator from her wardrobe and went back to her, she knelt down again and looked at the fanny in front of her, she would love to use her mouth and taste her but that might scare her so she licked the rubber cock and switched it on to vibrate, she then rubbed it along her slit,[this brought an instant moan from Stacy] she then rubbed her clit from side to side [this not only brought a longer louder moan, it made her lift her head up] Stacy was watching Sarah, eye to eye.

Sarah let her watch her as she put the rubber cock into her mouth and lubricate it, glancing down she put the cock to her slit and looked back at those staring eyes, she inserted the cock slowly Into that virgin fanny [this made Stacy bite her lip] she pushed it into Stacie's naked fanny taking her virginity in the process, as soon as she began to fuck her with that rubber cock, [Stacy's hips began to bounce] keeping the cock going in and out of her fanny, Sarah stood up and leaned over Stacy and looked deep into her eyes, Stacy lay there with her eyes closed, rocking her head from side to side moaning all the time, she chewed her bottom lip, her hips were bouncing wildly "go on Stacy relax, let it happen, just relax, that's it, it's coming" [she was whimpering continuously, she then pushed her head back hard into the bed and opened her mouth wide, holding her breath, as her first ever proper orgasm flooded through her] "that's it Stacy that's it, there ya go, that's it" Sarah kept the rubber cock going, using her right hand but now it was deeper and a lot slower, she looked down at the wet cock as it went in and out, licking her middle fingers on her left hand she placed the fingers onto her clit, and began to move them very fast sideway, she herself was so wet she would only have to touch herself to cum, Stacy looked up at her then held her arms out to her, Sarah bent over and Stacy pulled her close and said " thank you, that was so nice" Sarah knew that her fanny was less than an inch from Stacy's and the slightest touch would probably take her over the edge, Stacy then said " do you want me to do it to you now?" Sarah lifted her head and looked into the other woman's eyes, their lips were so close she would only have to pucker and they would kiss, Stacy made the move and lifted her lips to hers, within seconds the world changed, they were kissing, tongues doing a lovers dance, Sarah had lowered her pelvis and their fannies were rubbing together, both women came again and again, their hands were all over each other, Sarah rolled to the side taking them both onto their sides, Stacy followed her lead and when Sarah put her hand between her legs and pushed two fingers into her and began to finger fuck her, Stacy followed suite, they stayed like this until they had both came again.

Sarah pulled away and smiled at her "have you had enough?" the other woman looked lovingly at her, and shook her head, so Sarah got of the bed and eased Stacy down flat, leaning over her she began by kissing her long and hard before she moved her lips around her cheek to her ear lobe which she nibbled for a few seconds, moving down to her breasts she sucked her right nipple deep into her mouth, making her lover moan deeply, after sucking the other breast she moved down her body kissing her every inch of the way she reached Stacy's fanny, with one long motion she licked her slit from end to end, very slowly taking in all of the love juice the oozed from her slit, at the top she began to suck on her clit, which made Stacy cum instantly with shouts of " oh god please, oh god" Stacy reached down and ran her fingers through Sarah's hair and then gripping it in her fists as she came again, Sarah went lower again and pushed her tongue deep inside her lovers fanny, just by moving the tip of her tongue it took Stacy over the top again, Sarah pushed two fingers into Stacy's tight fanny and frigged her, as she licked between her fanny lips at the same time, Stacy gave out a shudder and a loud moan as she yet again climaxed, keeping her fingers deep inside the fanny of Stacy, Sarah lifted her mouth and looked directly at Stacy "are you happy now?" Stacy smiled broadly in response.

	Sarah kissed the fanny before standing up and walked back to her locker and after a bit of shifting of things she turned around with something in her hands, she stood in front of the other woman and strapped a rubber cock to her hips, Stacy's eyes were locked onto the cock, Sarah rubbed some lube onto it and pulled Stacy to the edge of the bed, Stacy opened her legs and waited eyes closed to be entered, Sarah put the end of the cock to her fanny lips and pushed forward, she took her virginity properly this time and sent her flying into womanhood, she fucked her, until she whispered stop, Sarah pulled the wet cock from her and looked down at all of the female cum that covered the rubber cock, she reached down to undo the straps that held the cock on but stopped and climbed onto the bed, Stacy lay there smiling up at Sarah, Sarah held the rubber knob to Stacy's mouth "lick it clean" demanded Sarah, Stacy looked at the cock and looked repelled, when Sarah pushed it onto her lips Stacy poked her tongue out and touched it with the tip of her tongue, she pulled her tongue back into her mouth and tasted her own love juice, deciding that she didn't mind the taste she put her tongue out and licked the tip of the cock, Sarah moved the cock around so that Stacy cleaned it all, when it came to the knob, Sarah said open your mouth, staring up at Sarah, Stacy opened her mouth, Sarah said " close your lips around it and lick all around the head" Stay did as she was instructed, when Sarah began to move the cock back and forth, Stacy's eyes became very big, as she felt that cock moving in her mouth, Stacy began to move her head on her own, taking a little bit more each time, but she took too much at one time and gagged, which made her spit the cock out.

     Lying on the bed now, side on to each other, both tenderly stroking each other, Stacy asked. "Will you tell me everything you did to me? Only you gave me so much pleasure that I want to give you the same pleasure in return" so Sarah explained what she had done, until the fingers in the fanny bit, Stacy smiled and pushed two fingers into Sarah's fanny and began frigging her "like this ?" asked Stacy, Sarah opened her legs wider, the two women just sat and stared at each other, Sarah reached over and returned the favour and pushed her fingers into her new lover, within seconds they were in a full blown kiss, both women moaned into each other's mouths as Stacy eased Sarah down onto her back, kneeling by her side both women frigged the other to orgasm, now that they had cum, Stacy began kissing Sarah around the neck and ears, slowly moving down to her breasts sucking the nipples in the same way that had been done to her, Sarah moved slowly down her body kissing her every inch of the way, when she reached Sarah's naked fanny she kissed all around the area before she began to lick up and down her swollen fanny lips, when she tried to find the clit she failed and looked up at Sarah, so Sarah lifted her pelvis and with her left hand she pulled her mound back enough to expose her female cock, she then pushed Stacy's head back down and held her head still while she pushed her clit to her mouth, Stacy began licking while Sarah directed her clit, as soon as she had found it Stacy licked and sucked that little button until Sarah came very noisily.

Chapter 9

With both women now spent, they lay together in Stacy's bed folded into each other, tenderly stroking each other and nibbling each other's necks. When they woke in the morning Stacy was a different woman, she was so excited about the changes to her life, and she knew that she had grown up at last and the changes were all down to her new lover, she climbed out of bed and began getting Sarah out of bed, when Sarah stood naked in front of her, Stacy then pulled her into the bathroom and turned the shower on and joining Sarah in the hot water, they wrapped their arms around each other, Stacy took charge and began things by lowering her mouth to Sarah's right breast and chewing her right nipple, she didn't waste any time at all, she went to her knees and put her lips to Sarah's fanny, as she began kissing and licking, Sarah reached down and put her hands onto the back of Stacy's head to hold her in place, as she opened her legs wide, then pushed her hips forward to allow her lover to lick the whole length of her fanny, Sarah came strongly and Stacy licked her fanny clean. They both jumped when there was loud knock on the door and a strong voice shouted "parade 10 minutes" the women were suddenly thrown into a panic.

Hurrying to get dressed Stacy began to cry because her hands were shaking so much she couldn't do the buttons up on her shirt, Sarah went over to help her, as she did the buttons up, Stacy lifted a hand to Sarah's breast, she rubbed her nipple until it could be easily seen through her shirt, when all of the buttons were done up, they kissed briefly then turned and left the room to begin another day in the navy.

Chapter 10

The day finished with a trip to the swimming pool and once it was known that all of the new intake could swim, they were made to tread water in full battle dress and also with various weights strapped to them, the two women passed with flying colours. Sat in the NAAFI eating their evening meal they agreed that what had happened between them, stayed between them and must never be discussed with anyone else. The future must also stay back in their room. Stacy had changed overnight because she held the door open for her lover. As soon as she was in the room Stacy locked the door to their room and in under a minute she stood naked leaning against the door, Sarah looked the woman over and studied her from head to toe, taking extra time on her swollen fanny lips, their eyes locked for a short time. That is the time Sarah slowly began taking her clothes off, making her partner wait by folding each item very neatly, and placing the clothes in her wardrobe, when she turned around she had a large thick purple vibrator in her hand, she waved the big purple vibrator at her lover "want to try this?" she asked, Stacy answered by lying flat out on her bed and opening her legs, Sarah walked over to her lover switching the lubricated vibrator on as she went, she stood there by the bed and rubbed the vibrator all around her lovers neck, then down to her breasts which made her nipples rock hard, down over her body to her pubic mound, Stacy opened her legs in expectation but Sarah carried on and rubbed the rubber cock slowly down both legs, as she moved the vibrator back up her legs, Stacy moaned on every breath as love juice oozed from between her swollen fanny lips.

Sarah only had to touch the fanny lips of her lover to take her over the top, she sat up and hissed at Sarah, Stacy held her legs high in the air as her hips bounced up and down, big loud oooozzzzzeeeeeddddd and aaaaaahhhhhssss came from Stacy, Stacy reached forward and tried to grab the vibrator, she was so desperate to get it inside her. When Sarah moved the rubber cock, out and away from Stacy she did no more than drop her fingers to her fanny and begin frigging herself, when Sarah tried to push the vibrator to her lovers fanny, her lover pushed it away and frigged herself to an orgasm, her legs were as wide and high as they could be, her body almost bent in two as her fingers went in and out of her fanny, the intense orgasm raging on and on, she held her free hand out to Sarah and groaned "please" Sarah positioned the rubber cock to her lovers fanny lips. Stacy grabbed Sarah's wrist and pulled it towards her, that big rubber cock slipped inside the well lubricated fanny, as Sarah began fucking her, Stacy groaned out loud and lay back down with her eyes closed, her mouth egg shaped with pleasure, her whole body jerked as the big cock stretched her wide and gave her unbelievable pleasure, she seemed to be in a state of continuous orgasm, Sarah stared into her lovers eyes as she rammed that big rubber cock as deep as she could, and as fast as she could into her body.

Stacy finally pulled Sarah's hand and vibrator away from her fanny, she lay back panting heavily, her body spread eagled on the bed, she had tears flooding from her eyes, she held her hands out to

Sarah who bent over and hugged her latest lovers trembling body, after they had hugged long enough for Stacy to calm down, they begin to kiss passionately. Stacy reached out for the vibrator that lay buzzing on the bed, she stroked it all over Sarah's body finally pushing it onto her fanny lips which brings a deep moan from Sarah. Stacy moves out from under her lover and stands by the bed, Sarah takes up position on her hands and knees, with her bum facing Stacy who rubs the buzzing cock up and down her slit occasionally touching her clit with the tip of the cock, Sarah is moaning deeply as her fanny is being teased, she is at the point when she needs that big cock inside her fanny, she begins to scratch at the bedclothes and groan deeply, Stacy reads the signs and pushes the rubber cock deep inside her lovers fanny and begins to fuck her with fast, deep strokes.

Sarah has begun her journey towards her orgasm by pushing back at that big cock as her lover keeps ramming it in and out, Stacy reaches underneath the vibrator with her free hand and rubs Sarah's clit as fast as she can, now Sarah is moaning and thrusting back as hard as she can, she is close as she feels her lovers finger tips on her clit, it is to much as her orgasm floods through her whole body, she is holding herself still with her eyes closed and her mouth wide open as that big cock is still being rammed deep into her fanny, as soon as Sarah lets her head hang down, Stacy pulls the cock out and replaces it with her tongue, after licking inside her fanny she moves up to her lovers clit, flicking it first with the tip of her tongue and then sucking it with puckered lips, Sarah held her lovers head in place as she sucked her sensitive clit, Sarah moved her hips back and forwards over her lovers mouth, she then felt her body tense as she finally reached the release of her orgasm.

Sarah moved her fanny slowly back and forth over her lovers mouth prolonging her climax for as long as possible, when Sarah lifted herself from her lovers mouth she flopped down onto the bed and lay there panting with her legs wide open, Stacy is stood by the side of the bed looking down at this beautiful woman whom she loved and wanted to so desperately please, she opened Sarah's locker and searched and found the big strap on cock, she snapped the dildo around her hips and approached her lover, she gripped her legs and pulled her around so that her bum was on the edge of the bed, Stacy pushed the cock into her lovers fanny, Sarah arched her back as the rubber cock entered her trembling body, she pulled her legs up and held them open as Stacy fucked her at a steady rate until she saw that her lovers climax was close, she then increased the pace at which she fucked her, smiling at the intense pleasure that she was giving her lover.

Later that day lay in Sarah's bed kissing passionately and grinding their mounds against each other, Sarah reached under her pillow and gripped the big purple vibrator, she moved her body away from her friend and pushed the vibrator against her lovers clit which had an immediate effect, Stacy began thrusting her hips back and forth moaning as she did so, her eyes opened wide and her hips moved faster and faster as she came, she looked at Sarah and said "please fuck me with that big cock" so Sarah changed position and knelt by the side of the young woman's open legs, she then switched the vibrator on and pushed it into her friends gaping fanny, she pushed it in deep and taking a good hold she began to fuck her as fast as she possible could to start with, she then slowed down, her right hand slowly moving and ramming the rubber cock into her lover she looked up into her lovers face to see a look of ecstasy, her eyes were half closed and her mouth hung open in the shape of a small egg, little moans escaped her gaping mouth, Stacy held her breath as Sarah began to move the vibrator round and round inside her fanny, this was enough to tip her over the edge, her orgasm seem to last forever as she held her hips as high as she could.

When Stacy had calmed she reached out and took the wet vibrator from Sarah's hand and put it into her mouth, she licked it all over and then she sucked it as if it was a real cock, Sarah stood with her hands on her hips and watched her lover, she said "I think you need a real cock to suck" Stacy looked up at her and asked" have you had a real cock?", Sarah shook her head" no, but I have thought about it lately, don't get me wrong I love what we do to each other, but there is always that thought * would a man be better*?, I will get round to it one day, but in the meantime, well at least until we get posted, I will want to fuck you at every opportunity" Stacy smiled up at her lover, "I don't think I could do it with a man, I mean, with you I know that I will cum, you already know what I like and I like what you do to me, you have changed my life Sarah and I will never forget it as long as I live" Sarah bent over and kissed her lover " what about kids, you will need a man for that, then there is marriage, a house and what about growing old, it could be a very lonely life on your own" Both women were deep in thought " will you write to me Sarah?" asked Stacy, Sarah smiled and nodded, but she doubted that she would keep in touch, the world is a big place and she wanted to live life to the full, and about a man, we will see.

The two women have fucked all night because this was to be their last night together, they have had their orders, Stacy will be land based and will train to be a navy doctor and Sarah will join the Ark Royal as a communications officer. On board ship

she is sharing with eight women, in a small grey
metal room with enough space for twenty bunks
and twenty lockers, one blonde woman named Ruth
James is a real stunner and is in the next bunk to
Sarah and she has smiled twice at Sarah "would it
be possible to fuck on board ship?". The ship has
set sail and is heading for America, Sarah finds the
work exciting and relatively easy, Ruth is on the
same course as Sarah and is struggling and has
asked Sarah for help, which pleases Sarah no end,
sat together on Ruth's bunk hips and legs are
touching, Sarah is very wet down below, as if
sensing this Ruth takes Sarah's hand and squeezes
it firmly, the two women lock eyes a moment to
long, Ruth leans over and kisses her friend briefly
on the corner of the mouth and say's " thanks for
helping me Sarah",

Sarah climbs down and gets into her own
bunk, she lays facing Ruth, the two women lay and
look at each other, it is when Sarah pretends to be
asleep, Ruth turns onto her back, her eyes never
leave Sarah as she spreads her legs and
masturbates, Sarah can see the sheets moving as her

hand bounces up and down, Ruth smiles as she cums and closes her eyes to dream whatever dream she wants, but Sarah is sure that it will be a nice dream. Sarah pushes her own hand between her legs, her fanny lips are swollen to their fullest, she hardly touches herself, all she does is use her middle finger on her clit to make herself cum, now she has a smile on her face as she drifts into a happy, contented sleep.

Chapter 11

Sarah and Ruth become nervous around one another as the sexual tension mounts, things take a turn when they have been volunteered to clean and disinfect one of the operating theatres. They have been given their strict instructions, the work is to take place overnight and the doors must remain locked during and after the work is complete. Sarah decides that she has got to take control of the situation, they have been at work for a couple of hours and Ruth is on her hands and knees and is singing a Searchers song. Sarah takes a flask and pours two cups of coffee, she calls Ruth who comes over and sits on the operating table swinging her legs, Sarah stands in front of her work mate and passes her the coffee. They stare at one another both taking tiny sips of coffee, Sarah looks into her cup and dips her fingertip into the foam, she then lifts the fingertip to Ruth's lips. Ruth pokes her tongue out and licks the foam from the fingertip, their eyes never leaving each other's. Sarah is holding her cup in her right hand. She slides her left hand to Ruth's leg and rests it there. She then dips the tip of her tongue into the coffee foam and pokes her tongue towards Ruth but holds it short of her mouth, giving Ruth the option to make the next move.

Ruth smiled and leaned forward and touched the foam with the tip of her tongue, Sarah lifted her tongue, they had a little touchy, feely sort of thing with their tongues before Sarah sucked Ruth's tongue into her mouth, within a second they were in a full on kiss, with tongues fighting and moaning on both sides, as soon as Sarah placed her hand on Ruth's right breast, Ruth pulled her overall open to reveal her light blue bra, in a heartbeat Sarah had lifted the bra and had her mouth on her friends right nipple, sucking it deeply into her mouth, Ruth slid her hands to the breasts of her new lover and rubbed the nipples through the material of her overalls, Sarah took a step away from Ruth and undid her overalls, one stud at a time. As she held the unstudied overalls in her hands, she looked at Ruth and asked. "Are you sure?" Ruth nodded and reached forward and pulled the overalls apart to see Sarah's naked breasts, Sarah let the overalls drop to the floor and stepped out of them, she stood there in a pair of plimsolls and a tiny red thong she pulled Ruth from the table, as soon as her feet hit the floor she removed her overalls, all she had on were her plimsolls and a pair of white pants. They moved together at the same time, to meet with their lips, but their hands were soon all over each other. Sarah pushed Ruth's pants down and let them fall to the floor, she slid her hand down over her pubic mound to her swollen fanny lips. She didn't hesitate, she pushed two fingers into her fanny and finger fucked her to her orgasm, Ruth groaned out loud as she soaked her lovers fingers, she clung onto Sarah trembling from head to toe, Ruth lowered her hand to Sarah's naked fanny to find her swollen fanny lips either side of her thong, she pushed the thong down and let it drop to the floor, Sarah opened her legs as Ruth pushed her fingers into her waiting fanny, she returned the compliment and made Sarah cum.

Sarah eased Ruth back onto the operating table, she moved her until she was laid lengthways but near the end, as Sarah moved towards Ruth,

Ruth opened her legs and let them flop open, Sarah leaned forward and reached up Ruth's body and gripped her breasts hard, she began kissing her around her stomach, slowly moving downwards kissing her as she went, when she reached her hairy mound she kissed her all around her thighs and hips everywhere but her fanny, this drove Ruth mad, so mad in fact that she pushed her hand down over her mound and began rubbing her clit, Sarah let her do this while she licked all along her fanny lips back and forth, until she dipped her tongue deep into her hot fanny, this made Ruth lift her head, she reached down and gripped the back of her lovers head and began moving her hips up and down , moaning all the time, Ruth was very close to her orgasm as Sarah sucked Ruth's fanny lips around her clit, Sarah reached up with her right hand and parted her lovers fanny lips, Ruth couldn't hold back any more as she called out in orgasm.

Sarah had difficulty in keeping contact with her mouth as Ruth squirmed around in ecstasy, how she stayed on the table Sarah didn't know, when Sarah came up for air Ruth reached out for her and pulled her to her, folding her arms around her neck and pushing her lips against her lovers. With Ruth holding onto Sarah with her left hand she lowered her hand to Sarah's naked fanny, she gasped out loud as she discovered Sarah's total nakedness, she ran her fingers along her oozing slit, when Ruth pushed two fingers inside Sarah all she had to do was hold her hand still while Sarah moved her fanny back and forth in desperation, Sarah was almost crying for the need to be touched, Ruth pulled away from Sarah and slid down from the table, she moved to Sarah and turned her around so that she had her back to the table, Ruth dropped down to her knees and pushed her mouth to her lovers naked fanny, Sarah placed her hands behind her and gripped the table, she then leaned back and spread her knees, as soon as she felt the warm lips on her fanny she closed her eyes and let her head go back, she could tell that Ruth had kissed a fanny before as she soon had Sarah on the brink, when her lips sucked her fanny lips into her mouth Sarah almost fainted with pleasure, Sarah made a lot of noise as she moved her fanny over Ruth's mouth, as Sarah came, Ruth put her mouth flat over her lovers entrance and sucked for all she was worth, as soon as she tasted warm love juice she buried her tongue deep into her lovers fanny and began lapping at the drink of the gods.

The women stood silently tit to tit and hugged, each could feel the others speeding heartbeat, softly stroking each other and running finger tips down eachothers spine. It was Ruth that began to rub her mound against Sarah's naked fanny, she put her mouth to Sarah's ear and said "let's make each other cum" from that moment on the next few minutes were fast and furious, it went from mound rubbing to tongues down each other's throats until they finished up in this position, they stood hip to hip, lips to lips, with one arm around each other's necks and two fingers inside each other's fannies, they made each other cum twice before pulling apart, Ruth reached up with her hands and cupped Sarah's face, " have any of your previous lovers touched your secret spot, it is commonly known as the G spot ?" Sarah shook her head and had a quizzical look on her face, Ruth smiled and said" let me show you, it will change your life" Ruth knelt down in front of Sarah, she pushed two fingers back into Sarah's fanny and frigs her as normal, but as she gets near her orgasm, Ruth pulls Sarah's hips forward and bends the tips of her fingers up towards the back of her mound, as soon as Ruth touches whatever is up there, Sarah's legs almost give way the spot is so sensitive, as long as Ruth's finger tips rub along the spot Sarah continues to cum, in the end she has to snatch the fingers away as she could take it no more, Ruth explains what to feel for up there, "it is a rigged place about half an inch long. Do you want to see if you can find it inside me?"

She went to speak again but Sarah put her finger to her lovers lips to quieten her and said "Lets get this lot finished first, we can talk after" and that is what they did, with the work done they walked silently around the deck, completely on their own, they stood looking far out to sea, Sarah spoke first she asked " do you regret what we did, or are you happy that we did it?" Ruth didn't look at Sarah and smiled, as she answered, "when I followed you up the ramp on to this ship, I wanted you then, I couldn't take my eyes from your tight ass" they stood looking at each other and laughed "so does this mean that we are an item?" asked Sarah "I hope so" smiled Ruth.

As you can imagine finding somewhere to be on their own on the ship with 600 personnel is very difficult, apart from the odd fumble here and there, not much contact had gone on between them. Now that they were due to dock in America first thing the next day, the lovers had agreed that the first thing that they would do when they left the ship is to find a room and fuck each other stupid.

After five hours in a room,[which included half an hour in the shower] the women were now sated, as they walked around the shops, Ruth kept whispering things like "my fanny is all tingly, I'm still wet down there" and Sarah would smile and nudge her " stop it", she would say, they had to return to the ship at night to sleep, the five days that they were in America they spent each afternoon in a room having sex, Sarah had introduced Ruth to all of her toys, and Ruth had shown Sarah how to locate the G spots, Ruth liked the strap on cock the best, both giving and receiving, they found a shop full of sex toys and bought a double ended cock in a purple colour, which when shared they enjoyed immensely.

Sarah had to buy a lock up box to keep all of her toys in, because the last thing that she wanted was for the other women on the ship to find out that they were lovers, but saying that there is another women who has been smiling at Sarah and brushing up against her, Lena was her name, she was over six feet tall, thin with a cropped hair style, she was pretty enough but she had no tits, well not anything that you would need a bra for, her eyes were a grey-green colour but her most striking feature were her teeth, they were the whitest teeth that Sarah had ever seen.

With the ship heading back to the UK, everything was fine until Sarah had to work three nights in a row in the communications room, on her dinner break she made her way to the female dorm to see Ruth. Sarah crept into the dorm to find that there was no Ruth, she checked the dorm to find that Lena was missing as well, before jumping to conclusions because it was just possible that they had been called back onto duty, but she thought that she would check the female showers just in case. Sarah opened the shower door quietly, all was quiet but the lights were on which was unusual, Sarah walked in and sure enough in the far corner both women were naked, Lena was leaning against the shower wall with her legs spread wide open and Ruth was on her knees in front of her with her mouth stuck to Lena's fanny, Lena had her eyes closed and her hands on the back of Ruth's head.

Sarah slammed the door as she ran out of the showers, in floods of tears she returned to duty. In the morning she returned to her bunk to find Ruth waiting for her, she came out with those famous words "It wasn't what it looked like, honest" said Ruth, Sarah stared at her for a long time before she spat out the words " fuck off" and stormed out. Sarah returned to the dorm and moved her bunk to the end bunk far away from everyone, she needed some time on her own, "what's wrong with her, is the same thing going to happen each time she forms a relationship, maybe she should try a man, she couldn't do any worse, could she?".

Chapter 12

Sarah kept to herself until they reached the UK, Ruth had tried to talk to her on numerous occasions as it turns out that Lena was already in a strong relationship with a female petty officer, and they lived together and had done so for a very long time, what had happened meant nothing to Lena and it wouldn't happen again, which left Ruth on her own, on the last night on board Sarah walked past Ruth's bunk to get to the kettle, Ruth was lay on her bed sobbing her heart out, when Sarah walked back past Ruth bunk, Ruth put her arm out and tried to stop Sarah, " please" said Ruth, Sarah put her mouth close to her face and spat out "slag" and went back to her bunk.

After they had disembarked, Ruth immediately put in for another course, one of which she would be land based for three months, after a week on shore Sarah boarded the ship again, she didn't know where she was bound and it didn't matter, all that she knew was that it was a top secret mission, she chose her bunk, she knew a couple of the women from the last trip, she got on alright with them, and swore blind that she would keep herself to herself in the sex department, the last woman to board ship was Lena, the dorm went quiet as Lena stood and looked around all of the faces of the women, she smiled and chose the bunk next to Sarah, there were eight spare bunks and as soon as Lena left the dorm, Sarah moved all of her stuff to one of the spare bunks, when Lena returned from the shower she looked for Sarah, seeing that she had moved, she just shrugged and climbed up onto her bunk and began to read a book ignoring all of the other women totally.

Nothing sexually happened to Sarah on this trip [not for the want of trying by Lena] although she did receive a letter from Ruth saying that she was very sorry, it was only a one-off and she didn't enjoy it, and it didn't mean anything, and what happened was a big mistake and could you Sarah give her another chance because I love you, and I miss you so much. Sarah read the letter again then ripped the letter up and tossed it into the bin.

The officer in charge of what Sarah did on board ship was named Terry Dawson, he was a chief petty officer, he was tall, handsome, with bright blue eyes, and he fancied Sarah a lot, and he asked her if he could take her out when they docked, she had replied "Maybe." he asked her out time and time again and each time she replied "maybe". As time went on Terry was getting more and more forceful, he kept brushing against her, he would lean over her to point to a piece of work, making sure that he brushed her breast, he would rub himself against her, it all came to a head one night when they were on their own, and were going to be so for the best part of an hour, as soon as the door had closed and they were on their own he went to her and pulled her up, he began kissing her, and she did respond, he fondled her right breast and rubbed his hard cock against her, she could hardly feel his cock so she pushed him away and looked at his groin, he stood there and said "what?" she moved away from him and went to her bag, she pulled that big purple vibrator, and said " Terry if you can match this then you can fuck me, if you can't then leave me the fuck alone" Terry looked at that big purple vibrator and turned away and without speaking he moved away from her and sat at one of the computers and began to do some work Terry didn't bother her again, but he started telling his friends that she was a lesbian, so Sarah mentioned to the same people that the reason she was a lesbian was because men like Terry with tiny cocks had driven her to it, Terry became very angry about this and tried to ignore her, but one day they had to work together and he then asked her why she had said what she had said, Sarah said simply " you started it Terry, you made a move on me and you started the rumours about me, what was I supposed to do, sit back and do nothing?".

Sarah and Terry only spoke when they had to, Sarah loved her job and her ship and she wasn't about to give it up because of one man. The ship docked in China and would be there for ten days. They had all been warned not to go ashore on their own, as there were a lot of dangerous gangs about, so all of the women went ashore together and had a great time, with no problems at all, on the last day Sarah was called before the captain and was told that a Chinese female officer was coming on board and Sarah had been chosen by her petty officer to look after her, Sarah was to move her kit into one of the officers rooms, where she would share with the Chinese guest.

Sarah had been briefed on what she was allowed to show their guest, and what she wasn't allowed to show her, Sarah was there when the Chinese officer came aboard, she was greeted by everyone, there was a lot of bowing and shaking hands , her name was Si Li and when she was introduced to Sarah she took her hand and said in perfect English " I am sure we will become great friends" she smiled just a fraction too long, and Sarah could feel herself becoming wet down below, when all of the introductions were complete Si took Sarahs arm and said " please show me to my quarters" Sarah led the way to the two man room, when she realised that she was in fact sharing with Sarah she was delighted, while Si put her kit away they talked just like old friends.

Si had brought some Chinese women's

magazines and sat on her bunk reading she showed
Sarah some Chinese fashion, Sarah moved across
the cabin and sat by Si and looked at the magazine,
they sat hip to hip, Si read some of the articles out
to Sarah who hung onto every word, Sarah couldn't
understand why she was as wet as she was, and she
thought that Si was in the same position, Sarah
decided that she needed some fresh air, so she stood
and took Si hand and said "come, let me show you
the ship" Si stood and held onto Sarah's hand at
every opportunity, the tour took about two hours,
they then had lunch, while they were eating Sarah
studied this beautiful woman, she stood about the
same height as herself, she had shiny black hair that
was hidden in her cap, her eyes were dark brown,
she was a slim woman with a nice hand full of tits,
Sarah now had her eyes fixed on Si's small but long
nipples as they stuck out against her shirt. After
lunch they made their way back to their room,
Sarah was laying down reading a book while Si was
doing what she was doing, Si moved to stand in
front of Sarah with her shirt unbuttoned to the
waist, and said "I saw you watching me in the
restaurant, did you like what you saw Sarah?"
Sarah closed her book and laid it down, she then

looked up at Si and then reached up and pulled Si's shirt open, her white bra stood out against her olive coloured skin.

Sarah reached up and stroked the warm olive skin of this most beautiful woman, her hands gently squeezed her firm breasts through her white bra, Si looked down at the hands on her breasts, Si pulled her shirt off and reached behind her and undid her bra and took it off and dropped it to the floor. Sarah fondled those perfect breasts, when she rolled those long thin nipples, this brought the first moan from the Chinese woman who reached down and pulled at Sarah's shirt, Sarah undid and removed her shirt, Si watched her new lover removing her shirt, as soon as the shirt was open she reached out and fondled her breasts, Sarah removed her bra and watched the olive hands fondling her tits, Si pushed her lips to Sarah's lips, their first kiss was long and very passionate, they kissed as their tongues tangled, the lust building so much that Si pulled away and began to strip herself naked, while she did Sarah was just as busy removing her clothes, both women were down to their pants Si had black pants on and Sarah has red they looked at each other's bodies both marveled at what they could see, Sarah put her hands to the side of her pants and slid them off, Si did the same to reveal a single line of trimmed pubic hair about half an inch wide in a direct line with her fanny lips.

Si gasped when she saw Sarah's naked fanny for the first time and moved forward and put the flat of her hand to her lovers fanny lips, when Sarah looked down she moved her fanny against the olive hand, Si looked her lover in the eyes and bent her middle finger up and slipped it inside her fanny, Sarah groaned out loud and parted her legs inviting this beautiful Chinese woman to do whatever she wanted to, Si dropped to her knees, with her right hand she pushed two fingers deep into Sarah's wet fanny, she leaned forward and licked the naked lips, her fingers were frigging her at a fair rate and her tongue had now found her lovers clit, Sarah stood with her head back and her hands pushing the Chinese head against her fanny, Sarah began to moan out loud, saying " oh yes, oh yes, that's it just there, oooohhhhh yes, keep going I'm coming, yes

yes ooooooohhhh, fuck that was good" as she moved her hips back and forth over the mouth of her Chinese lover, Si pulled away from her fanny and stood up and put her salty lips to the lips of Sarah, they kissed deeply, they stood there mound to mound, tit to tit, there mounds moved against one another, Sarah could taste her own cum in the mouth of Si, Si pulled away and said " please make me cum Sarah".

Sarah turned her lover around so that she stood next to the bed, Sarah eased her down onto the bed, Si opened her legs as she laid back on the bed, Sarah went down to her knees, she kissed all around the olive thighs before she kissed the fanny lips, she sucked the lips deep into her mouth making the Chinese woman moan loudly, Sarah inserted two finger into the gaping fanny, she began to frig her, she reached up with her left hand and parted the fanny lips so that Sarah can do whatever she wanted to, Si has had her first silent orgasm and is building nicely to her second, she looks down at this woman who is watching her that is licking her fanny, eye to eye she smiles down at her new lover, she closes her eyes and pushes her head back into the bed, she feels her hips begin to bounce up and down as she came again, she now leaned forward and gripped Sarah's head and eased it gently back and forth as she is close again so soon, she is moaning out loud "yes yes, oh yes, please don't stop" Sarah bent her finger tips up in search of her hidden spot, as soon as she stroked the ridged spot Si came again and she soaked Sarah's fingers which were slowly still doing their thing in between those swollen fanny lips ,Si lay back on the bunk with her legs spread as wide as they can go, totally at ease with this beautiful woman who is giving her untold pleasure, as she is on the verge of another beautiful orgasm.

The young lovers are lay on the hard bunk in the after glow of good sex, wrapped around each other totally spent as they stroke each other and move there mounds slowly, lovingly against each other.

Chapter 13

Sitting on Sarah's bunk, the lovers at different stages of their periods, flicking through magazines and chatting, Si stops, lays her magazine down and says "Tell me about your first time" which makes Sarah say "My god, Ria, I haven't thought about her for a long time", they turn and face each other. Si watches her lovers mind travel back in time, Sarah says" if I tell you about my first time you must promise to tell me about yours " Si agrees excitedly as they hold hands, so Sarah begins " It was at boarding school named The Regal school for girls, in a town called Hastings, which is on the south coast, I was 15 years old at the time and as we are now I shared a room with a pretty English girl, but she was mixed a bit of oriental, which gave her lovely olive skin, the same as yours, the girls name was Ria, as I said she was very pretty, she was a few inches smaller than me. She had long jet black hair and eyes to die for, they were a chocolate brown colour, she had a slim olive coloured body with nice shaped tits that had small hard nipples, her fanny hair was fine and like soft down, almost velvety to the touch, we did everything together and as girls do we were always hand in hand or arm in arm and we told each other everything.

Ria and I were walking down Hastings high street one Saturday afternoon, again we were arm in arm when Ria said " I love you Sarah" well I didn't think anything of it, I remember squeezing her arm and saying " I love you to" she seemed very happy at this and leaned over and kissed me on the cheek, I remember blushing and feeling a bit funny, not strange but a little bit tingly, it was something I had not felt before, when we arrived back at school and I went to the loo I noticed that my pants were very damp and I didn't know why, I suddenly became very confused.

The next thing that I remember is one evening we were sitting in our night clothes on a bed much the same as we are now and Ria kept pointing at things on the models in the magazine we were sharing, and saying things like" she has nice boobs or she is pretty and she is beautiful, girlie things, but I noticed that she kept moving a little bit closer until we were pressed against each other, we stayed like that until we said good night to each other, she leaned over and kissed me on the side of the mouth, I was confused even more and didn't know what to think, when I lay in bed later I found that I was wet between the legs again, well I pushed my hand down there to find out what was going on just in case it was my period, what I found surprised me, not only was my fanny wet but my lower lips were different, they seemed a lot bigger, I sprang out of bed and went to the bathroom, when I lowered my pants they were soaking wet, but I didn't know why, well I wiped myself but it felt different somehow, well I wiped myself a few more times and suddenly became very embarrassed I had to change my pants, when I climbed back into bed I was even more confused but very excited.

The next day at break Ria took me to one side and asked me quietly " did you do it to yourself last night?" well I didn't know what she meant, well I ran away from her flushed, embarrassed and even more confused, later that evening we were sat in our room, on our own beds not looking at each other, you see I had become nervous to be around her, it was then that she took the bull by the horns and asked me" Sarah, do you know anything about sex?" well I knew about periods but very little else, I shook my head and said " no, should I?" she laughed and said you must be the only girl in the whole school that hasn't tried it, look Sarah I want to be more than friends with you, I want to be your lover" I remember I felt myself blush deeply, I felt more embarrassed because I didn't know what she meant, in the end I just lowered my head and rung my hands in my lap, she came and sat close to me and placed her arm around my shoulders and said " I'm scared as well Sarah, I can show you what I know if you want " I remember sitting there and cursing myself as I nodded, she turned my face to hers and kissed me on the lips. We both held our lips tight together for a little while, we were both trembling like mad, I remember I jumped when she touched my left breast, she moved away and asked if I wanted to stop, by this time I was hot, trembling, scared but somehow excited as well, I said "no I don't want to stop."

She stood up and pulled me to my feet, we were standing toe to toe. She then reached down and gripped the hem of my nightshirt and lifted it up and over my head, I immediately crossed my arms over my naked tits, even though she had seen them loads of times before but this seemed different, she removed her own nightshirt, I don't know why, it was just the sight of all that olive skin, like with you now it sent shivers down my spine, back to my story she gently pulled my arms from in front of my tits and pushed her tits against mine, we kissed again this time our lips parted a tiny bit, this time when she touched my left tit I didn't jump and when she rolled my nipple I almost passed out, I nervously touched her breast, I basically did what she was doing to me, while she fondled my boobs she dropped her other hand to my bum, when she pulled me hard against her I was shocked when a deep moan escaped from me and I had this nice feeling between my legs that I had not had before, I felt so hot down there, we were rubbing ourselves against each other when she stopped and took a step away, she took her pants off, then reached to my pants and pushed them down, I was shocked but all of a sudden I did not feel embarrassed anymore, we stood looking at each other's young virginal bodies, her body was beautiful and her fanny hair had been trimmed to a perfect V.

RIA eased me down onto the bed and lay by my side, she began with the kissing again only now her hands were all over me, each time her hand brushed my mound I would moan out loud, I wondered how this gorgeous young girl knew what she knew, and how to do what she was doing, but to be honest I was past caring, she tried to push a finger between my legs, she did manage to rub the tip of her finger along the top of my fanny but that was enough to make moan, Ria whispered " open your legs for me" and without thinking I opened my legs, she rubbed a finger along my fanny lips, I was trembling like mad, having feelings I couldn't explain, when she pushed a finger into my fanny, it was when she moved it in and out it suddenly felt wonderful, when she entered a second finger the feelings just grew and grew, she was rubbing her wet fanny up and down my leg, I could feel her trembling just as much as me, " do the same to me " she whispered, as I reached down she opened her legs for me, her fanny was so hot and so wet, as soon as I touched her she shuddered and said do it quick, I pushed two fingers into her fanny and pushed then in and out but I obviously wasn't doing it right as she rolled onto her back and opened her legs as wide as she could, she then grabbed my wrist, she had her eyes closed and was moaning out loud, she moved my fingers faster and deeper, I watched her arch her back and make this strange gurgling noise, she then lifted her hips as high as she could, it was then I felt this hot wet stuff drenching my fingers, she still held my wrist tightly but she wasn't moving it as fast, she opened her eyes and smiled at me " fuck, that was good" she said, she pulled my wet fingers from her fanny and looked at them closely, she wiped them clean and said " your turn".

She pushed me down onto my back she opened my arms and legs wide, she then positioned herself between my legs, she then said " close your eyes and relax" she placed her hands either side of my chest and dangled her tits against mine, rubbing her hard nipples against mine, she kissed me all around my neck and ears before placing her mouth onto mine, she pushed the tip of her tongue against my lips, I only parted my lips a fraction and her hot wet tongue was deep in my mouth, our mounds were now rubbing against each other getting faster and faster, she pulled her mouth from mine and moved her mouth to my tits [oh how she sucked my tits] her mouth moved slowly down my body until she reached my spread thighs, she teased me by kissing me all around my thighs and all around but not on my fanny, she finally pushed two fingers into my virgin fanny and moved them back and forth quite quickly, something nice was happening I didn't know what but whatever it was I liked it a lot, she pressed her mouth against me down there and moved her fingers faster.

I had my first ever orgasm, it was the most frightening, beautiful thing ever, I knew that I was shouting out loud but I couldn't help it, she lifted her mouth from me but kept her fingers slowly moving, I jumped when other girls began knocking on the door and cheering, I didn't care I lay there my body open to the world, my life had just changed forever, I could feel my fanny glowing and tingling.

At that particular time there was one video going around our school and Ria managed to get hold of it, the video was called " Pussy eats pussy", I must at this point that each two man dorm has it's own video recorder for homework. We sat on my bed and watched the video, it was a bit grainy from too much use, but we got the gist of what was happening, the thing that stood out for me was that both girls had shaved fannies and since that day I have had a shaved fanny.

There is a saying in England and that saying is "practice makes perfect", well Ria and I practiced at every opportunity, things took an upward turn when one of the older girls began to sell vibrators, they were great fun until it was time to leave that place, we cried as we watched each other walk away. I often think about Ria and where she is and what she is doing now, Sarah's first time wasn't quite as she told it, I think this was more of a sexual fantasy than reality.

"OK, Si your turn to tell me about your first time." Si begins " I will tell you but my story is not as interesting as yours, if I am honest I seriously thought about telling you a lie but in the end I decided to tell you the truth, Ria blushed at this point, I was a year older than you I was 16 years old and I attended a private school that was far away from my home and like your school mine was for girls also, but unlike your school the 30 girls all shared one dormitory, you could if you wanted to pull curtains around your bed [that was when things to do with sex happened] but not that many girls bothered.

English Literature is the subject that I had a lot of trouble with, the school had written to my father informing him of my weakness in this subject and making him the offer to send me to a private tutor, my father agreed to pay for the service and the out of school visits were arranged, the lessons were to take place in the English teachers home that was not far from the school, on the first day that I arrived at the tutors home. I rang the doorbell and a young English woman of maybe 18 years old, a couple of year older than me, she was stunningly beautiful with long blonde hair and sparkling blue eyes, she stood the same height as me and her build was the same as mine, she had a western dress on and unlike my culture her breasts could been seen quite clearly.

Sat in her study she introduced herself as Alice Jay, Alice told me that she had a masters in English Literature and she has been teaching for two years and to her way of thinking teaching should be fun and to be honest the private lessons were fun and I soon got to grips with the subject, Alice would wear lots of different colourful clothes in lots of different styles, some days she would wear her hair up and other days she would let her hair hang down, I liked to see her hair hanging down, I don't know why but I liked it best when

Alice did not wear a brassier under a see through blouse, when she caught me looking her nipples would become hard, I liked this a lot but I didn't know why, after maybe a year we had become very good friends and also very relaxed around each other, Alice had always left English magazines lying around for me to look at, some of the magazines were becoming more and more daring with topless women, even some naked women, when I would turn the page and see these things I would quickly put the magazine down.

Alice asked me If I was embarrassed by nudity I explained that in my culture nudity is a thing between husband and wife and only ever in the home, Alice said "So if I was to say lift my top and show you my breasts, would you be offended?" I felt myself blush down to my toes because I really wanted to see her tits but I began to answer "in my culture no, and that was as far as I got as she lifted her top and showed me her naked breasts "Does that offend you Si?" I blushed and looked away but i was instantly wet between the legs, Alice lowered her top and took me by the hand and led me into the bedroom, she closed the curtains and the door and moved to me, I was so scared I didn't know what to do.

Alice opened her wardrobe and shows me all of her clothes, "Take your pick, whenever you come here I want you to dress in English clothes, do you agree?" I nodded eagerly as I looked at all of the bright clothes, as you know all Chinese clothes are dull and grey but I changed my mind when she said " take your clothes off" I didn't want her to see my basic under garments, she wouldn't understand, seeing my reluctance she came to me and lifted my top from me, I stood there with my wrapped breasts on view Alice said " take that off" I had never shown my naked breasts to another living soul, but I unwrapped my breasts and stood there in front of Alice, she stood in front of me and placed a hand under each breast, I felt hot and embarrassed as my nipples were as hard as they could be, using her thumbs she gently rubbed my nipples but only for a second, I remember it clearly just that simply action was almost enough to take me over the edge, Alice crossed the room and went

to a chest of draws, she searched through the top
draw and found what she was looking for, she came
back to me and slipped on my first ever brassier,
she touched my breasts as she adjusts the straps, it
instantly felt better than the wraps we use.

She then put her fingers in the sides of my
uniform bottoms and pulled them down, I stood
there in my sopping wet grey school drawers, Alice
knelt down and went to pull my draws down,
seeing how damp I was she said" someone is a little
excited" she ever so slowly pulled my drawers
down to the floor, I lifted my feet one by one as she
slips them off, she looks at the dampness and
moves to the chest of draws again and searches
again, finding what she wanted she moves back to
me, she has a pair of pink pants in her hands, she
bends down again and holds the pants for me to
step into, she pulls them slowly up my legs I have
to spread my thighs so that she can finish pulling
them up, she then turned me so that I am facing a
long mirror, she stands close behind me, the pink
pants are instantly soaking wet as she releases my
long hair and spreads it over my shoulders, she

stands with her hands on my shoulders and looks in the mirror, she undid the bra and pulled it from me, she went back to the draw and chose a bright yellow one, she came back to me I had to hold my arms out straight in front of me, she slid the straps along my arms and placed the cups onto my tits, her eyes burned into mine, she moved closer to me and pushed her tits into mine and reached behind me to do the straps up, her lips were half an inch from mine, our breaths were blowing hot into each other's mouths.

My legs were about to give way, this most beautiful woman was pressing her tits into mine, her eyes bored into mine, I knew that it was me that had to make the next move so I closed my eyes and pushed my lips forward, as our lips touched, Alice melted into me, the pink pants that I had on were sopping wet, my legs had gone to jelly now that we were pushing our mounds against one another, she dropped her hands to my bum cheeks and pulled me even harder against her, I was absolutely terrified, I didn't know what I had started but whatever it was it felt bloody good, Alice pushed her tongue deeper into my throat as she pushed her right hand into the pink pants, she squeezed my bum cheek before pushing her hand under my bum to my fanny, the tip of her finger just reached my most intimate part, my legs parted on their own which shocked me deeply, her finger now slipped easily into me, which brought a deep moan from somewhere deep within me, my hips began to move on their own but in time with her finger, when she entered a second finger I pushed my hips back and her fingers slipped deeper inside my fanny bringing forth my virgin orgasm, when she felt me cum it was enough to bring forth her own orgasm, we shared a most intimate moment, my legs sagged but she held me tight and frigged me to another climax, I was in a complete state of shock as Alice stepped away from me she held my hands briefly and smiled before letting me go and removing her clothes slowly bit by bit, I stood there and stared at her hairless fanny as my eyes widened.

Alice dropped to her knees and slid her fingers into the side of the pink pants, she slowly eased them down my legs and off, she ran her hand back up the side of my legs and placed her mouth to my fanny, the tip of her tongue just touched the top of my slit as she eased my legs apart, at the first long firm lick my legs spread even further apart, I lowered my hands to the back of her head I then did two things at the same time I pushed my fanny forward and harder onto her mouth and the second thing was to push her head harder against my fanny. I threw my head back and came for the third time as I felt her tongue deep inside me searching for my virgin cum, my legs finally gave way and I slipped back onto the bed with my legs wide open, I thought to myself "what's happening to me?" the next thing I know she has her mouth to my fanny again sucking the warm cum from me.

When Alice had drunk her fill, she slowly moved up my body kissing me every inch of the way bringing me out in goose bumps all over, my nipples felt as if they were going to explode, when her lips touched mine it was me that pushed my tongue into her mouth, she moved higher and lowered her right breast into my mouth, she looked down and watched me suck hungrily on her hard nipple, I was sucking hard when she pulled it from me and swapped it for the left nipple, I looked up at her as she smiled down at me which made me suck harder, my inexperience showed as I placed my hands onto her bum and tried unsuccessfully to reach her naked fanny, she moved further up my body and knelt either side of my head and placed her fanny onto my mouth, I looked up into her eyes needing to be told what to do, she smiled and said " first of, lick it as if you were licking an ice cream" my eyes never left hers as I licked her heavenly fanny, she began to move her hips back and forth and said " push your tongue inside me and taste me, taste my cum" when I had done as I was told she told me to suck her fanny lips, she was very close again by the noise that she was making, she stared down at me and said " keep your mouth still" she reached down and parted her fanny lips and placed her clit onto my mouth and shouted " suck that fucker hard" she had her head thrown back as she pulled her nipples as hard as she could.

Alice groaned out her orgasm and sank her fanny down harder onto my mouth, she looked down and said "lick it " I began licking she moved her fanny back slightly and looked down into my eyes as I licked her clit, I was now drinking her cum from her fanny, Alice was loving every second of it, " get ready I'm coming again " she said, she closed her eyes and I watched her whole body as it shook, I felt her offerings hit my tongue and now that I had the taste, I licked up every last drop of her cum and Alice was loving it.

Lying on the bed sated for the moment, we lay tightly in each other's arms gently stroking each other, our mounds touching but not moving when Alice asked " are you ready to try something else?" having enjoyed everything that we had done so far I naturally said "yes, I'm ready", she moved around the bed and positioned herself as thus, she lifted my right leg into the air, she then straddled my left leg, kneeling she placed her fanny onto mine, she moved her fanny back and forth very slowly, she looked down at me, and said " can you feel what I am doing [I nodded] well you move the same only when I go down you go up" we began to move against each other "oh my god, oh my god" I shouted, you can't imagine the pleasure that I was receiving, as we began to move faster against each other, I could never have imagined such pleasure, I had cum twice and was heading for a third time, Alice had cum I don't know how many times but now she had slowed down, she eventually climbed from me leaving me with my legs spread wide open, I lifted my hands and brushed the hair from my sweaty face, Alice searched in the bottom of the wardrobe I heard her moving stuff around she eventually came out with a white shoe box with red roses all over it, she place the box onto the bed and looked at me and said " I'm going to make you a woman" she pulled this rubber thing from the box and threaded it up her legs to her waist she was facing away from me at the time, she turned around to show me this big purple cock, she reached back into the box and pulled out a plastic bottle, she squirted some stuff onto the rubber cock, using her hands she rubbed it all over the cock, as I looked at it, it sort of sparkled and looked even bigger, to big even but it was too late now Alice pulled me to the edge of the bed, I watched the cock as it swung and bounced, she gripped my right leg and with her left hand she positioned the cock to my entrance, she looked at me and said "take a deep breath" I took deep breath and she pushed it into me but only so far the cock was now against my barrier " take another breath" she said as I breathed in she pushed forward " ouch, fuck bloody fuck" as I became a woman, I will never forget the way that rubber cock stretched me and when she began to fuck me, well it was glorious, I closed my eyes and went to a special place, a place that I could go to forever and ever.

Alice stopped and adjusted her grip on my thighs, she then rammed that rubber cock into me, the feeling was like nothing that I had felt before, when I closed my eyes and arched my back she rammed it harder and faster, I came on that big cock but she kept ramming that cock into me until I came again, I had to tell her to stop, I was sore and my insides hurt, I reached out and pushed her stomach to make her stop. She finally slowed down and stopped, I gasped when she pulled that big rubber cock from my sore fanny, she moved around the bed and showed me the blood on the base of the cock and the cum all over the shaft, she pushed the cock to my mouth and said " lick it" I poked my tongue out and Alice rubbed the cock along my tongue, I looked up at her, she opened her mouth, I gradually opened my mouth, she pushed the cock into my mouth, I still looked at her as she closed her mouth so I closed my lips around that rubber cock I still looked at her waiting for further instruction " lick your spunk from it" it tasted better than I thought, I became nervous when she began to fuck my mouth, seeing that I wasn't happy she removed the cock from my mouth.

She placed the cock on the floor and went back to the box, when she turned around she had this huge black cock in her hand, my eyes went huge as she moved towards me, I gave a sigh of relief when she began to run the straps up my legs, I slid from the bed and let her strap the huge black cock to me, when she had the cock in the right place she spread lubricant all over it, the cock must have been 9 inches long and as thick as my arm, she eased me back own onto the bed and climbed onto the bed by my side she straddled me her fanny hovering over the cock, she reached between her legs and gripped the thick cock and guided it into her fanny, she sank all the way, taking it all inside she looked down at me and proudly said " when I go down you push up, all the time she spoke to me her hips were moving back and forth, now I'm going to fuck myself first, when I place my hands either side of your chest I want you to ram this big fucking cock into me as hard and as fast as you can" I nodded in agreement, she then pulled her knees in tight to my body and began her journey, on the first downward stroke she closed her eyes, she began slowly making a high pitched "Oooooohhhhhaaaa" sound, on and on she rode that big thick cock giving herself a lot of pleasure, twice I watched her sink down an rub herself to orgasm with glazed eyes she flopped forward and placed her hands either side of my chest, she stared into my eyes " fuck me with this big fucker" it took me a few seconds to find the right rhythm, her eyes were still staring at me but she could not see me she was in some secret place, she suddenly began to move with me each stroke going deeper, each stroke brought a grunt, she sank down to full depth and shouted " pull my nipples" she startled me with the outcry I pulled her nipples hard and she suddenly went perfectly still, I continued to fuck her hard fascinated by her actions, she finally sank down and used her hips to finished herself off.

Sat on that cock looking down at me Alice asked me "Have you had enough or can you do some more?" I smiled at her " I can try" she lifted herself from that thick cock, I watched her female spunk run down its length, Alice moved around and lowered her mouth to the base of the rubber cock and licked all of her offerings from the shaft leaving the knob, she moved again and placed her fanny over my mouth, I dipped my tongue into her fanny as her head went up and down the cock, I had to grip her ass to pull her down lower so that I could go deeper, now I could drink her cum. When Alice lifted her fanny from my mouth I thought we were done but no, she pulled me up onto my feet, we did a lot of fondling, she pulled me down to my knees and on her hands and knees she placed herself in front of me, looking back at me she said " fuck me with that big black cock" I positioned myself behind her not confident in what I was doing, but I was desperate to please her, I looked down at her fanny and I could see where the cock had come from, so I put the cock to the same place and pushed forward, I watched that black cock disappear into her body, Alice groaned and moved her knees and began to ride that cock, I fell into her stride, we fucked for an age until she shouted " harder, harder" I rammed that big cock into her as hard as I could Alice had her orgasm and finally told me to stop, I was just about fucked but my fanny had stopped hurting.

Alice stood up and took my hand "come my new Chinese lover, lets lie down" she said as they moved back to the bed, after a while she asked if I was ok with what had happened, I said that ", I was fine with it, but will you make me cum again with your fingers?" as her long finger fucked me I had the orgasm that I so desperately wanted.

And that was my very first time but not the end of the story, I surprised myself two weeks later when I took that big black cock, I couldn't take it all but I took most of it, I must say that Alice fell in love with me, when it was time for me to leave she wanted me to live with her and help her teach, I said that I could not do that, Alice became desperate towards the end and fell to her knees and begged.

Sarah had undone Si's blouse and had set her breasts free, she was absently playing with her left nipple " that is one hell of a story Si, it has made me as randy as fuck, it's a pity we are both bleeding" Si looked at Sarah and kissed her long and hard, she suddenly stood up and pulled her lover to her feet, she went to the locker and took out two strap on cocks and said " lets take a shower and fuck each other rigid with these rubber cocks" at one stage it looked like a murder had been committed with the amount of blood that was in the shower tray.

Chapter 14

Six weeks had passed from the day where they had told each other their tales of their first experience of sex. They were sitting in a café in Denmark, Si had been a bit quiet for a few days and Sarah had asked her what was wrong on numerous occasions. Si had said that she was just being silly and she would tell her when the time was right, it seemed that the time was right and this was the time. She began "Sarah can I tell you what has been bothering me recently, I would have told you sooner only you would have thought I was being childish and stupid". Sarah said " yes, please tell me, only you have been driving me nuts" Si lowered her head and said " when I was with Alice and we would shave each other, well she had this electric razor and after each time she would use the razor on me to make me cum by holding it to my button [she looked coyly looked at Sarah] it is so nice Sarah I want us to have one" Sarah laughed and said " is that all, I thought that you were going to finish with me" Si looked at her lover "there is one more thing Sarah, Alice pushed a vibrator up my other hole, I liked it at first, but after a short while, I didn't like it and asked her to stop, but since that day I have thought about it a lot and it was just the size of the vibrator that was the problem, it was much too big, I thought that we could buy a couple of small ones and try it again, I don't want you to think that what we do together is not working. Sarah I love what we do together and I love you" Sarah stood and said "c'mon lets go shopping".

No-one took any notice of them as they shopped, they laughed as they came out of the adult shop, because the lady behind the counter had invited them to a very private party, ladies only, she had promised that she would take special care of them, Sarah had bought to 2 small vibrators and in another shop they had great fun with another young woman who made it obvious that she fancied Si, they even managed to get her opinion on which electric razor she uses, the young woman didn't hesitate " trust me it has to be this one, she switched the razor on and placed it on her arm and moved it up and down, she then placed the razor on to Si's arm, she ran it slowly up and down as she stared at Si, she moved the razor up her arm to the spot by her breast, when she looked at Si's hard nipple she almost came on the spot, the woman was so close to coming we could both see that, Si then did something that not only shocked me but surprised me, [we laughed about it later]. Joe the sales girl wore a skirt that had a long open slit in it, she was wrapping our razor when Si pushed her hand into the slit and ran her hand up the naked trembling leg to discover a soaking wet thong, she pushed it to the side and pushed two fingers into her swollen fanny, deep into her wet fanny, Joe pushed her legs apart and stared at Si, they watched Joe close her eyes and had her orgasm, when it was all over Joe looked at Si and whispered thank you, as she took our money and gave us our shopping she said " I finish at 6, I have my own flat, not far away from here, we could all have some fun, I have lots of toys" she looked from me to Si and back again. Si said " maybe" and we left the shop, as we walked past a fountain Si washed her hand, we sat on the wall of the fountain and Si said " did you see her, she was so desperate, she was so wet up there, you didn't mind did you Sarah only I felt sorry for her, I couldn't leave her like that" we had bit of a laugh about it but I knew that Si wanted to go back, I had never tried sex with three before, maybe it could be fun, I knew that Si would not mention it again because she knew that it could offend me, we would have to be careful as we were due back at the ship at 10.30pm.

We walked around the town and bought some clothes, I kept an eye on the time to make sure that we were back at the shop at 6pm, I had made up my mind that I would not get involved, I would sit and watch. Joe came out of the shop and looked around for us, when she spotted us she ran over to us, she led us down a back road and pointed to a large building in the distance and said " I have a flat in there, what are your names?". We told her our names but her eyes never left Si, we arrived at the flat, it was well kept and Joe had some nice things, she gave us a quick tour of the flat, when she opened the bedroom door, she stood to the side and let us walk in, she opened the wardrobe and took out a shoe box, when she opened the box it was full of vibrators. She took Si's hand and said "Thank you for earlier" I sat on a chair by the dressing table, Joe already had Si practically naked. When Si was naked she looked at me and held her hand out, I smiled and blew her a kiss but did not move, Joe was naked by now, she did not even glance at me as she took my lover to her bed. I sat and watched my lover make love to another woman. Could we survive this? I didn't know.

I watched them pleasure each other for 2 hours, I was as wet as a sponge, but I remained sitting on the chair. Joe strapped a big red cock to her hips and fucked my lover from behind making her cum countless times. Was I jealous? Yes I was, was I enjoying watching them? Yes I was, when Joe had fucked Si, she went to the box and pulled out a purple double ended rubber cock, Joe inserted it into both fannies and gripping it in the middle she fucked them both to their final orgasm's, Si got off the bed and dressed, Joe came to me and tried to pull me to the bed, when I refused she slid her hand up my skirt " But you are so wet" she said, she went to the box and took out a thick blue vibrator, she came back to me and lifted my skirt and pulled my wet pants down, she went to pick up the vibrator but Si had already picked it up, she licked the head and went to her knees and pushed that thick blue vibrator up inside me, as Si fucked me Joe had her hand up my sweater and had my left tit out and her tongue down my throat, Si made me cum, over that thick cock, she pulled it out, I put my tit away, Joe looked at me and said " please let me taste you before you leave" she put her mouth to my fanny, I had to admit that she was very good, she licked me clean and then sucked my clit until I climaxed. When she came up for air, I finished dressing and put my coat on. Joe gave Si her phone number and told her to ring her anytime. As we were about to leave Joe kissed SI deeply" please ring me, you are a beautiful woman and I already love you" she said, we left the flat and took a taxi back to the ship. We boarded the ship and went directly to our room, not a word had passed between us, Si got undressed and got into bed and turned her back to me.

I went to her and sat on the bed as I rubbed her shoulder, she cried and tears ran down her face" what have I done, oh god what have I done?" she sobbed, I tried to turn her over, but she would not let me, she just sobbed her heart out, " I spoke quietly to her "Si you did what you wanted to do, it was obvious that you wanted her in the shop, who am I to stop you, you are a free spirit, you can do what you want" I sat there for a minute or two, when she didn't answer me I shrugged and stood up and went to bed. "Will you ever forgive me?" she whispered, I rubbed her back "You are already forgiven my love" I said and went to bed.

I lay in bed playing back in my mind what I had seen, the way Si and Joe had kissed, it was very intense for someone that she had just met, I asked myself if we could survive what has happened, the answer was " I doubt it very much" we both began our periods over the next few days which was a good thing as it took pressure off our relationship, the more I thought about what had happened the more doubts I had, if we were going to come through this then we would have to talk, if Si wants to be with Joe then so be it, I wouldn't stand in her way.

Two days later we came off duty and went back to our dorm, we were getting changed and I said " we need to talk Si" she didn't answer she just nodded, I sat on my bed and when she looked at me, I beckoned her over and patted the bed by my side, she came and sat down, her head hung down and she rung her hands in her lap" have you fallen in love with her?" I asked, she nodded. "Have you kept her phone number?" I asked her, she nodded "Well then there is nothing else to say, will you move out or shall I?" Si burst into tears "I don't want to move out I love you Sarah, you know I do, why should we split up, I may never get to Amsterdam again" I only had one thing to say "you kept her number Si, that's enough for me" she burst into tears and lay went and down on her bed.

We remained civil to each other until we reached port, I went and looked at the recruitment board and saw a vacancy for a HGV Driver, so I applied, 2 day later I had the interview and had been given the job, I packed my kit and leaving the new razor on her pillow, I left.

Chapter 15

I passed my HGV driving test at the first attempt, the depot that I would be working out off was in Portsmouth, I enjoyed the work a lot as I could be sent anywhere in the country to fetch anything from boat engines to explosives, the only problem I had is a man named Adam Parks. Now Adam Parks thinks he is a real ladies man and he had a habit of touching me somewhat inappropriately but he always seems to go a bit too far. He was always making comments, sexual comments, when I threatened to report him for sexual harassment, he laughed out loud in front of all the other drivers and loaders "I have all of these witnesses" as he waved his arms and boasted. I had to think up a plan to put a stop to Adam Parks.

Two days later I had my plan, there was an element of risk, but I was quietly confident, I just had to choose the right moment, and that moment came two weeks later in the naffi, on this particular day the naffi was fall of drivers and loaders, and at the back of the room were a lot of officers including the commanding officer. I walked in and picked up a tray and moved along to select my meal, I heard him say " watch this" he shouted " that Sarah is a fine piece of ass, I think she has the finest ass in the navy and the biggest nipples" this brought a big laugh from all of the men, I turned and walked over to where he was sitting, I slammed the tray down in front of him, I could see the commanding officer stood up at the back watching what was going on, the room was deadly quiet, " Adam Parks, I have just about had enough of you, I reached into my bag and pulled out a my big purple vibrator and dropped it onto the tray, it was at least 9 inches long and as thick as your arm, I let him get a good look at it before I switched it on, " now Mr Parks if you can match that you can fuck me here and now in front of all your mates, if not leave me the fuck alone" his eyes were on the vibrator as it buzzed around the tray, he looked up at me and went bright red then stood up and walked out of the room to a round of applause, the commanding officer closely followed him out.

I went back to the counter and got my dinner and when my chicken dinner was on my new tray I walked across the room and sat in the chair that the disgraced Mr Parks had vacated, the vibrator was still buzzing on the tray". "Can I have a look at that" asked Ray a driver mate, I nodded and the vibrator was passed from man to man, each man making some sort of gesture with it, there were two other women Jill and Alex in the room, both drivers, both fed up with Adam Parks, Jill held the vibrator and pretended to wank it, which raised a big laugh, she then stood up and put the knob end into her mouth and gave it a blow job which got her a round of applause, she came over to me and slapped me on the back " fucking well done, it is about time someone put that bastard in his place".

When I had finished, I left the naffi with Ray, outside the canteen the C O was waiting for me Can I have a word please?" I stood to attention and said " yes sir" he took me by the arm and said "yes, yes" he then led me back into the naffi to sit at a table, he was known as bit of a ditherer, he was a man of retirement age, he had on thick glasses, he had a thick grey moustache that matched his grey hair, he placed his hand onto my shoulder and said " bloody well done, I knew that I had to do something about our Mr Parks but I have never had any real proof, as things stood it would have been difficult to make a case against him, but now thanks to you our Mr Parks is now in the guard room, under arrest and he will be dismissed in due course, I can only apologise for the way that you have been treated by that man, I must say that you did bring him down a peg or two.Sarah isn't it?", when I nodded, he looked around the empty room, "do you think I could have a look at that thing?" I reached into my bag and took the vibrator out and held it in his hands, he looked at it from every angle" rather life like, isn't it" I took it from him and switched it on to full speed and gave it back to him, he immediately burst out laughing as he held it, he put the knob to his cheek and began to laugh again. "Where does one buy one of these, I ought to buy one for the wife" he laughed and slapped his knee.

On a return journey from Newcastle, I called in at the services for a pee and a pie, as I exited the services there stood a young woman hitching a lift, we are not supposed to pick hitch hikers up, but rather me than some big bloody bloke like Ray Parks, she opened the door. Where are you going?" I asked her, she climbed in "Wherever you are going" she undid her coat to take it off, she sure had a big pair of tits, she took her hat off and let her dark hair fall down to her shoulders, she looked me over, I could feel her eyes all over me," where are we going love ?" she asked " Portsmouth, what's your name?" I asked her "Jade, what's yours?" " Sarah" I said "hi Sarah thanks for picking me up, I'm bloody fed up with men, they give you a lift and expect a fuck, they give you a sweet and they expect a fuck, well fuck all men fuck the lot of them" " amen to that" I said, I could feel her eyes stripping me naked, I looked at her and said " what?" it took her a full minute to ask me " don't you like men then?" I shook my head and looked at her tits, she looked down to where I was looking and began to undo the buttons of her tartan shirt, she pulled it open and pulled her bra down to show me her big tits, I looked at them and she had the biggest nipples that I have ever seen "Can I touch them?" I asked, she leaned closer to me and I fondled her big tits, I rolled her right nipple as it grew in my fingers "When are you stopping?" she asked, I looked at her big tits and said. "In about 5 minutes" she looked at the bed in the back of the cab and climbed onto it and began taking her clothes off, my hands were shaking the steering wheel, and my fanny seemed to have started without me.

Jade reached over my left shoulder and fondled my left tit and said "Nice tits, she then undid the top two buttons of my uniform and reached down into my bra and gripped my tit, she immediately began to roll my nipple driving me mad, I pulled into the lay by and pulled the curtains round, in under a minute I had my army boots off, and my uniform. In my bra and pants, I crawled into the bunk and her hand went straight into my pants "Ooohhh, I love shaved fannies " said Jade, she had me naked in seconds and those long fingers deep Inside my fanny, in no time at all she finger fucked me to orgasm, I soaked her fingers which she pulled out and sucked clean, lay on top of her I had my face and hands on those big tits Jade was a big strong woman, she put her hands on my shoulders and pushed me down her body until my face was on her hairless fanny. I buried my face between her legs, I sucked her long lips and flicked my tongue at her clit, she reached down and using two finger she parted her fanny lips and pulled them up slightly, I licked and sucked her clit, I then pushed two fingers into her opening and frigged her slowly at first, Jade suddenly became very vocal and thrust her hips as high as she could get them, I frigged her faster and took her to her orgasm, I pulled my fingers from her fanny and placed my mouth over her opening and then pushed my tongue deep into her fanny and lapped up her cum, she pulled me up so that I lay on top of her again, her eyes bore into mine when she said" you certainly know how to lick a fanny" her mouth was back on mine and her tongue was down my throat, her hand reached down to my fanny again, when she pushed those long fingers into me I returned the compliment and pushed two fingers into her fanny, we frigged each other to another orgasm, it was what it was, desperate, urgent sex that we both obviously needed badly.

We watched each other as we dressed and carried on our journey to Portsmouth, I dropped her off on the edge of the town with a promise to ring her, I watched her watching me in the wing mirror, I threw her phone number out of the window, it was what it was a good quick fuck, the first that I had had for months, "maybe I should start looking again", Sarah could feel the tingling in her fanny, " yes maybe I should".

Chapter 16

The gym is always a good place to make friends, I had been on a running machine for maybe 5 minutes when a young fit blonde woman, her hair cut really short, stepped onto the machine next to mine, she was soon matching my pace, "I'm Usula, are you new here?" she asked in a Polish or Czeck accent "I'm Sarah, and yes this is my first day" I could feel her eyes looking me up and down "you are very fit Sarah" she said " thank you" without looking at her " maybe we can get a drink later ?" she asked " maybe" I answered again without looking at her, taking the hint she moved off to try somewhere else, I moved to the steps, I was happy doing step ups when a woman two steps away said " I see that the dyke was trying to chat you up "I looked across at her, she was maybe the same age as me, slim and fit with her long black hair caught up with an elastic band, her hair bouncing each step she took, her tits were caught up in a sports bra" don't knock it until you have tried it"I said with a smile, she looked me up and down "do you mean that you are that way?" she asked "would it matter if I was?" I asked her, I could see her thinking about it, and said " no I don't suppose it would, I'm Ashley" she said "Sarah, nice to meet you " I answered, Ashley was deep in thought " can I ask you a question Sarah?" she asked, I looked over at her "you can ask me anything that you want" I said opening the door for her, she carried on " I can't imagine having sex with a woman, well what's it like?", I smiled at her and moved onto the next step to her so that I could speak quietly, "you see Ashley I can't imagine having sex with a man, when two women are together they have a fair idea what each other wants and what the others needs are, and a woman will keep going until her partner is satisfied, from what I have seen of men, with their rough faces and rough hands, the only person that they think of is themselves" she looked at me "so what you are saying is that you always, you know cum?" she asked I nodded " always" she went quiet for a good few minutes deep in thought " but how do you do it if you haven't got a cock?" I studied her closely, she could only be twenty or twenty one, the same age as me " if I ask you a question will you be honest with me, I have been honest with you" she nodded, guessing what I was going to ask her.

"How many times have you actually cum with a cock?" I asked, she blushed a deep red that travelled all the way down her chest " well never, but I can't see how you could do any better" I looked at her "Ashley, I could guarantee you multiple orgasms, probably more in one day than you have ever had" she was so embarrassed she walked away from me and began to lift weights but still facing me. We kept looking at one another, at one stage her nipples were rock hard when she looked down at them, she seemed to be shocked, but she looked at me to make sure that I had seen them, I had had enough so I went and got changed, I didn't see Ashley again which was a shame. I slung my bag over my shoulder and left and began walking down the road, when a white sports car pulled up by the side of me, the door opened and I looked in to see a smiling Ashley.

I got into the car and told her the way to my flat, when we were inside Ashley looked very nervously around, I went over to her and led her into the bathroom she stood there and let me undress her, her body was fit and hard from hours in the gym, her lower hair was trimmed and shaped like a strawberry, I stripped my clothes off and turned the shower on, I pulled her gently into the hot water, we stood tit to tit but not touching, I reached up and took a breast in each hand and rubbed the nipples until they were hard. I lowered my mouth to her to her right nipple and sucked it deep into my mouth, I then did the same to the other nipple When I pulled my lips from her hard nipple I reached down and took her hands and put them onto my breasts, Ashley watched her hands as they fondled my tits, I reached up with my left hand and put it to the back of her head and pulled her lips to mine, at the same time I pushed my tits into hers, she was very nervous for a second or two, when I pushed my tongue at her lips, she gave in and opened her mouth, she had reached the point where curiosity had got the better of her, we kissed for a very long time I had lowered my hand and now pulled her mound against mine, within seconds she was grinding against me, I turned the water down and went to my knees, her fanny was the most beautiful fanny I had ever seen, I pushed my mouth to her fanny, I reached behind her and pulled her hips forward, on my very first lick her legs opened and she gasped out loud, her hands came to the back of my head, I reached between her legs and pushed two fingers deep into her wet fanny, Ashley groaned out loud, her legs had become weak and were shaking, I frigged her and licked her to her orgasm, she rewarded me with her warm cum. When she had stopped shaking, I stood up and dried her hair, and then took my time drying her very fit body.

I enjoyed it when she dried me, I took the towel from her and dropped it to the floor, I then took her to the bed, as soon as we were in bed we were kissing hard our tongues fighting, her body telling me that she wanted more, I pulled her mound to mine and we ground against each other, after a minute or so I put my hand between her legs and rubbed the flat of my hand along her swollen fanny lips. Her fanny was very hot and I could feel on my hand where her fanny juice had seeped from her slit, I pushed two fingers deep into her and finger fucked her to orgasm number two. I began kissing her neck slowly making my way down to her tits, I spent a lot of time on her tits and then moved slowly down her stomach, I moved around and placed myself between her legs, I pushed her legs up to her chest exposing her beautiful fanny to the world, she moaned out loud as her fanny was now at my mercy, I placed my mouth onto her fanny I flicked my tongue up and down her slit, I then pushed my tongue as deep as I could into her fanny, I flicked my tongue up and down inside her fanny then pulled my tongue out and reached up and parted her fanny lips. I licked up and down with long slow strokes and looked up at her face. She had her eyes closed but she was in a state of ecstasy, I located her clit and as soon as my lips touched it I saw her head come up and look down at me. I sucked it hard and watched her cum again, that was orgasm number three.

I leaned over to my drawer by the bed and pulled out my thick purple vibrator. Turning it on and placing it to her clit, she moaned and lifted her head again to see what I was doing to her. I rubbed it all over her fanny, she was almost there again as I licked the head of the vibrator before I pushed it into her fanny, her whole body shot up momentarily and she flopped down onto the bed and lifted her hips as high as she could, her hips were bouncing up and down in time with her moans, orgasm number 5, I said to her " turn over Ashley" she rolled over onto her front, I rubbed my hands all over her beautiful body, before getting off the bed and strapping on my favourite 9 inch black cock. After I had lubricated that black cock I picked up the purple cock and pushed it into my own fanny, I climbed back onto the bed and lifted her bum into the air, I put that big black knob to her entrance and pushed it in, she gasped at the thickness as it stretched her, I gripped her hips and began to fuck her, she turned her face to me her eyes were closed and her mouth was the shape of a large egg, I rode her hard, I fucked her all the way through number 6 and was heading fast towards number 7. I pulled her back as I rammed that big black cock into her then eased her to number 7. I would have kept going but she had gone a bit limp so I eased that cock from her and let her slide down to the bed, she lay still, I stayed where I was and watched her cum seep from her fanny, she almost jumped from the bed when I rubbed my finger up her slit to get some of her cum, I licked my finger. I lay with her and we folded our arms around each other lovingly. I rubbed her back as she calmed down. She suddenly looked at me and said "But Sarah what about you, please show me how to pleasure you".

Chapter 17

We sat on the bed knee to knee and I showed her all of my strap on cocks and vibrators, she was shocked when she saw then size of the rubber cock that had been inside her fanny, I showed her how to touch a fanny, and how to lick a fanny and how to suck a clit. Ashley was fascinated by it all, she looked into my eyes all excited and asked. "That one you used on me, can I put it on and use it on you?" I smiled and said."Yes of course you can but you will have to lubricate it first." I helped her to put the straps on and showed her how to lubricate it, I leaned over and grabbed the end of the bed and spread my legs, Ashley moved up behind me and put that big cock to my slit, she pushed that big cock all the way in, which made me moan out loud, I told her to grip my hips, she gripped my hips and gave me a good fucking, I told when I had had enough and she stopped, when I turned around and looked at her, she was standing there with her eyes closed and her legs spread wide, her hips still moving back and forth, I picked up the purple vibrator and went behind her, I placed my hand onto her back and whispered " bend forward" she bent forward and I pushed that rubber cock into her fanny and fucked her to orgasm number 8. She stood up and hugged me "Thank you Sarah, I don't know how many times I have cum, but I want to cum some more, can I see you again?" all this was said with her naked body pressed into mine, and her mound pressed to mine, both of us moving gently against one another.

Ashley was ready for some more, her mound moved against me so I pulled away from her and strapped that big cock back on, I turned her around and told her to grip the bed the same as I had, I put that big black knob to her slit and pushed it in, I gripped her hips and gave her a good fucking, her face was turned to mine her eyes were closed and her mouth was stretched into a snarl, she began to shake the end of the bed, I rode her to yet another climax, what number I can't remember, when I pulled that cock from her fanny she turned round with tears running down her face " oh Sarah, I can't believe it I have cum so many times I have lost count, never in my life have I received so much pleasure, please tell me that I can see you again".

I said "You can see me anytime you want, I will give you my number you only have to ring me" we arranged for her to come back around the next evening at 7, I walked her to the front door, we kissed long and hard before she finally left. At work the next day I had numerous texts from Ashley the funniest was this one "I have been shopping today, in the shop they had these white balls on a piece of nylon, I could not for the life of me figure out what they were for so I asked the assistant. She told me what they were for and even offered to put them in for me, she must have been 70, see ya later X". The text brought a smile to my face, I couldn't wait for later, I had bought a bottle of red wine and a few nibbles and I counted the minutes`

Ashley arrived just before 7, when I opened the door she almost threw herself at me, her tongue was down my throat, she wore a long gold necklace under a beige mac, in her right hand she had a white carrier bag "I've bought you a gift. I don't know what some of them are but I am sure that we will figure it out". We sat in the living room with a glass of wine and I asked if I could take her coat, she stood and undid the buttons slowly one by one, when she pulled her mac open to show me not only her naked body but also her naked fanny " I thought I would bring you a surprise" she said, I held her coat and looked her over, I looked long and hard at her fanny, she parted her legs and pushed her hips forward, I dropped her coat onto a chair and dropped to my knees in front of her, she leant back against the wall and parted her thighs, I licked her naked fanny from end to end, she almost sank to the floor, she was so aroused, I made it quick for her by exposing her clit and sucking it hard, she pushed her hips at me and let go, I lapped up her offerings with relish. When I looked up at her she was almost in tears, the way her pelvis was moving and the vacant look on her face, she was either still coming or coming again, I reached forward and pushed two fingers into her fanny and frigged her hard and as fast as I could, her knees parted even further, she could see nothing as her eyes were glazed over, her hands were clenched by her side, her cum was running down my hand and dripping off my wrist there was so much of it, she whispered something, I didn't know what and she then grabbed my wrist and whispered "please stop" when I pulled my fingers out she sank to the floor and her head slumped to her chest, silent tears fell to the floor.

I stood and fetched her wine, when I offered it to her she just looked at me, her eyes just stared at me "I've never cum like that ever before Sarah, you have changed me into a desperate woman, you would only have to touch my hand and I would cum again" I took her hand and led her to the settee, I put a towel under her bum as she was still oozing cum " please kiss me" she whispered, I stood and undressed in front of her, she watched each and every move that I made, I sat back down and we fondled a lot, until she pulled away from me and reached for the carrier bag" I've bought you a gift." She hid it behind her back and stood up and said "Open your legs and bring your bum to the edge of the settee" I did as I was told, she brought this bright silver implement from behind her back. I called it an implement but it was nothing like I had ever seen before it was 9 inches long with silver balls inside it, on the base was a square box, the whole thing looked like a rocket, protruding from the top was a stiff piece of rubber about three inches long, slightly angled upwards on the end was a rubber, V she pushed it to my fanny lips and said "the woman in the shop said if you don't cum with this then you are dead" she pushed it into me and switched it on, I felt my eyes open wide, it turned round and round the same as a drill would, the silver balls vibrated inside the vibrator and the rubber thing, well every time she pushed it forward it rammed into my clit, I pushed forward so much my ass was hanging off the settee, this was very rare for me, I came in under a minute, she let me calm down and switched it off but left it buried fully inside me, she reached for the bag, she looked at me and put her finger to her lips as if thinking and dipped her hand into the bag, she turned her back to me and did something, she looked back at me " close your eyes and put your bum back onto the settee and pull your knees back" I did as I was told, I felt her hot breath on my fanny which told me she was between my legs.

I felt her hand below the vibrator, I jumped when she touched my bum hole "relax Sarah" she said as she pushed something into my bum hole, it was quite thick but not too thick, it was the length, it was a long way inside, I felt her changing her position "apparently this will blow your mind" she said, my eyes were still closed as she switched them both on at the same time, The thing in my fanny went around and around, but the thing up my ass, well the deepest two inches were going around and around as a finger would, the thing in my fanny began to go even faster, I felt myself gasp out loud, she fucked me slowly but deliberately with that spinning thing up my fanny, I came again, I looked as Ashley, she was smiling broadly as she watched my face. After the third orgasm I had to tell her to stop, she pulled the thing out of my fanny, the bottom three inches by the handle was covered in thick white cum, the thing up my ass still moved around and around, I thought she had forgotten it, but she did turn it off, when she pulled it out and it was as thick as a broom handle, she showed it to me, the end two inches moved slowly in a circular motion, she pulled a tissue from a box on the table and laid the implements onto the tissue, she reached

for then carrier bag and asked " are you ready for
some more" I nodded and she pulled out a string of
white balls, "stand up and bend over," I did as she
said " spread your feet" I looked back as she
lubricated the balls, they were just a bit smaller than
a table tennis ball, she held my fanny lips open and
rubbed the ball up and down my fanny before
slipping the balls deep into me, she pushed four
balls deep into me, she then squirted some lubricant
onto my bum hole and slowly pushed a ball up my
ass, and then a second ball went in, she told me to
stand up and I burst out laughing, she gave me a
string of balls for herself and bent over.

I did to her as she had done to me, she giggled
as she stood up straight, she took my hand and we
walked around the room, we giggled out loud, she
then grabbed me around the waist and jumped up
and down, it was great fun, I wanted to walk up and
down the stairs, but we couldn't do that naked so I
had a brainwave and got the step ladders out, that
was great fun, we took it in turns, after a short
while we had to stop, things were tricky for us
when we tried to getting the fuckers out, the ones

from the fanny came out ok it was the ones up the ass, it was like pulling a cork from a wine bottle, when we were both free of balls we sat on the settee and relaxed. We drank some wine before I picked the new vibrator up and examined it. I switched it on, it was a clever piece of kit and very well made, I put it to Ashley's nipple, we both sat and watched her nipple as it grew, I looked at my lover and said "would you like to get onto your hands and knees madam?", she placed her glass on to the table and dropped to the floor, I pushed the vibrator inside her to its fullest, I had to make sure the clit bit was in position but when I finally got the thing going I could see that I didn't need to, when I switched it on the effect was instant, her knees seemed to give way as she said " oh, fuck, oh fuck", I used it as I would use a normal vibrator in and out, she came twice before asking me to stop,

We spent the night together and made love at various time throughout the night, we parted in the morning with a kiss that made us both sopping wet. When I arrived at work I was called into the main office and was told that I was going to Denmark for two weeks for some special duties, and I would be leaving that morning. I sent Ashley a text and told her, I was a bit disappointed but wish me well and I would count the hours until I returned home.

Chapter 18

I enjoyed the work in Denmark, I like the people and the new open roads. Ashley texted me all the time for the first few days, she sent me one text telling that she went shopping with all of the white balls inserted in her lower holes. She said that she went on a bus ride and the speed humps made her laugh out loud, over the next few days the texts were not so regular. She also said that she had begun going back to the gym to pass the time. The text messages stopped all together halfway through the second week.

I arrived home on the Monday evening and rang Ashley to find that the number was no longer in use, so I changed and went to the gym. When I walked in the first thing I saw was Ashley helping the dyke with the blonde hair, Ashley looked at me and mouthed "Sorry" and ran into the toilets, the dyke stood and smiled at me. I don't mind losing, it has happened before a few times before and it will probably happen in the future, what pisses me off is arrogance. I walked over to the dyke just as she opened her mouth to speak, I caught her with an uppercut to the chin, she went down on her ass and then fell backwards, and lay spark out. I was banned from the gym, but when I walked out, I left to a round of applause.

Chapter 19

I decided to take up running so she joined a group of women that went out running two nights a week and they ran 6 miles both nights, perfect. The women were friendly enough, it was on the third night that I noticed that the same woman had ran behind me each time that we had gone running. She was black and tall and wore a hoody and a baggy top. The next time I was getting ready to go running when the phone rang. I answered it to find a nervous Ashley on the line " Sarah I'm sorry for what I have done to you, she wouldn't leave me alone, she kept on and on, it happened on the Thursday night after gym, she waited by the car for me, she began kissing me and she got my tits out and well, I stopped contacting you because I felt guilty, I want you back Sarah, I love you." What could I say? "if you loved me you would not have cheated, goodbye" as far as I'm concerned it was all over.

Back running on a Tuesday evening yet again I was being followed by my black stalker, it was a bit strange, "Do I ignore it or do I say something?"

I knew that I would have to think about it. That's what I did and after half an hour I had a plan. On the Thursday evening I arrived late, I waited for the women to set off and she then I followed, catching up slowly I dropped in behind my stalker. She was tall and slim but that is all I can tell you about her, after a while she glanced back to see who was following her so closely. She tried speeding up, but I stayed right behind her. The stalker then moved out to the outside of the group, again I stayed right behind her, she gave up trying to loose me and dropped back into the inside and I dropped in behind her.

When we had all finished the run and we were doing our stretching I walked over to her and stood directly in front of her "unnerving isn't it, being followed" I said. She looked at me and asked "Can we get a drink?" We walked to the nearest pub and I went to the bar and bought a bottle of red wine, with two glasses and sat down opposite her. She pulled her hoody back to show me that she was a really beautiful woman. Aged around mid twenties, her eyes were chocolate brown and her teeth were the whitest I had ever seen. "Tell me then, why you were running behind me?" she looked at me and thought about her answer, she began. "First I will tell you my name, my name is Wilin, and I do not know how to tell you what is going on in my head, simply because I am not sure myself, but let me try. You see I was engaged to a man who I had been with for five years, even though I had some pleasure from the sex that we had it was still disappointing. I then went to a house party at a friend of mine, and at this party. I call it a party there was no dancing, it was just standing around talking. A woman arrived later in the evening with all of these women's toys, I had never seen anything like it before, I handled some of the toys, it was when a film was put on the television involving two women that I began to doubt my sexuality. You see just watching those women made me so wet, I had to go to the toilet and, well you know. Anyway I bought one of the toys, I then looked on the computer and found various sites where I could strip naked and watch the women on the computer, I would then use the toy on myself.

Using the sex toy was better than any sex I have ever had with a man. I talked to a friend who has lived with the same woman for years, the things that she told me, well, she certainly made me think. As for following you so closely, I think you are a beautiful woman. I also think that your body is perfect, but if you had not done what you have done tonight, I would never have had the nerve to talk to you." I sat and looked at her and poured her another drink. "My name is Sarah, what makes you think that I like women?" I asked, she smiled at me. "I do not know if you like women, I do not know how I can tell, the last thing I want to do is to make you angry, I can only hope" she said. I studied her closely but did not speak for a while, I then said "if I said I had a bottle of red at my flat, and would you like to help me drink it, what would you say?" she looked me in the eyes and said "when are we leaving".

We were sitting on my settee, I had taken off her hoody and her nipples were rock hard. I reached over and stroked her left nipple, the nipple grew even harder, she looked at me " would you like me to take my top off" I nodded, she gripped her top and pulled it over her head, she then removed her sports bra, her tits were perfect, they were firm to the touch, her nipples were long and thick, I put my mouth to her left nipple and sucked most of her tit into my mouth, I moved to her other breast and did the same, when I looked into her face, her eyes were closed and her mouth was slightly open, I stopped what I was doing and said " Wilyn would you like me to strip you naked and pleasure you, that way you won't have to worry if you are doing the right thing ?" She nodded and said "Call me Wyn please" I stood up and pulled her up to her feet. I knelt down and undid her laces, she kicked her trainers off then lifted each foot as I removed her socks. I pulled her joggers down and took them off. She had on some skin tight running shorts. I put my fingers into the top of her shorts and pulled them down an inch, then placed my mouth to her fanny through her running shorts, her thighs instantly parted and a deep moan escaped her throat and her hands gripped the back of my head, I used my teeth through the material as I chewed her fanny, I looked up at her and she was so close I decided to keep going, only I lifted my hand and rubbed my finger hard along her lower fanny, I felt her cum as she pushed her fanny at me, I kept her going until she was through it. I stood up and took her to the door. I leaned her against the door and went onto tip toe and pushed my lips to hers, her thick black lips were soft and warm, her tongue was small, pink and hard, we began to rub our mounds together, I took a boob in each hand and fondled them roughly, moans and groans were escaping from her all the time. I lowered my hands and gripped the tops of her remaining clothes and began pushing them down. I pushed them down far enough so that her mound was exposed then pushed my mound to hers. She went mad.

"Please make me cum." I pushed her shorts and pants down to the floor, I looked at her fanny, I must say that I had not seen a prettier fanny, her short black curly hair has been trimmed to leave a tiny patch at the top of her fanny, her fanny lips were short and crinkly, I pushed her thighs apart and put my mouth to her lower lips, at my first touch she shuddered and moaned out loud, I reached up and parted her dark fanny lips, I put my tongue to her pinkness and flicked the whole length of her fanny, her hips were being pushed further and further towards me. I flicked her clit as fast as I could. I puckered my lips and placed them onto her long clit, I sucked it between my lips, there was enough clit, that I could flick it with my tongue, she was on the verge of screaming, I felt her body tense as she came, her knees were moving in and out as she moaned, she gripped the back of my head and fucked herself against my mouth. I reached forward and pushed two fingers into her fanny, I finger fucked her as fast as I could, she came again, her whole body was shaking, I lifted her left leg up and pushed my mouth over her fanny and sucked for all I was worth, her legs were gone now, if she had not been leaning against the wall she would have been on her knees on the floor. I pulled away from her and looked at her, she was in a state of complete disarray, she looked like a spider that had been squashed against the wall, I eased from the wall and took her to my bedroom and she flopped onto the bed. I left the room and stripped naked put the big black vibrator on and lubricated it then walked back into the bedroom. She had not moved a muscle, I took hold of her legs and eased her round towards me pulled her body towards me and opened her long legs. She didn't even look at me, she was totally relaxed as I pushed that thick black cock into her, the only response from her that that rubber cock had entered her body, was a grunt and as soon as I began fucking her, she gripped the bed clothes and then did something I had not seen before, she spread her long slim legs as if she was doing the splits. I rammed that cock into her as hard and as fast as I could, I watched her cum at least three times before she whispered for me to stop.

As soon as that black cock had left her fanny, she reached for me and pulled me down to her, she pushed those thick lips against mine and kissed me passionately almost sucking the soul out of me. She trembled as she held me, tears ran down her face, and her chest began to heave. When she began to settle down, she looked at the black cock that had been inside her, she pushed me onto my back and licked it clean, she finished up by giving it a blow job, she kissed me upwards from that cock to my lips, paying a lot of attention to my tits on the way, she reached her left hand to the base of the cock and stretched her fingers between the straps and stroked my wet fanny lips, she changed position and undid the straps that held the cock on. She pulled it off and then eased my legs apart she lowered those soft lips to my fanny, for someone who has never licked a fanny before she certainly made a good job of it, when she pushed her fingers into me she made me groan out loud, they were the longest fingers that I have had the pleasure to have inside me, I could have those fingers inside of me for the rest of my life, they were better than any rubber cock ever made.

She picked the cock up and strapped it around her hips, she lay me on my back and pulled me to her, she used her own spit on her hand to lubricate the cock, she gave me the fucking of my life, she turned me over and kept going until I surrendered, she pulled out of me and turned me onto my back

and licked me dry, she finished me off by licking
me from end to end, her tongue seemed to be rough
like that of a lion, over and over that tongue licked
me, I was covered in goose bumps, this was an all a
new experience for me. We lay in bed together and
Wyn seemed to take control now we were in bed, I
seemed to be spell bound, she seemed to be doing
things to me that no-one had ever done to me
before, I seemed to be in a permanent state of
orgasm. I don't know what happened but when I
woke up in the morning, she was gone, my clothes
were folded and left on a chair, the black cock had
been washed and put away, the glasses had been
washed up, it was as if she had not been there at all,
I had no contact number for her, nothing.

I went running for the next three weeks on the
dark winters evenings without seeing my tall dark
lover, I began to believe that it was a dream, that
the whole event did not happen at all, I turned up
late for the next meet and had to run fast to catch
up, we had done maybe three miles before I heard
the familiar sound behind me, I glanced behind me
to see a brilliant set of white teeth, as she smiled at

me from the dark, when we passed the entrance to the car park she reached out for my hand and pulled me off the pavement. We went down a short lane to a row of cottages. Wyn dragged me into the third cottage, pushing me before her and closed the door. "Have you just kidnapped me?" I asked, she pulled her hoody back and smiled at me, " I had to talk to you, and I was not sure that if I had asked you, whether you would have come or not" she led the way into the living room and opened a bottle of wine, " please take a seat" she said and passed me a glass of wine, we looked at one another as we held our glasses to our mouths " well, what do you want to talk about?" she swirled her wine around in her glass "Sarah, you have confused me, sexually you see I had thought about lesbian sex for a long time, I have been sort of engaged to Greg for over a year now and I think that I would have been happy being married to him, that is until our night together, you see the problem for me is this, when I think of Greg, not much happens but when I think of you, I am instantly wet, and I want to come over and let you fuck me to death and for me to do the same to you" she said.

I looked at her "that's all well and good, but do you think that you have treated me fairly? You go out of your way to pick me up and fulfill your wild fantasy but what about me? You leave without a word, without leaving any contact details and you have dragged me into here and what now? We end up in bed and fuck each other, is that what you have in mind, well if that is the case, then it ain't going to happen." She looked down into her lap, and reached out and lightly brushed her finger tips along my arm, I was instantly covered in goose bumps, when she did it again my nipples were the hardest I have ever known them, and my fanny was so wet I would have to go to the toilet and sort myself out, Wyn reached out and rubbed the tip of her finger around my left nipple, a loud moan escaped from me, I reached up and pulled her finger from my nipple and stood to go, she looked up at me and reached out one of her long fingers and touched the top of my fanny and slid in down my slit, my legs opened on their own as she did it again, once more and I would cum, I moved away from her even though I wanted her badly, I will not be treated like this, I turned around and walked out of the front door, and out of her life forever, saying that I did give myself a good seeing to with my purple vibrator as soon as I reached home.

Chapter 20

The commanding officer called me into his office first thing Monday morning and asked me if I would be prepared to travel to Germany for three months and teach an intake of recruits hgv 1driving. I jumped at the chance and made my plans to fly out in two days. I was greeted at the airport by SGT Heather Thorne, she drove us back to the base. Heather was a good looking woman with blue eyes and curly brown hair with blonde highlights, she seemed to have a lot of muscle for a woman, but there was no doubt she was fit. As you read this you may think that I am bit of a tart, well maybe I am but be honest if you were writing these words wouldn't you make yourself out to be lucky with women, even if it meant making yourself out to be a tart.

I helped SGT Thorne to set up the reversing course, we then drove around the local area mapping out routes. We stopped in a café and decided we would need to take the candidates on a nine hour drive taking two candidates each. We spent the rest of the day sorting out paperwork. When it was time to finish for the day SGT Thorne said "bring an overnight bag tomorrow we are going on a trip". When I asked where we were going, she said simply "Berlin." Wow I couldn't wait, I was suddenly like a little school kid, "oh, and wear civilian clothes" she instructed. When I arrived at work the next day with my overnight bag. SGT Thorne was standing by a brand new black Audi A6 and when I looked at the woman standing by the side of the car I couldn't get my breath. Her hair hung down her back and she had on a blue summer dress and a pair of blue slip on shoes. I couldn't swear to it but I don't think she was wearing a bra, "Morning Sarge" I said. She smiled and said "My name is Heather when we are in civvies" she was a very confident driver as she drove the powerful car along the Auto Bahn, we chatted like old friends on the journey to Berlin. She drove around the city with ease and pulled into a large car park, looking at me she said "Time for some shopping." We spent four hours shopping, she made me buy a dress which I didn't want, but she insisted, she drove to the hotel, [a very good hotel] and she said "when you have showered and done your face, put your new dress on".

I waited in the foyer for her and had to look twice when she walked towards me, she had her hair bunched on the side of her head, she wore a white dress that I could see through, she wore a white thong and no bra, we looked each other up and down both smiling at what the other saw, she walked up to me and kissed me on the lips and said " you look bloody good" she took my arm and led me from the hotel, I went to ask her where we were going, but she put her finger to my lips " surprise", she took me to the best show in town where we ate five courses and drank champagne all night. Heather took my hand halfway through the evening and held it until I went to the loo two hours later, when I returned to sit back down she had moved my chair so that it was touching hers. As soon as I sat down she placed her hand on my leg, as the show went on she moved her hand higher, she looked at me as her little finger stroked my fanny, " do you mind ?" she whispered as she licked my ear, we were surrounded by other people so I wasn't sure how to answer so I parted my legs, she slid her finger the length of my fanny, I then pulled her finger from my fanny and held her hand, she put her mouth to my ear and said " come to the loo with me" I turned and looked at her and said " can't you wait?." She looked hurt and sat quiet for the rest of the show, we travelled back to the hotel in silence. We went back to our rooms and slept on our own, the next morning I left her a note in reception and caught a train back to base.

As soon as I returned to base I asked to be returned to the UK I was called into the C.O's office and asked why I wanted to return home so soon, when I said that I would rather not say, just that it would be better if I returned home, he asked me to wait where I was for a few minutes, he then left the room, a few minutes later there was a tap on the door and a Captain Eva Jennings entered the room " hello Sarah do you mind if I join you for a chat?" she said and without me answering she sat opposite me. "Now Sarah I understand that you want to return home after only three days, can you tell me why?" I looked at her and said "I would rather not say", she said " we know that there is a problem with a certain member of staff, because there have been things said about a female person in authority. This person has put new female recruits under pressure to sleep with her and we are looking for someone strong willed enough to put a stop to this, you see the problem with new female recruits is that they can be influenced to change their minds.

We know that you went to Berlin with this person in her car and came back alone on the train, so it is obvious that something has happened that has upset you, so will you be prepared to help us out with this problem". I thought about it for a few minutes, and said I needed time to think about it, Eva Jennings shook her head, " we have been trying to remove her on for a long time Sarah" I stood up and said that I would think about it and get back to them the next day, I left the office and went to my room, when I opened the door Heather was sat on my bed, she jumped up " Sarah, I'm sorry for the way that I acted, I sometimes get a little bit impatient, and I can't help myself, I'm so sorry for the way I acted" I looked at her "you only had to wait until we got back to the hotel and I would have slept with you willingly, but you can't bully people Heather, it's just not normal." Heather went and looked out of the window "I can't help myself Sarah" I knew then that I had to do something " please tell me you are staying Sarah", I shook my head and pushed her out of the door.

The next day I made a complaint and Heather was arrested and charged with sexual assault, she was shipped back to Portsmouth for a court marshal, and I was promoted and asked to take on the training of the new female drivers. It was after maybe 6 months that I felt a little bit sorry for Heather because here am I in her position and two new young women every two weeks, who look up to you, it would be easy to become involved, sexual offers have been made towards me but I have always refused because at the moment all I want to do is to concentrate on my work.

Chapter 21

How time flies I am sat on a train heading north to Perth in Scotland to collect a new lorry, deep In thought I think back to the last time I had any sex [with another person] and it must be getting on for 9 months, to be honest the last twice I've had any female contact, they have gone dramatically wrong and to be honest I'm not sure that I can be bothered, I am brought out of my depressing thoughts by a slightly older army sergeant, by older I guessed her age to be 30 years old, who has dropped into the seat opposite, she asked "fancy a bit of company?", she put her hand out "I'm Stella" with the introductions out of the way , we chatted about all sorts of military stuff from our uniforms to the latest computers, we seemed to get on well and when she was about to leave she asked if we could keep in touch and I agreed as I found her to be fun, I didn't think it would be anything other than friendship, and I was fine with that, we spoke on skype every week for the next5 months and when Stella asked me if I wanted to go on holiday with her, when I said "yes " I sort of shocked myself after I had kept myself to myself for so long, it had been a long time since the last time I had been on holiday, Stella said that she would sort everything out and all I had to do was pack for the sunshine, she arranged everything, all I had to do was give her a check at the end of the holiday.

I arrived at the airport in plenty of time and when Stella walked towards me she looked completely different, she had lost some weight and dyed her hair blonde and had it styled, she was braless in a thin yellow dress, we air kissed as she looked me over, I had a blue skirt and a white tea shirt, sandals and just looking at each other was enough we were full of smiles for each other, she suggested we get a coffee, it was when we were drinking our drinks that she told me that we were going to the Caribbean, I became very excited as I had never had such a holiday before, we were sat on the plane and she took my hand as she was so excited, she gripped my hand firmer as the plane lifted off, it was at this point that she hinted at some sort of relationship which was fine with me as I liked her a lot, we sort of skirted around it for a while when she said "I've booked us a double room, I hope that is ok with you?" I said that I had hoped that she would have, we had a few drinks on the plane and Stella became a little bit frisky, as we were in a twin seat at the back of plane, I suppose that if we were very careful we may be able to get away with certain things, Stella whispered " can you undo your skirt?" my skirt did up at the back, so I had a good look around, I pushed my shoulders into the seat and lifted my bum, I twirled my skirt around and undid it, when I sat back down Stella put her cardigan into my lap and pushed her hand inside my skirt and down to my fanny, she ran her fingers along my slit, she tried all ways to get at my wet fanny, she finally whispered " move your bum forward" I moved my bum forward slowly, as soon as she could get to the top of my pants she pushed her hand inside my pants down to my naked fanny, as soon as she touched my nakedness, her eyes went very big, she whispered " I can't wait to get my tongue into your naked fanny" she then pushed her tongue into my ear and her fingers as far as she could inside my fanny, and then began to frig me.

My legs were at full stretch, well as far as my skirt would allow, she watched me closely as I came on her fingers, she kept her fingers moving inside me as she whispered " do you want me to make you cum again?" no-one was watching us so I nodded and pushed my lips to hers, briefly and felt her right breast, we stared intently at one another, she said quietly " I wish I could fuck you properly" I pulled her hand from my skirt and looking round and seeing no-one looking I put my hands up my skirt and pulled my wet pants down and off, Stella grabbed them and shoved them into her pocket, I spread her cardigan over my lap and hitched my skirt up, my fanny was now easy for her to get at, she searched in her bag and came out with a silver tube that holds a cigar " for emergences" she said she reached under the cardigan and rubbed that tube up and down my slit, she dipped the tube into my fanny and fucked me with it, I came silently on that tube, she then left it inside me.

Stella moved round on the seat and lifted her right knee up onto the seat, she hitched her dress up her right side, she reached under the cardigan and pulled the tube out of my fanny, she pushed it into her mouth and sucked my cum from it, she then passed it to me and lifted her dress up. I pushed my skirt back down and put the cardigan over my arm as I sought out her naked fanny, as soon as I touched her fanny she lifted her hips up, i pushed two fingers into her, watching that no-one could see us I proceeded to finger fuck her to her orgasm, we almost got caught as she grunted when she came, I pulled my fingers from her and sucked them clean, we decided to behave for the rest of the flight and giggled like a couple of innocent school girls.

The hotel called The Golden Sands was rated 5 star and first rate, the first place that they were on their own was in the lift, as soon as the doors were closed they had their tongues down each other's throats, when the bell in the lift rang they pulled apart, they found their room and entered they dropped their cases and stripped each other naked, Sarah pushed Stella back against the door and I dropped to my knees and pushed my mouth to my new lovers swollen fanny, Stella grabbed the back of my head and ground her hips into my mouth, she was a very vocal lover, as she came she almost screamed out loud, I sucked up what she had to offer, and then stood and pushed my salty lips to hers, she couldn't wait for me to do anything else to her, she pushed away from the door and grabbed my hand and took me to the bed, she pushed me onto the bed and pushed her mouth to my fanny, I can honestly say this about Stella she sure knows how to suck a fanny, it was as if someone had turned the spunk tap on inside me, I came, and came again and again, I would say something else about Stella, she has the longest tongue in the world, the time was about 11 am, we finally stopped fucking at 7 pm, I think that that was only because we were so hungry.

We left the hotel and searched for somewhere nice to eat, we found a fish restaurant on the golden beach, that was really very special, the staff were great and the food was brilliant, the chef Bradley cooked the food at our table, and when we had finished eating, we were the last customers and the three staff member came and sat with us and brought some bottles of rum, we sat and chatted about England, and what it is like to live there, they all said that they wanted to live in England which I couldn't understand, as where we were sat now, with the deep blue sea and the golden sands, Bradley had the deepest sexiest voice I had ever heard, he said " there is tings going on around here that you don't understand, all the drugs and the drug dealers coming around every day trying to get us to sell the drugs for them, and we ain't going to do it" by the end of the evening we felt really sorry for them as we walked shoeless, hand in hand along the beautiful sand, back towards the hotel, sat on a wall we watched the sun go down, even though it was getting dark it was still hot, this was pure paradise.

Lay on top of the bed because of the heat, Stella took control and made love to me for hours, what made it even more special was the glass in the ceiling, I could see more stars in the royal blue sky than I had ever seen back in England, the next day we swam out to a pontoon that was a long way from the beach, we stripped naked and lay in the sun, Stella lay with her arm lazily draped over me, we made love under the hot sun and clear blue sky's, if there is anything better than this, I hope that I find it one day.

The holiday as ever was over to quick and when I offered to pay my share of the holiday Stella smiled and said " I don't want your money my love, I have more money that I know what to with, I live in a big house and if you want to live with me, you are welcome my love, we kissed at the railway station as Stella boarded her train to Oxford, we agreed to speak in the week, and we would spend our weekends together, yes I was in love again, in my head I made plans for the future, I had a year left to do in my service, but I had the option to stay on if I wanted to, but I could live with Stella and be happy.

I had a parcel arrive for me a week later, I left the parcel on my bed until I finished work that day, I was totally shocked when I opened the parcel, inside were three best seller books, books that I had seen on the book shelves, all with the picture of my lover on the back cover, I could not get my breath, all the books were signed " to my lover, whom I love deeply, Stella. I picked up the first book called " Love under the clear blue skies" and began reading, I would not normally read this sort of book, but to be honest, I really began to enjoy it, the way that she described the female sex scenes was very clever, and reading between the lines this book was in fact a true story, which make me wonder if I will be the star in the next book, I can see the title now " love in the Caribbean".

Contact between Stella and I had been restricted to the phone and computer, but I have become excited as I am about to head of to Oxford to see my lover, I have packed my overnight case, the first thing into my case were my sex toys, I have bought a double ender, having seen one used by Si and Joe, I quite fancied trying it out myself, I have left it in the wrapping so that Stella could see that it was brand new, on arrival in oxford, I was about to get in a taxi, when I bought a large bunch of flowers for my lover. When the taxi pulled up outside her house, I was shocked as the house was huge, standing on its own the house had three stories and a most beautiful garden, Stella opened the door and smiled broadly at me, the taxi left and I went to my lover, she looked good in a light blue dress, as soon as I entered the house she took my case and then took me into her arms and kissed me deeply, " god I've missed you" she said, as she took my hand and gave me a tour of the ground floor, Stella had spent a fortune on her house, the kitchen for example had been hand made. She hesitated at the foot of the stairs and said "I will show you up there later, I have a little surprise for you up there, but that is for later" she smiled and took me into the conservatory which was full of cane furniture, the view out of the windows were of a large well kept garden, that was walled in, Stella took me in her arms and eased me back against a glass topped wicker table, she put her hands to the bottom of my cream top and pulled it up and over my head, she dropped it on to a chair and rubbed my breasts through my bra before reaching behind me and released my tits.

She fondled my tits and lowered her mouth to

my right tit, she sucked my nipple deep into her mouth, her hands went to the button at the back of my skirt, she undid it, then undid the zip, I eased myself forward and let it fall to the floor, my tiny white thong was sopping wet as she eased the thong down my legs, standing there naked she eased my bottom onto the cold glass, we kissed deeply I had my hands on the back of her head, our tongues were dancing with one another, she pulled away from me and said" lay back for me, let me pleasure you", I lay back on the table and opened my legs, Stella buried her face between my legs, her tongue licked my fanny from bottom to top, very slowly at the top she sucked my lower lips and flicked he tongue at my clit, I reached down and using two fingers I parted my fanny lips, she took full advantage of this and sucked my clit for all she was worth, she pushed two fingers deep into my fanny and finger fucked me to orgasm, as soon as I drenched her fingers, she then pulled her fingers out and licked them clean, she then pushed her long tongue deep into my fanny searching for more of my cum.

Stella stood up and lifted her dress over her

head to reveal her naked body, she then did something that I had not experienced before, she lifted her right leg and put it over the top of my left leg, she then pushed her fanny against mine, she began to rub her fanny up and down mine, I moved opposite to her so that our fannies were pushed hard against each other the faster we became the louder we both became, I have to admit that I came noisily sooner than Stella but i kept going for her, she closed her eyes as her hips moved even faster, loud moans escaped from her throat, I lay there and watched her going through her orgasm, she finished herself off with slow deliberate movements, finished she stood there with her throbbing fanny pressed to mine, she looked down at me, and said "I want to take you upstairs to my special room and fuck you stupid" I smiled up at her and said " lead on".

She took my hand and led me upstairs, we reached a door and Stella stood with her hand on the door handle, she looked at me and said " I have never shown another living person into this room, so that will tell you how special you are to me" I smiled at her as she opened the door and led me inside. The room was covered in narrow shelves and on each shelf lay a different type of vibrator, whip, restraints, lubricants and above the fireplace the shelves were full of strap on cocks, Stella smiled at me and said " you choose" I looked all of the cocks over but my eyes were drawn to this really thick purple cock with a big knob on it, I reached up and took it off the shelf and passed it to her, " good choice" she said, as she eased the straps up her legs and clipped it on, when she adjusted the straps she said " I think we had better have some lubricant for this big cock, we moved around the room to another set of shelves, there was every kind of lubricant that you could think of, there must have been 12 different flavours, a few different colours and lots of bottles that all do different things, I chose a strawberry flavoured lube, which made Stella smile she put some of the lube on her hands and rubbed the lube all over the rubber cock that she had strapped to her hips, she pushed me down to my knees and pushed the cock at my mouth, I did the best that I could and sucked that cock, as she began to fuck my mouth, pushing deeper all the time, when she was getting close to choking me, I pulled away from her, she took me to the bed, and said " are you feeling adventurous ?" I shrugged, so she took me to the end of the bed and placed me in between the two posts of the bed, the first thing she did was say " if at any time you want me to stop just say so" she put a blind fold around my eyes first, she then tied each ankle to the bottom of the bed posts, she then bent me over and tied my hands to the posts at the top of the bed, I must say that I was a little bit scared, but excitedly so.

I heard her moving around the room, whistling to herself, I heard her picking things up and putting them down again, I heard her walk back towards me, I felt her mouth by my ear " have you ever been punished before?" asked Stella, I shook my head she then asked " would you like to be punished ?" now when she spoke her lips were touching my ear, I nodded nervously, not quite knowing what to expect, she moved away from me, all went quiet as she stood still, my body was trembling all over, I eventually said "Stella, are you there?" she never spoke for at least a minute " I was stood looking at you, I cant make up my mind whether to fuck you first, I'm just rubbing some more lubricant on this thick cock, I don't think I could take this thick cock, but I will happily fuck you with it," she then pushed the cock to my fanny lips, I was disappointed when she pulled away, I jumped when I was struck across the ass cheeks with some sort of whip "ouch" I shouted her mouth came to my ear "did that make you jump my little lover?" I nodded, she then whispered " you can punish me after" she moved away from me, I jumped again when I felt her tongue on my exposed fanny, she licked me twice and I almost came on the spot, If I am honest I was beginning to feel a little bit scared, she must have sensed this as she put that thick cock to my fanny lips and pushed forward, I was stretched wide when that thick cock entered me, Stella reached over and undid my hands, I immediately felt relieved, she gripped my hips and began fucking me.

Stella gave me a real good fucking, I came a lot and eventually I had to tell her to stop. She stopped and released my feet, I slumped onto the bed and curled up Stella folded herself around me and held me tight, "I'm sorry Sarah, I didn't mean to frighten you" I slept for a short while, when I stirred she was there, she seemed worried " are you ok Sarah?" she asked me, I nodded " I'm sorry I was such a wimp, only this is all knew to me" she pulled me from the bed and taking my hand she led me from the room and down stairs, into the kitchen she sat me down on a stool and put the kettle on, she made us both a coffee and sat opposite me, " I'm sorry Sarah, do you forgive me?" she asked, I reached out for her hand and said " you are already forgiven" i smiled. Stella then said "shall we forget my special room, and be normal lovers " I looked at her and said " oh no you don't, I want my revenge up there" as soon as we had finished our coffee she took my hand and led me to the stairs, she ran up the stairs dragging me closely behind her, she walked into the room and stood there, " where do you want me?" I looked around the room and spotted something I had not noticed before, there were two hooks on the wall, and when I reached up and they were the right height for my lover, so I moved a chair to the hooks and tied Stella wrists to the hooks I looked at her and could see that something was missing so I walked around the

room looking for something, not being sure what I
was looking for.

I left her hanging there and ran down the
stairs, looked in all of the rooms until I found
something that I could use, I found a golf club, just
the one, why she had one golf club I didn't know, I
went back up stairs, seeing the club she said
nervously "What are you going to do with that?" I
ran the cold metal down her hot body, she shivered,
I put the head of the club in line with her fanny and
told her to open her legs, she parted her legs, when
I pushed the cold steel onto her fanny and she
pushed herself onto her tip toes trying to get away
from the coldness, I dropped down to my knees and
placed the club between her ankles, I found some
restraints and tied her ankles to either end of the
golf club, that done I began walking slowly around
the room, seeing Stella watching me, I found the
blindfold that she used on me and returned the
favour and placed it around her head, i think that
this had been the worst part for me, the not
knowing, I selected a long thin white vibrator, I
selected some lubricant and went back to her, I tried

to part her ass cheeks but she was having none of it,
so I went and selected a whip, I walked back and
ran the whip slowly down her back, Stella shivered
all over, I asked her if she was going to resist me
again, when she didn't answer me, I stood back and
gave her a sharp crack across the ass with the whip.

I put my mouth to her ear and said" are you
going to resist me again?" she never answered me,
she just trembled " I stood back and gave her four
cracks with the whip, this time when I put my
mouth to her ear and asked her, tears ran down her
face, I reached around her and gripped her nipples,
I rolled them first and then I pulled them hard,
Stella groaned out loud "are you going to resist
me?" I asked her, she shook her head, I picked up
the vibrator and this time when I tried to ease her
ass cheeks apart she did not resist me and when I
pushed that vibrator to her brown hole she clenched
it tight, " do you want me to whip you again ?" I
asked, she shook her head and unclenched her
brown hole, I pushed the vibrator up her ass, which
made her moan again, when I turned it on, she
almost came on the spot, I moved around the room

and looked for something special, I spotted
something I had seen before, the bunny rabbit, I
picked it up and carried it over to Stella, "I have
something special for you, guaranteed to satisfy" I
put some lube onto the silver cock, I had to tell her
to push her hips back so that I could get at her
fanny, with her hips pushed back I managed to push
it into her fanny, and when i switched it on Stella
went wild, I switched it onto fast speed and gripped
the handle and fucked her hard, Stella groaned and
moaned and came so many times her cum was
running down my hand " stop, please stop, I've had
enough " I stopped the vibrators but left them inside
her, when I looked at her, she was crying, I undid
her wrists and she slid down to the floor and rested
her head on her knees, her back heaved as she cried,
after a while she undid her ankles and went to the
bed and got in between the sheets.

Lay on top of the bed I hugged Stella, she
gave the odd sob, I went down stairs and found a
bottle of wine, I went back upstairs and sat on the

bed "Wine ?" I asked, she looked around at me and took the glass from me, she drank a little bit and smiled at me, "that was great Sarah, that was just what I wanted to happen, that is why I built this room, I wanted just what you did to me, thank you Sarah, thank you" we sat and smiled at each other, we went to bed together and we fucked normally for two women, Stella asked me to fetch the bunny rabbit and fuck her with it again, she said that it was the best vibrator she had ever had inside her fanny. And this is how the rest of the weekend went, the only other strange thing that happened was when Stella went and fetched a very thin cane and asked me to whip her, I gave her a total of nine firm strokes, and while her ass was hurting, I had to fuck her from behind with the biggest cock in the room, all and all it was a good weekend, and I looked forward to going back again.

My fanny was a little bit sore and maybe a little bit tingly as I sat on the train back to Portsmouth, I sat and thought about Stella and wandered if the relationship would last, thinking about it I hoped it would, I could see myself living with Stella and her shagging room. Back at work the next morning there has been a change to my brief, I now have to train male recruits, there is a huge difference between men and women when learning to drive, men are definitely more confident and more aggressive there happened to be one such driver name Phil Johnson, and I knew that he would be trouble, when I teach drivers I take two at a time and they take it in turns to drive, I sit in the middle so if need be I can assist or correct the person that is driving, which is how it should be, Phil Johnson knew everything and was of the opinion that women should be in the kitchen or in bed with their legs wide open, private Johnson had touched me inappropriately on three occasions on the first day of a weeks course, at the end of the day I asked Johnson to wait as I wanted to have a word with him, when we were on our own he thought that he had pulled, big mistake as I laid in to him good and proper, I made him realise that touching me was off bounds and if it happened again he would be off the course and on a charge for sexual harassment, private Johnson had gone very quiet, but he had a smirk on his face, and I knew that I would still have trouble with him, he may think he can still control

the situation, if he does think this then he has got a
big surprise coming.

      The next day we had been on the road for five
hours and we had stopped at my usual truck stop,
for lunch when he started up again, he was trying to
show me up in front of all the other drivers, I let
him carry on as he became louder and louder and
fair play he had the attention of the drivers that
were sat close to our table, when he bragged that
he would have me before the week was over, he
had gone to far, now it was my turn. We left the
cafe and walked towards the lorry private Johnson
was supposed to drive now, he headed for the
driver's door, I said " you take one of the passenger
seats, I fancy driving " I drove the lorry and my two
passengers that were suddenly very quiet, I headed
for the army camp, I pulled up at the barrier by the
guard house, I set the hand brake and took the keys
out of the ignition, I jumped down and walked into
the guardroom, ten minutes later I emerged from
the guardroom with a sergeant and two guards from
the military police, the sergeant opened the
passenger door and ordered both passengers out,

they arrested private Johnson for sexual harassment and defamation of character, private Johnson began protesting and shouting that there was no proof.

I had to file a report, which I did, I went to see Johnson in the cells, he called me a cold bitch and said that there was no proof, I finally got a word in and told him that I had warned him what would happen, on camera he told me to fuck of you, you fucking lesbian bitch.

At the trial private Johnson was court marshalled, when the recording that I had made on my mobile in the transport café was heard, private Johnson lowered his head and shook it from side to side, he was sentenced to an undetermined time under lock and key, he would then be discharged from the army and would be reported to the civilian police, as a danger to women.

Chapter 22

Stella had arranged for us to meet in a hotel at a golf club that was miles from anywhere, she had promised me that we would be pampered. I arrived first and waited in reception for my lover to arrive, a young fit oriental woman brought me a cup of coffee and biscuits, she touched my hand and said that if I wanted anything else, I was to ask for her at reception, the smile and look that she gave me made it obvious what she meant, maybe if I was single I would have been tempted. Stella turned up and was openly pleased to see me and kissed me on the mouth, in the room we sat on the four poster bed holding hands, she said that this was a special hotel and the hotel did these special weekends, and this weekend was a lady only weekend, if you had not noticed all the staff were ladies, we are here to be pampered and pampered we will be, she looked me in the eyes and said " do you want to fuck first or shall we go to the spa, I said " spa, I think" but that changed when we began to get changed into our swim suits. Stella reached out and tweaked my left nipple, the next thing, we had our lips pushed together, Stella took me to the bed and made love to me, when she had finished with me I turned her over and made love to her, sated we finally went to supper, we were now too late for the spa. I was stunned when we were served by a topless black girl, when I looked around all of the waitresses were topless.

The waitresses all had a pair of bikini bottoms on under a see through plastic apron, Stella was loving it, when I looked at her she was stroking the black girls tight brown ass, I looked at Stella and raised my eyebrow, she kissed me on the cheek and said " lighten up, have a little fun, this is why I brought you here, the girls come in the price, help yourself" at this point Stella had her hand inside the black girls bikini bottoms stroking her bum cheeks, I looked around the room and each waitress seemed to have someone fondling them in some way or another. I wasn't happy with this situation, not at all. I ate my meal and watched the room, at one table there were four women customers and each one had a waitress either sat on their laps or kneeling down sucking their tits, this was getting out of control, I began to worry when a waitress walked around the room closing all the curtains and doors, a olive skinned waitress came up behind me and reached over and pushed her hands down my top and fondled my tits, I pushed her hands away and gave her a stern look, she walked away to another table, as I looked around the room, on one table the waitress was naked and lay on the table, all four customers were involved in pleasuring her, one woman had her face between her legs, the waitress had a woman kneeling over her face, the other two women had a tit each.

I was suddenly uneasy with what was going on, Stella was trying to get my tits out, but I would not allow her to, from what I could see every waitress was now naked, some women were stood up and watching, their eyes were all over the room, Stella was stood up clapping to the music that had suddenly been turned up, all the doors were now closed. I could see what was going on, in the end the whole room will turn into an orgy, and that is not for me, I watched and slapped away hands that reached for my tits, and lips that tried to kiss me, next to me Stella had her tongue down a naked waitresses throat, and her hand between her legs, the waitress had her hand up Stella's skirt, well it looks like another relationship over.

Stella was now naked and the waitress had her mouth to her fanny, Stella reached out for me, I glared at her and stayed where I was, a woman customer from the next table stripped naked and got onto the table and squat over Stella's face and from where I was sat I could see Stella's tongue flicking at the unknown fanny, not ten minutes later, I was the only person in the room that was dressed, one of the women left the room and came back with a cardboard box she placed it on one of the tables and opened it and began passing out vibrators and strap-on cocks, there was now a full blown orgy going on, one woman that had caught my eye had on this big black cock and was fucking any fanny that she could get to, and she could get to quite a few, women quite a bit older than all of the waitresses were having the time of their lives. I mean where else could they get so much young fanny without any effort on their part, after 45 minutes women began sitting down and resting, there were maybe a dozen women left in the centre of the room still sucking and fucking and Stella was one of them, when a few more women dropped out, one being Stella, she came and sat down by me and tried to kiss me.

I pushed her away, she pouted at me and turned away, now in the middle of the room on a table the woman with the big black cock had a young girl on her hands and knees and was fucking her hard, the young girl had her mouth wide open and her eyes were very big, the woman behind had a look of determination, she gripped the young girls hips and rammed that big black cock full depth into the girl, I felt sorry for her, she was too young to be treated like this, I could see that she had had enough, but the woman still pounded her with that big cock. I don't know who she was but a woman stepped up and told the cock rammer to stop, the woman with the cock pulled out of the young girl and stood with her hands in air expecting a round of applause, the room was silent as the woman who had put a stop to the entertainment helped then crying girl from the room, women began chatting again and the bar was reopened by naked women, the drinks came in the price paid for the weekend, I stood up and left the room.

All packed up and ready to leave, Stella had still not left the orgy room, I carried my case down stairs and headed for the exit, I had a quick look in the room to try and catch Stella's eye but I was out of luck as Stella was lay on her back across two tables and there were a gang of women all around her by the action of the women she was being pleasured from every angle, a woman hovered over her mouth, she had a woman sucking each tit, a woman holding each leg wide and a petite blonde woman with her fist inside Stella's fanny and the women standing watching were clapping in time with the blonde woman's thrusts, I closed the door and left, I will admit that I did shed a tear as I drove back to camp, half way home my phone rang , 4 times, I ignored the phone and did not look at the phone until I stopped, all 4 calls were from Stella asking where I was, and was I with another woman in the hotel, if so what room number. I did not answer her and would not be speaking to her again, yet another relationship bites the dust. Oh well back to my purple vibrator and lots of work.

Chapter 23

Stella has phoned me a hundred times but it was too late for me, she can't understand why I was so upset, she said that I could have joined in and had fun, I told her I was not a slut, meaning that she was. I still see the scared look on that young girls face, she knew that she had got into something she could not handle, but that episode in my life is well and truly over, well, that was not quite true, a few months later I saw Stella's new book that was on sale, and sure enough our time in the Caribbean was in the book, even the time we fucked on the pontoon, the bitch.

Work was my priority for a few months, I had decided not to bother anymore with women, at 28 years old it was a sad place to be in. I received a letter from Dr. Stacy Drew who was an old lover of mine, it seems that she had been holed up, in Kansas training for all these years, she had only had one lover in all the time in America, and she wandered if I was free for a meal som time in the next two weeks, as she was on leave in the UK. Stacy had sent her email address, and a photograph. I was shocked, Stacy had become stunningly beautiful, I contacted her on skype that evening, as soon as she saw me she lowered her head and cried, I asked her why was she crying, she looked up at me with tears streaming down her face, " when we parted Sarah, it broke my heart, I cried silently for months, I ended the one relationship that I had, because I realised that she looked a lot like you and I was just wishing that it was you, I have come back to the UK just to see you, please say that you will meet me, Sarah" I looked at this beautiful broken woman, I said that I would apply for annual leave and come to see her where ever she was staying, I knew that the navy owed me a lot of back leave, so that would not be a problem.

I arrived in London the next day and headed for The Park Lane hotel, Stacy was sat in reception with a bunch of flowers, on seeing me she almost ran to greet me, she hugged me tightly and I hugged her back, she stood back and looked me in the eyes and said " god, I've missed you" I kissed her under the ear and hugged her again, she took my hand and led me into the dining room " I have a table booked for us" she said. We sat and ate a fine leisurely lunch, I told her about my love life and she told me about her sad life, yes she had passed all of her exams and is a fully qualified doctor, and has volunteered for a tour of Afghanistan simply because she can lose herself over there in her work. Stacy asked me if I wanted her to book me a room, or we can share, she said hopefully. I told her that I would love to share with her, I mean who wouldn't want to sleep with such a beautiful woman, we took my bag up to her room we were both very nervous around one another, we both wanted to fuck the other, but we both knew that it would be too much too soon.

Sat on top of an open topped bus taking in the sights of London, it was somewhere near Buckingham palace that we found ourselves holding hands, we seemed to notice at the same time and we both looked down at our hands and smiled at one another, the rest of the day was spent looking at theatres to see what shows were on and what we would like to see. We ate supper out and walked around Soho late into the night, which in itself was an experience. We finally headed back to the hotel in a taxi, holding hands all the way, I suggested having a drink before we went up to our room as I had to ask her if this was what she wanted " oh yes, more than anything, I wanted this for the last five years, many nights I have cried myself to sleep thinking of you " I wasn't completely comfortable as she sounded a little bit desperate to me and what if I didn't satisfy her, she would be absolutely crushed, well there was only one way to find out, I emptied my glass and held my hand out to her.

We lay in bed with the lights on facing each other, both in our nightdresses both holding hands, we were looking into each other's eyes, both trembling just a little bit, I moved my head forward and gently touched her lips with mine, Stacy smiled at me and said " make love to me Sarah, just like you used to" and that is what I did, I made soft passionate love to her over the next two hours, it was just like it used to be only now we were more confident with each other, I sat up and looked down at this beautiful woman, with her hair spread across the pillow, " would you like me to fuck you with a cock?" I asked her, she smiled up at me" you can do whatever you want to me, my love it can only make a perfect night even more perfect" I got of the bed and went to my case and took out a new red strap on cock 7 inches in length and quite thick. The reason that I bought it was all the veins were very pronounced, I lubricated it well and Stacy watched every step, she sat up and took my hand " I've had vibrators inside me before, but I've never been fucked as you say, how do you want me?" she asked, I pulled her round so that her bum was on the edge of the bed and opened her legs, I used my hips to rub the red cock up and down her slit, " I want you to watch me fuck you Stacy, I'm going to fuck you until you cum again" I gripped the rubber cock and held it at her entrance and pushed it forward Stacy gasped as it stretched her insides, she arched her back as I buried the cock to its fullest depth, as I began to fuck her she smiled up at me " I love you Sarah" she whispered, I rode her at a steady pace, when she closed her eyes and moved her hips in time with me I slowly began to move a little bit faster, she kept in time with me perfectly, when she suddenly lifted her head up and stared at me with a snarl on her mouth, I began to ram that cock into her as hard as I could, she began making long hissing sounds as she came long and hard, all the time she held her head up, I rammed that big cock into her.

Stacy lowered her head to the pillow and said " Jesus that was good" I asked her if she wanted me to carry on she nodded enthusiastically so I pulled out and told her to turn over, she placed herself onto her hands and knees in front of me, I parted her thighs and pushed the red cock to her entrance, when I pushed forward to full depth, she looked back and went "Oooohhhhhhhhhh, that's much deeper" Stacy met every single stroke that I made with a stroke of her own, she came but asked me to keep going so I rode her to another orgasm, after her second climax she asked me to stop, I stood there with the cock buried deep inside her, she looked back at me and asked " do you want me to do it to you now or can you do it to me again?" I said if you want me to do it to you again, I will" she smiled and pushed me back, I pulled out of her, she smiled and got of the bed, she ran across the room and sat in a big leather chair, she stretcher her legs over the arms of the chair and pushed her bottom forward, I stood and looked over at her, Stacy had this stupid smile on her face, I walked over to her, her eyes never left mine for a second, I stood between her legs and looked down at her, I leaned forward and pushed the sticky cock at her face and said" lick it clean" her eyes were still locked on mine as she pushed her tongue out and licked the rubber cock, I rubbed it all around her mouth before pushing it at her mouth, she opened her mouth and I pushed it in just far enough that it didn't make her gag, I fucked her mouth which she seemed to enjoy immensely, when I pulled the cock from her mouth she kissed it on the tip before I lowered myself down to my knees and pushed it back into her open fanny.

I fucked her until she told me to stop, she said that she was too sore to carry on, but she wanted to suck the cock again while it was still all sticky, she licked it clean and then sucked it, she expected me to fuck her mouth again but I just held the cock still and she used her head back and forth to give her the pleasure that she wanted, finally done she stopped and let the rubber cock slip from her mouth, she looked up at me and said " that was the best sex that I have ever had, thank you, can I do it to you now?" I unclipped the red cock and let it slide to the floor, Stacy picked it up and pulled the straps up her legs, she clipped it around her waist and lubricated the cock from end to end, she told me to bend over and grip the end of the bed, which I did, she pushed that red cock into me and rode me expertly, she gripped my hips and rammed that rubber cock into me like it was going to be her last time, I came twice before I began to sink to the floor, she followed me down and continued to fuck me from behind, when I had had enough I asked her to stop, when she pulled the cock from my sore fanny, I sat back and leaned against the bottom of the bed, she moved forward on her knees and pushed the cock at my mouth" lick it " she smiled, I opened my mouth, and after I had licked it she pushed it into my mouth and fucked my mouth.

We woke early the next morning and showered together, it took almost 1 and a half hours to have the shower, we had a full English for breakfast and spent the day doing touristy things. We did manage a snogging session in Hyde Park at lunch time over a sandwich and a paper cup of coffee, and basically that is how we spent the next five days until Stacy had to report back to her barracks to get ready for her tour in Afghanistan, we spent our last night together in a hotel near Heathrow, I said goodbye to her at the hotel and we had agreed to meet up when she came home on leave, we had sort of talked about the future, as we both had about the same amount of time left to serve in the forces, we had decided to leave and move in together, we would find a practice up in the Cotswolds for Stacy, as for me I can drive a lorry from anywhere, she sent me a text which I received on the way back to Portsmouth, saying simply " thanks for a great week, I love you, Stacy".

Stacy and I skyped every two weeks, we always had a lot to say to one another, she always told me how dangerous it was out there, she was a little bit worried as from the next week she would be going on patrol, apparently it was part of her duty as a doctor, she passed one comment which brought everything home to me and that was " I've put you down as next of kin, so everything I own will come to you" I told her not to think like that, and I tempted fate by saying " if you get blown up, who will fuck me from behind?" we both laughed at that, I saw her look around both ways and she leaned in close and said " show me your tits" I lifted up my top and showed her my naked tits, she put her lips to the camera and pretended to suck my nipple, " I can't show you mine, there are too many people around" when we had said good night, I sat on my bed and thought to myself, " yes, I do believe I could be happy with Stacy".

I had it in my mind that when I next spoke to Stacy, I would tell her "yes, I will move in with you, when we have finished our service" there was no contact for three weeks, I did receive a postcard from someplace that I had never heard of, saying basically that she was on tour and wouldn't be back at base camp for at least two weeks, and that she would contact me then, the days passed slowly by and I had to admit that I did miss her a lot. I was roused from a deep sleep by my phone ringing, I looked at the clock, it said 4.20am, I knew something was wrong when I was asked for by my full name, the man on the phone said that he was a Major Kemp and he was ringing from Afghanistan," I have your name as next of kin for Capt Stacy Drew, [when I said that was correct] I have to inform you that Capt Drew has been killed in action, her belongings will be forwarded to you in the near future" and that was that, I took some compassionate leave and met her from the plane, she was given a military burial with full military honours.

It appeared that she was killed instantly by a roadside bomb heading back to base on the last day of her deployment with the troops, the rest of her tour would have been based at camp Bastion, I cried and I cried. I attended the funeral but they would not let me see her because she was too badly damaged, I received a box two weeks later which

contained all of her belongings, in her diary there
was a letter addressed to me, it read:

My Darling Sarah

*I have written this letter
just in case anything bad happens to me, well if you
are reading the letter then I guess that something
bad has happened, I have it in my head that I do not
deserve to be happy for whatever reason, and I
know that I would have been happy with you as I
know that you were about to tell me that we were to
be together for ever and ever. As that will no longer
be the case I have to tell you that if I have died then
I have died happy, our last week together would
have made anyone happy. I love you Sarah, but
then you know that don't you. As I can' share the
future with you and make you happy, then I hope
that what I have left you in my will, will in fact
make life easier for you. It is only right that you
have what I have left you as we would have shared
it anyway, I want you to be happy Sarah and I want
you to find a new love. You must think that you are
not meant to be happy, from what you have told me*

*about your past loves and now this. Sarah my
darling, you will find happiness, I will watch over
you and find the right person for you to love and
send her to you.*

*Goodby my darling
Sweet dreams*

*Your ever loving
Stacy.*

As I reread the letter for the tenth time, I cried
and cried, I asked to see a female naval vicar and
showed her the letter, I sat down and told her every
detail of our short relationship, she re ashured me
by telling me that I had to believe what Stacy had
written, and that she would watch over me, and she
would find me love.

I received a solicitors letter asking me to
attend a will reading in Brighton. I arrived at the
said time and sat in the waiting room, my

appointment was with a Mr Grattan. When I was called into his office Mr Grattan stood to greet me, he was getting on in years, his half rimmed glasses were sat on the end of his pock marked nose, he was a portly man that had trouble breathing, he welcomed me to his office and asked me if I knew the contents of the will, I shook my head nervously, as I had never been in this position before, I didn't know whether I was excited or not and why were the rest of her family not here. Mr Grattan began "you Stacy are the soul beneficiary to the last will and testament of one captain Stacy Drew, I don't know how much she had told you about her upbringing but she was an only child to Miss Nancy Drew who died some years ago, now Nancy Drew in her own right was a very wealthy woman, and that wealth now passes to you, congratulations Sarah you now own several large properties here in Brighton, which are rented through a letting agent Dobbs and Dobbs on the high street You will have to discuss what you want to do with the properties, on top of that there is a car showroom that you now own also rented through Dobbs and Dobbs, out at the back of these offices there is a black Audi A6 motor car that belonged to Stacy, that is now yours,

we have sorted the insurance for you so that you
can drive the car away when you leave, in hard
cash, that is money that you can transfer to your
own account or with a little notice you can draw out
in cash there is a total sum of £2.875.442.97 I
almost fell from the chair. Me a millionaire, me!
When I add my own little fortune to it there is well
over three million quid. Mr Grattan was still
talking, about what I hadn't got a clue, I had to say
pardon and he passed me a case full of papers,
when he asked me if I wanted him to continue to
act for me I was mighty relieved, when I said yes,
he told me to leave everything to him and he would
do the necessary, all I would have to do would
come and see him once a year and sign any papers
that needed signing, apart from that I was to go
away and enjoy my life.

<h1 style="text-align:center">Chapter 24</h1>

I decided to leave my fortune until I had left the Navy. I was offered the chance to stay on for another 6 years but decided against that for the obvious reasons. I had looked around the car show room that I now owned and very impressive it was too. I had been to look in the window of the letting agency, it seemed to be quite a busy agency and I had to find somewhere to live, should I buy or use one of my own buildings? When my demob date was certain I made an appointment with Dobbs and Dobbs as I had decided to live in Brighton and that was where all my assets were. I looked around different estate agencies and had found a flat that I quite liked, it was a top- floor flat with an outlook over the sea, a snip at £375.000. I decided to wait until I had seen all of my own properties before buying it. I finally left the navy and when I handed my uniform in I hoped that my love life would change, with a change in my lifestyle. Things looked up on Monday morning when I went to Dobbs, I asked to see my portfolio, I was shown into Miss Nancy Dobbs office. There was an instant

bond between us as she offered to take me to see
my buildings herself, we travelled around Brighton
in her little yellow car. The buildings that I owned
were all four storey buildings on the sea front.
Nancy took me to lunch, to a very nice restaurant
out of town as we shared a bottle of wine, I asked
how much my four properties would realise. She
thought about it for a while, then said "just under £
3 million, but you're not thinking of selling are
you?"

I reassured her with a shake of the head and
she seemed very relieved. I mentioned the flat that I
had seen, "Oh, leave that to me I will sort that out
for you, I may even save you a few quid?" I said
that if she sorted things out for me I would take her
out for a meal as a thank you. She seemed to be
touching me at every opportunity, only lightly but
nevertheless, any contact is better than none, I
watched her walk up to the bar to pay the bill, she
was an attractive woman with red hair, greeny grey
eyes, a nice slim figure with firm titsand she had
nice legs as well. She glanced back to see if I was
looking at her and smiled when she saw that I was

scanning her. In the car heading back to her office I asked her if she belonged to a gym as she looked so fit, she placed her hand on my leg and said "Thank you, yes I belong to tone and drone, in Walter street it is very exclusive but I can recommend you for membership if you want me to." She gave my leg bit of a squeeze as she lifted her hand back to the steering wheel, I said "That would be very helpful, thank you." She said that she would ring me as soon as she had sorted things out. As she parked next to my car, I got out of the car and went to air kiss her but she kissed both of my cheeks, she lingered a little bit too long and breathed my perfume in deeply.

Nancy rang me a few days later to say that she had my application form for the gym, maybe we could meet at Nanno's on the high street at say 7 for a bite and we could fill the form in then. I agreed but not to enthusiastically, I didn't want to drive up her hopes too much too soon. I arrived early and sat at the back of the restaurant so that I could watch her walk towards me. As the reader you may think that in times gone by I would have had herk nickers down by her ankles by now but you must take into consideration that I have an awful lot of money, and she knows that, so is she after my money? Nancy arrived in a white suit, through which I could see her white thong. She walked towards me using her modeling training and smiled as I watched her, I had a bottle of red wine on the table, and I poured her a glass from which she took a long swallow." Hard day?" I asked, she nodded "We had to evict a tenant today, not easy to do " she said, " not one of mine, I hope" I said jokingly, she shook her head and touched my leg again " oh no, not one of yours. " We chatted about life in general and about property. Nancy moved really close to me, when it was time to fill in the form for the gym and as soon as our thighs were touching Nancy had a touch of the hard nipple attack when she looked to see if I had noticed, I smiled and looked at them again. It looked like it was down to me again, I looked around the room and checked that no-one was watching us. Seeing that I was in the clear I reached out and rubbed my finger around her right nipple, she looked around the room and undid a button on her blouse, the one between her tits. I slipped my hand to her naked breast when I pulled my hand out and looked at her, "Are we going back to yours ?" I asked. She finished her drink in one gulp and stood and said "ready then?".

I followed Nancy back to her flat and parked next to her car, we got out at the same time and I followed her to her flat. She was obviously well practiced as she was in no hurry to get into my pants. I looked around her flat, she had a nice place, well decorated. As we sat on the couch with a glass of wine, there was a little bit of tension between us, I had done my bit by getting us this far, now it was up to Nancy to get us into bed. I had let her know that I was game, I decided that I would give her ten minutes and then go. She placed her glass down onto the coffee table, then reached over my shoulder and pulled me to her. As she pushed our lips together I reached up and undid the buttons on her blouse and fondled her naked tits. She seemed to be a little bit reserved so I lowered my mouth to her left tit and sucked most of her tit into my mouth then did the same to her right breast. Still she made no effort to touch me so I asked her "Is this your first time?" she blushed all the way down to her tits " with a woman yes, will you teach me?" I stood up and walked around the room and finally stopped in front of her. "Have you any toys?" she shook her head, I picked up my coat and said " do you want to come to mine and I will teach you how to love a woman, or you can stay here and stick to men?" she picked up her glass, that was enough for me I left and went back to my purple vibrator.

The next day I was at a viewing at the flat that I liked the look of when my phone rung "Hello" I answered , Nancy said " hello Sarah, I think I owe you an apology for last night, I acted like a young virgin, I wanted to ask, if I get some toys would you come back?" I thought about it for a second and said "I don't think so Nancy, to be honest I don't need the hassle" and rang off. You see your mind may not work like mine. Why should she want to go out and buy toys when she could have come to mine and have all the toys that she could have wanted, my suspicious mind says ENTRAPMENT, hidden cameras, it could be anything these days, there is no point in having money if you don't use it. I hired a private detective that had been recommended by Mr Grattan and asked him to check out the flat that I was in last night for anything not quite right. I waited for the detective to meet me at my flat that I was renting, he came in and said "I think you have had a very lucky escape, there are three cameras and two mics in the living room, he tossed a disc down on the table " that's from last night" I paid him and gave him a little bonus, I then rang Mr Grattan and asked him to contact the police and get the accounts checked out and then to change the agents.

I was sitting in the flat reading a magazine when there was a ring at the door. I opened the door to be pleasantly surprised, a woman with short brown hair and green eyes was stood smiling at me "Miss Briany?" I nodded she held her hand out" I'm Sgt. Oaks from Brighton CID, can I come in please?" I stood to the side and let her enter the flat. I offered her a seat and asked her if she wanted a coffee then sat opposite her with a mug of coffee I waited for her to begin. " we have received a phone call from Mr Grattan your solicitor about your dealings with Dobbs and Dobbs, we have made contact with the Dobbs and after our initial contact we could see that things were not right, so we have taken them to the station for interview, their computers have been seized and the premises have been locked down tight, the question that I have for you is, what made you suspicious ?"

I sat and looked at her for a while and asked her "is what I say next between us, or will it be on record?" she smiled at me and asked simply "Why?" I rubbed my chin and sat forward and said" If what I have to say is between us, then I will tell you why I became suspicious and I will show you proof" she thought about what I had said and said " let me make a call and we will see." She made her call from the kitchen and came back after a few minutes " At this point, what you say will be between us, ok?" I nodded and told her how Nancy Dobbs had gone out of her way to pick me up, I told her how she had flirted with me and when it came down to the sex, she had not got a clue what women do together, I made a pass at her and she was terrified, she was shaking like a leaf. I asked

her if she had any sex toys and as she seemed
shocked. As I had a selection I asked her if she
would like to come back here, she was frozen in
terror, so I left, then today she rang me and asked
me a question and that question was the telltale for
me. She asked me this "if I go out and buy some
toys will you come back tonight?" Why would
someone want to go out and buy some sex toys
when they could come here and use mine for
nothing." Sgt Oaks nodded and said "Makes sense."
"What about this proof?" I said and played the disk
for her. She sat and watched it and shook her head,
it was when a man emerged at the end and began
shouting at Nancy that clinched the case.

When sgt Oaks gave me her card I found out
that her first name was Helen, she assured me that
she would do her best to keep what I had told her
strictly between us, she was about to leave when
she turned to me and asked "just a thought, I
suppose you acquired the disc by legal means." [I
smiled] "I thought so, I will be in touch." Helen
asked me to go to the station three days later and to
bring the disc. She collected me from reception and

took me to her office. When she closed the door to her office she sat opposite me and said "Due to the sensitivity of the material that you hold, we have decided to set up a team of women officers to deal with the case, we have already made inroads into corruption and have discovered a second set of accounts. If you are agreeable I will call the other two women into my office to watch the disc." and that is what happened, they watched the disk a few times, before the trio of women left the room and had a discussion outside. One of the women left the room and came back ten minutes later with Nancy Dobbs in handcuffs. Nancy entered the office and sat down but she wouldn't look at me. Sgt Oaks repeated the caution, and told Nancy about the disc, her head shot up "How did you get that?" she asked. The sgt said "It appears that you left your front door wide open this morning, and when miss Briany entered the flat trying to fiind you she accidently discovered the disk" Nancy said " accident my ass, it was hidden so it was some bloody accident" she said sarcastically. Sgt asked "Would you like to watch the disk, Nancy?" she shook her head.

Chapter 25

When Helen came to see me a few days later she informed me that Nancy had told them everything, even down to where all the money was hidden, "It appears that they owe you a lot of money Sarah " the case was very complicated and it lasted five weeks in court, brother and sister Dobbs were both found guilty and imprisoned. I received over £160.000 that they had stolen from Stacy's estate. I felt a little bit guilty and gave it all away to charity. Now I could finally sort out my new flat. I purchased it for £350.000 cash and had it fitted out exactly how I wanted it. Finally I could move in.

I had just stepped from my sunken bath and picked up my dressing gown, it was maybe eight o'clock in the evening when the doorbell rang. I wrapped my wet hair in a towel and went to the door. When I opened the door I was pleasantly surprised to see Helen Oakes standing on my doorstep with a bottle of red in her hand and a smile on her face, I stood to the side and let her enter. While she removed her coat I took two wineglasses from the cabinet. she looked around and said "Nice flat" "I like it, it's perfect for me" I answered with a smile. We sat on the settee and sipped our wine, I asked about Nancy and she told me that she was suffering from depression, I was curious why she had called round so I asked her outright "To what do I owe this visit?" she blushed and stood up and walked across the room and stood looking out of the window at the sea. "Do you remember when I first came here, and you had something to say but you didn't quite know how to say it?" she said as she looked at me, I nodded and then she continued ." Well what I have to say is a lot more embarrassing than what you had to say, if I tell you, will you promise me that you will keep it to yourself." [again I nodded] she came and sat by me again. " I am 31 years old and I decided when I enrolled in the police to concentrate on my career and that is what I have done, I have never been out with a man and the only sexual experience I have had was when I was at boarding school at the age of 15, her name was Jessica and I called what we did as a sexual experience, well it was more like teenage fumblings, don't get me wrong Sarah I haven't missed what I haven't had" she stopped in mid flow, she was looking at her hands in her lap, I reached over and took her hand and said "and?" she looked at me and said " I can't, you will think that I am stupid." I said "Spit it out Helen" she stared at me and said "Can I look at your toys please?" I smiled broadly at her "Is that all, I thought that you were going to ask me to fuck you or something." I walked into the bedroom and took my box from the wardrobe.

I placed the box between us and removed the lid, Helen gasped out loud "My god, they are huge" and put her hand over her mouth, I said " What you have to remember is that they all do something different." She looked at me waiting for me to carry on, so I picked up a normal 6 inch straight white vibrator and passed it to her, she reached out and almost didn't take it but finally she did. When she held it in her hand and looked at it from all angles, I reached over and switched it on, she dropped it into her lap and giggled, with the vibrator laying in her lap she looked at me. She was dying to ask me what it was used for, so to save her embarrassment. I said "Undo your top" under her top she had a thin white blouse. She undid her top and I looked at her and said " do you mind if I touch you ?" she shook her head excitedly, I reached over to her chest and pushed her blouse tight over her breast, she looked at my hand on her breast, when I pushed the buzzing vibrator against her nipple she blushed as her nipple became hard, I moved it around and around her nipple and then the other nipple. She had suddenly became very flushed. I said "Helen undo your blouse" She looked very nervous as she undid the buttons. When the blouse was open I leaned across and pulled her bra down then rubbed the vibrator over her naked nipple. Helen moaned out loud and exposed her other breast, I passed her the vibrator and watched her using that buzzer on her tits, she put her hands in her lap and whispered "Show me another please" Helen was close to orgasm, I could tell just by looking at her.

I picked up a thick 8 inch lookalike vibrator, not only had it got a big knob but it had thick veins down the shaft, I switched it on and passed it to her, she held it in both hands and looked at me, I said " look Helen do you want me to make you cum?" she blushed and became nervous, I stood up and removed my dressing gown, standing there naked in front of her, her eyes were locked onto my naked fanny. I pulled her up to standing, and said " I will only touch you if you want me to, you can touch me anywhere you want, as you are can see I am at ease with my body. " She was like a rabbit in the headlights, she just stood there, so I lifted her hands and placed them on my breasts, her eyes went from hand to hand as they moved over my tits, I removed her right hand and placed it between my legs and rubbed it along my fanny, I stood and looked at her, looking at my body, her right hand moving over my fanny. The only sound in the room was the vibrator as it buzzed away on the settee.

I sat her back down on the settee and she folded into herself, I picked up my dressing gown and went to put it on, but she stopped me " please, let me look at you, you are beautiful" I sat naked by her side her eyes moved over my body, she reached out to touch my fanny again, I turned to face her and opened my legs, she stared at my fanny then picked up the vibrator and pushed it against my fanny, I took hold of her hand gently

and showed her where to touch me, she had a line
of sweat under her nose, she was getting hotter and
hotter, I parted my fanny lips and explained
everything to her, I pointed out my clit and how
best to use the vibrator on it, I opened my legs wide
and pushed that rubber cock into my fanny, I
showed her how to hold it and how to use it, I was
close myself now, so I asked her " do you want to
watch me cum?" she nodded without taking her
eyes from that rubber cock that was buried inside
me, I gripped her hand and laid my head back, I
used her hand that held the vibrator and took myself
to orgasm. Helen was so excited as she watched me
cum, I slowed her hand down until we eventually
stopped, I pulled the cock from my fanny and she
was fascinated with all of the cum that covered the
whole thing, as normal it was down to me to make
the first move. I got off the settee and pulled her up
again, I went behind her and slowly removed her
top clothes, until she was stood there with her tits
out naked from the waist up.

I undid her skirt and let it fall to the floor, I did the
same with her slip, she had on a pair of black pants.
I put my fingers into the sides and pushed the pants

down, she took a step out of everything and stood naked before me. I placed my hands on her shoulders and turned her around then looked her in the eyes and said" Helen it is decision time, I can use the vibrator on you or I can make love to you, it is entirely up to you?" she looked at me "Will you make love to me first?" I smiled at her "Why don't I make you cum first, then we can relax?" she nodded, I put my hands behind her ass and pulled her to me, we were mound to mound, I pushed my lips to hers and kissed her, she was trembling, I pushed my tongue to her lips, which she opened and we had a slow tongue dance. Helen was now rubbing her mound against mine now, tiny moans were coming from her throat, I turned her sideways and put my hand onto her fanny, she opened her shaking legs, I ran my finger along her slit, when my finger slipped inside her she tensed, I went for gold and instantly pushed a second finger into her and finger fucked her to her first orgasm, she growled in her throat as she soaked my fingers, I kept my fingers moving inside her as deep as I could, I took her to her second orgasm, she pulled my fingers from her fanny as she gasped for breath.

Helen gripped me around the neck and cried openly, I rubbed her back and stroked her hair and let her get out of her system whatever it was that was upsetting her, even though she was crying she still rubbed her mound against mine, as she pushed her lips to mine, I tasted her salty tears. I took her hand and led her into the bedroom, we climbed into bed and held each other, I took control and made love to her, she came as I pushed my tongue through her pubic hair to her clit. I made love to her for good hour until she was done, I talked her through making love to me. Helen was an enthusiastic learner, she made me cum and I had fun, I left the bed and went back into the living room, and selected a strap-on cock with a fair length but not too thick. I walked back into the bedroom and stood by her side and lubricated the cock from end to end. I pulled the bed clothes from her and eased her legs to the end of the bed, I held her legs and asked her " shall I make you a woman?" she smiled at me so I put the cock to her fanny lips and told her to take a breath, as she breathed in I pushed the head of the cock into her fanny, she took another breath and I pushed through her barrier, she gasped her way to womanhood but enjoyed every second from then on, I fucked her gently as it was her first time, her orgasm made her shudder and grip herself, now that she had cum I then proceded to fuck her properly. As she neared her orgasm for the second time with a cock, I rammed the cock into her, this time her orgasm was a lot stronger.

Helen asked me to stop, so I pulled out and walked back into the living room and selected the big black strap on. I took it back into the bedroom and strapped it onto her, I showed how to lubricate it and then I went down to my hands and knees and talked her through shagging me, after a few prompts she did very well on her own, she even rode me harder as I neared my climax. Sitting on the settee in dressing gowns drinking coffee, Helen is leaning against me and is full of smiles " I wonder now why I waited so long, I think the main problem I had was that I listened to my mother who I now realise was a man hater, men only ever think of themselves, as long as they are satisfied that is all that matters, but now with you and what we have done tonight. I am so pleased I came here tonight and thank you for being patient with me" I leaned over and kissed her on the lips and said "You're welcome". We sat quiet for a while and I asked her if she was staying or going, she looked at me "Staying if that's ok?" I stood up and took her back to bed, our love making was more practiced now on both our parts as we pleasured each other. In the shower in the morning she asked me to shave her, which I did and just that simple gesture built her confidence a hundred fold and when I went down and licked her naked fanny for the first time, she was so happy and as I looked up into her face she came on my tongue and I was happy as well.

Yes, I was in love again, Helen lived in a one bedroomed flat in the back streets of Brighton, within two weeks she had moved in with me. We were deeply in love and did everything together, I even took her to Paris for fashion weekend, we shopped for two days solid, we spent the nights in the Paris Hilton making love and planning for the future. Taking my past record with women I still expected things to go wrong, if they didn't then I would be pleasantly surprised. I knew that things were too good to be true. Helen had mentioned a man named Trevor from work on quite a few occasions, telling me that they had joined up on the same day and ever since that day he has been trying to get her into bed, reading between the lines, I think that now she has tried sex with a woman, she now is thinking about having sex with a man just to see if she is missing out on anything. As her Christmas party loomed ever closer, Trevor's name seemed to crop up more and more, on the night of the party she was dressed up to the nines and when I dropped her off at the station she had a definite sparkle in her eye, I went and ate at my favourite restaurant and call me suspicious but I thought I would take a ride past the station just to see what I could see. I knew where her office was situated so I sat across the road in the shadows and waited and sure enough about an hour later, I saw her walk into her office with a man, I could see them kissing in the lamplight, when she stepped back from him and put her hands in the air he lifted her top up and over her head then she put her hands behind her back to undo her bra. I drove away, back in my flat I packed her bags and wrote her a simple note, please leave the keys as you leave. When I woke in the morning the cases were gone and the keys were on the table, not a word of apology, nothing.

Chapter 26

I had my shower and made an effort as to my outfit. I wore a turquoise two piece suit and decided to treat myself, I walked down the main street to the travel agents. I had no plan as to where I wanted to go, I just wanted the warm sun on my back and some fun. I sat in the travel agents looking at all the different holidays, when a young woman of 19/20years old said "We do holidays to cater for certain tastes, like this one" she put a brochure in a brown paper bag for me to take home with me, I thanked her for her help, I wasn't looking for any sex or female contact, but the brochure was very interesting. It was called "Holidays without a man" I flicked through the brochure and one holiday took my fancy, the holiday was for women nudists on a Caribbean island, the hotel held 100 women and was run by women. I went straight back into the agents and spoke to the young woman who had given me the brochure and booked a week's holiday. "A good choice, I can recommend this holiday, I usually go myself once a year, it's good if you are not looking for anything too serious." I sat and looked at her name tag, which said "Amanda" I just happened to look at her nice tits at the same time! I gave her my number and said quietly "Ring me" she smiled and said that she would.

Amanda Holder rang me that evening and we arranged to meet for a drink. Sitting in a wine bar across from this pretty young woman, I asked her to tell me about the holiday that I had booked. She told me about the sundrenched beaches, the free wine, female entertainment and there is so much flesh everywhere you look. Not wishing to be to crude but I was wet every minute that I was there, "Why don't you come with me, Amanda? My treat?" She looked shocked, "I couldn't possibly" she said, I asked her "why not?" she looked a bit flustered and said "But I don't know you" to which I answered "I don't know you either, but you are a nice friendly woman, who has done me a favour and I want to repay that favour." She took a long drink and looked at me and her eyes dropped to my tits, seeing my hard nipples swayed her. " ok, I will, but I must pay for myself", I placed my hand on her leg and said " I have more money than you, please let me pay" with that I took a brown envelope from my bag and passed it to her " that should cover it, now I want you to come round to my flat before we leave and choose some clothes to take, you see I have just come back from Paris, and I have bought some delightful dresses, you are the same size as me, it will be fun" she agreed to come around the next evening.

With the holiday booked and something to look forward to, my evening was somewhat spoiled by a phone call from Helen, she wanted to know why I had thrown her out as she had not done anything wrong, I explained that I had seen her in her office with a man, and I had seen him removing her clothes. She stammered something about curiosity, but she now realised that she had been wrong and sex with me was much better, I said simply "maybe you should have thought about that first" when she went quiet, I said" goodbye Helen" and put the phone down on her.

Amanda arrived on time and kissed me on the

cheek "Hi Sarah, isn't this exciting?" we sat and had a glass of wine, and arranged where I would pick her up and what time, she was desperate to say something. So I waited, she took her cheque book from her bag " please let me pay for my holiday, only I feel like a prostitute and when we have sex, which we both know that we will, I will feel even worse" I smiled at her and said " look Amanda, I am a millionaire, I have more money than I know what to do with, I do not have any friends and when I find someone I like, well I like to help them simply because I can" she smiled and kissed me on the cheek again, " now let's look at some clothes" I led the way into the bedroom and opened all of the doors to the storage space, she gasped out loud as she looked at all of the designer clothes. She selected a flowered dress and held it to herself. looking in the long mirror she said " wow, this is beautiful." I went behind her and undid the long zip on the back of her dress and pushed it off her shoulders, she opened her arms and let her dress fall to the floor. We stood and looked at each other in the mirror, she was standing in a white thong and nothing else. When she saw me looking at her slim body she began swaying from side to side, " your turn" she said very sexily.

I removed all of my clothes and stood behind her naked, she moved slightly so that she could see my nakedness. She looked at my naked fanny and reached out and touched it as she ran her finger along my slit, I parted my legs for her and she pushed her finger inside my fanny and began to slowly frig me. I reached around her and fondled her tits, making her nipples hard. She turned around and pushed her lips to mine and inserted a second finger into my fanny and took me to a gentle orgasm. I slid slowly down her body kissing as I went, my eyes were level with her naked fanny, I could see her lower lips either side of her thong, I pushed my mouth to her fanny biting into her thong, I pulled her thin material down and placed my mouth to her fanny sucking in her crinkly lips, she parted her thighs and held my head in place, when she pushed her hips forward I could lick her from end to end. She liked me sucking her fanny lips, her hips began to move back and forward. Locating her clit, I flicked the hard little button with the tip of my tongue then reached up and pushed two fingers deep into her fanny and began to frig her fast, her eyes were closed tight as she enjoyed her orgasm.

We spent the next hour on top of the bed, I would fuck her and she would fuck me, we tried lots of clothes on and had our own little fashion show, at the end of the evening there was a pile of designer clothes on the bed, we stood there hand in hand and looked at the clothes, " that is the best night ever, thanks Sarah" later, lying in bed again in each other's arms I asked her " how did you know that I was gay?" she looked over at me and smiled " that's easy, you see I never wear a bra to work, when I catch a customer looking at my tits, my nipples get hard, then your nipples get hard, but believe it or not you are the first woman that I have ended up with from work. Well I will rephrase that, you are the only woman that I have ever wanted to end up with from work". We spent most nights together and packing for the holiday was good fun. With the holiday being nudist holiday, we only packed a few clothes for the evenings and the trip over there. It took all of ten minutes, the rest of the evening we spent at the spa, getting shaved and pampered, we decided to abstain from sex until we were naked in the sun.

As we entered the luxury hotel, we were shown to our room. We stood on the balcony which overlooked the pool and the beach and everywhere we looked there were naked fannies. We strolled down to the pool and by the exit that led to the pool, there was a sign "No clothes past this point" so we removed our dressing gowns and went for a walk. I have to admit I had never seen so many hairless fannies in one place, in my life, every twenty yards you would see a couple of wrinkly elderly women, their eyes were everywhere, and they would nudge each other when a fit woman walked past, the elder one on the left had the tits of a forty year old, only they were down by her waist, she was well over 80, her body had had so many tucks that she looked like a manikin, her face was pulled tight which left her with a permanent smile. When we walked past, we would get the odd wolf whistle, when we looked they would flash their fannies at us. I thought that I had gone to heaven, we had a shock when we were sitting in the bar later in the evening and a young fit black woman came around selling all manner of sex aids, she had some curved strap on cocks. She only had one bunny rabbit vibrator left, so I bought that and a selection of other stuff.

Amanda asked me about the bunny rabbit, I hid it under my napkin and said it was for later, and it came with a guarantee to thrill, one or two women were taking walks along the beach, none were removing their evening wear so I suggested that we take a walk, we drained our glasses and. went for a moonlight stroll, some women were swimming naked, other women were making love on beach towels, the whole scene was relaxed and no-one bothered anyone else. A little way further on we passed some swings, we sat on the swings and dangled our feet looking at the view, the heat at this time of the evening was just perfect. I stood in front of Amanda and pushed her a few times, she grabbed me around the waist and looked up into my eyes " make love to me, here now" she had a dress on that did up on top of the shoulder, I undid the ties and let the dress fall to below her tits, I went to my knees and sucked her tits as I ran my hands along the outsides of her legs, I reached the top of her pants and pulled them down, she had to lift her bottom so that I could pull them down her legs and slip them off. I reached under her bottom and pulled her bum forward and placing myself between her thighs she spread her legs as my mouth neared her fanny, and even though people were walking past and looking at us I was past caring. I licked and sucked and jabbed at her clit with the tip of my tongue. I made her cum by sucking her clit, this really was paradise, Amanda cried out in orgasm as she came against my mouth.

Amanda did her dress up and grabbed my hand " take me back to the room, I want to fuck you" as we walked back along the sand, my fanny was so wet, I stopped and pulled her to me" make me cum, please" she pushed me back against a palm tree, she fell to her knees and looked up at me as she pulled my pants down, I held my dress up as she pushed her mouth to my fanny, I closed my eyes and drifted off to another universe. That is what her tongue did to me, when her lips closed around my clit, I felt my legs go weak, I came and came, I felt her tongue enter my fanny as she licked up my cum. On shaky legs we walked back to our room, as soon as I closed the door I pulled her dress from her fit body and pushed her playfully back onto the bed and unwrapped the bunny rabbit, I pushed it into her fanny and switched it on to slow speed. As I began to fuck her with it and she sat up to see what I was doing to her, her mouth hung open and she made a strange noise, " is that good?" I asked her, she nodded as I said "try this then" and switched it to full speed, her legs spread wide open as she held her weight up on her hands " oh fuck, fuck fuck" she gasped out loud as that thing spun inside her fanny, every time I hit her clit with the ears she made a tiny yelping sound Amanda came so many times, she finally flopped back on the bed with her arms and legs spread wide with that thing still spinning in her fanny. She lay there moaning as her cum gathered all around her fanny lips, I switched it off and left it inside her, "I have never cum so much in one go before, my fanny is still spinning around" I reached up and brushed her hair from her face, her eyes found mine, " I love you

Sarah, I really do" I leaned over and kissed her hard on the lips " I love you to, my darling Amanda" .

I opened one of the curved strap on cocks and strapped it on and walked to the bed, Amanda looked up at me as I spat on my hands and lubricated the cock. I pulled the bunny out of her fanny which left a gaping hole and pushed the cock into her while lifting her legs. I eased her into the position that I wanted her in and began to fuck her at a good rate, I was concerned that she had had enough sex for one day and slowed down and eventually stopped, " are you all right Amanda, do you want me to stop" I asked her, she shook her head " don't stop now" she said in a concerned voice, so I began fucking her again, but I kept a close eye on her. I rode her to her calm climax, which told me that she had had enough, I pulled out of her and lay by her side, she sat up and fondled my tits " I think it's my turn to fuck you now my love" she picked up the bunny rabbit and pushed it into my fanny, but she didn't switch it on, she then got of the bed and pulled the strap on up her legs and clipped it up, " turn over Sarah" she instructed so I placed myself in front of her, she lubricated the rubber cock and also my bum hole, she switched the bunny rabbit on and then put the strap on to my bum hole, I didn't resist her as she pushed forward, whatever she wanted to do is fine by me, with that cock buried up my ass, she flicked the switch on the bunny to full speed. She fucked my ass at the same time. I had to admit that I was in complete heaven, as she pulled me back to meet her forward stroke, the rubber cock went in to full depth, if someone had looked at my face they would have thought that I was in a lot of pain, but it was ecstasy, complete and utter ecstasy, this was one of the best fucks that I have ever had the pleasure to receive.

Chapter 27

We swam naked in the sea at first light to one of the huts that were static but out from the shoreline. A woman came out on a canoe and brought us breakfast. We were in paradise, completely on our own. In nets that were attached to the base of the hut were bottles of drink in the sea and bowls of fruit on the table that we were leaning against. Although it was quite early the sun was warm, the blue sky was cloudless and a beautiful naked woman not only next to me but also deeply in love with me, as I was with her. We both dozed in the sun, the only sound to be heard was the lapping of the waves against the hut. I moved over to Amanda and ran my fingers through her damp hair, she never opened her eyes but just sat there and let me pamper her. None of my actions had any sex in them, this was just love and tenderness. A woman swam towards our hut, she hung onto the side and watched us for a few minutes and swam away again without saying a word. She was obviously single and looking for someone to play with. We spent the day at the hut, occasionally taking a swim or having a drink. Amanda was more than happy to lie along the bench with her head in my lap, this was all that she required to be contented. Lunch came out by boat again it was different breads, cheeses and meats. We assumed that it was mid afternoon when the sounds of a steel band drifted out to us, I asked her if she wanted to go back to the beach and her only answer was the shake of her head.

Amanda and I swam back early in the evening, we walked along the beach and had a hotdog from the barbecue. We strolled back to our room and showered and Amanda sat and watched the people by the pool while I took my credit card and went for a walk. I had only been gone maybe fifteen minutes but when I returned she was asleep with her head resting on her arms as she had been when people watching. As I sat and looked out to sea I had a thought, this must be the longest that I had ever been naked in my life, I poured myself a drink of rum with lots of ice and sat by my partner and watched naked people playing volleyball. I noticed that the deck chairs that were around the court were filled with all the older women. Was that the future for me watching pretty young things playing volleyball " what ya thinking about lover?" asked Amanda, I told her what I had been thinking about and she looked down at the players " I wouldn't mind watching them play, especially that fit blonde woman" she looked at me and smiled, I flicked a towel at her in jest, I took her hand and took her to the bed, I laid her down and laid down beside her and put my arm under her head " Amanda, can you get Christmas off?" she said " probably if I book it early enough, why?" she said "well, you have enjoyed this holiday, haven't you? I asked." she still didn't look at me "I could stay here forever with you, Sarah, this has been the best time for me" she said. I smiled and said "Good, because I have just booked us two weeks here at Christmas" Amanda jumped up with the biggest smile on her face ever " Oh my god. Oh my god, really?" I nodded and she grabbed me around the neck and kissed me all over, she was so excited. Her kissing led to other things and we licked each other's fannies at the same time, both of us coming on the tongues of our excited lover.

Our last night in paradise ended with a disco, we danced and drank and danced some more Finally we fell into bed and made love to each other passionately. Most people are unhappy when they have to return home, but for Amanda and I, hopefully this is the start of the future for us, this time I trod softly and kept her at arms length, not in a nasty way. It's just that I didn't want to get hurt again so soon. We saw each other twice in the week and all weekend. I had booked and paid for our flights for our Christmas holiday, and all was well.

The begining of November held a shock for Amanda as things didn't look too good at work, the holiday business seemed to be in a bad way with a lot of small companies going under. I told her not to worry, I would sort something out for her but she shook her head and said " I don't want charity Sarah" I smiled and said " I have something in mind, that I have been thinking about for a while now, if I go ahead with the idea, do you think you could you run a business?" she looked at me and said " with a bit of training, yes I don't see why not" I smiled and asked "do you have you a friend at work that you can trust ?" she smiled and said " yea, Debs" I suggested that she brought Debs round one evening so that I could meet her, I had a plan that could keep us all busy for a good while. Things were arranged for the two girls to come around for a meal and a chat. Debs was a nice person, she was short and a little bit dumpy, her dark hair was straight cut, but her brown eyes were to die for. I had found out what I had wanted to know without asking direct questions. The two women were to go on an intensive business course which consisted of three evenings a week and a Saturday each week for four weeks. That would leave us plenty of time for our holiday in the sun.

Debs and Amanda did well at business classes, they spent a lot of time together going through text books and flow charts. The travel agency where they both worked was on its last legs. Amanda finished work the day before we flew off to the sunshine. For the last five weeks both women had been asking me constantly what business we were going in to but I had kept the plans to myself as I needed to talk to the hotel manager in the

Caribbean to get things straight in my head. If things worked out right, this could be the final piece to the puzzle, we had the same room as before, and if anything, the sun was even hotter now. We stood and looked down at the pool and as before there were naked fannies everywhere. We donned our dresssing gowns and went for a walk Both naked again, we felt free, we looked out to the hut where we had spent one of our best days ever and seeing no-one we swam out to the hut, after ten minutes sitting there in the peace and quiet it felt as if we had never been away. We made love in the sun, we drank rum in the sun and watched as a boat rowed out to us with our lunch.

Our holiday as ever was perfect, we made love in a lot more places this time, it became the norm for people to walk past while we were making love, this time we even had single women asking if they could join in with us, I have to say that we declined each offer. On the sixth day it was the day for our meeting, I had not told Amanda about the meeting on purpose, if she didn't know about it she couldn't worry about it. I picked a case up and placed it on the bed and took a briefcase out of it and passed it to Amanda. I took another briefcase out for me. In both cases were writing pads and pens, calculators and a few brochures. I told Amanda that we had a meeting with the owner of the hotel and as this was our first business meeting. I wanted her to take notes and hoped that I had got the nerve to carry this off. We stood outside the owner's office and when we were shown in we were both pleasantly surprised. A woman about the same age as myself introduced herself as Lena Shore. I introduced both of us making it obvious that I was to be the spokesperson, Lena asked what she could do for us.

I took a deep breath and began "Well Lena, I have a proposal for you that may make life a lot easier for you. What I propose is this, we have a company in England that distributes sex toys all over the world, what we want to offer is this. We will set up a web page and take all of your bookings and organise everything, from flights to the sex toys. We will take the orders for sex toys when we confirm the bookings and airmail the toys to arrive a few days before the guests making sure that every guest is aware of the nudity. In fact we intend to make this the main selling point, also we have noticed that you have a fair number of single guests. We have a plan in place to match these single women with each other, therefore making everyones holiday a more fulfilling experience. All enquiries to our webpage will receive a package containing all of the relevant information.

Now, depending on your trust, I am prepared to place in a bank account a certain amount of money that will guarantee your payments. Our company is called "Women on Women holidays !" I sat there looking at Lena, I could feel Amanda's eyes boring into the side of my head in total disbelief. The next hour was all about percentages, costs and availability. As Lena had shown some interest I invited her over to England to visit our business and assured her that the web page would be up and running in a week to ten days from the time we returned home.

Lena agreed to look at our webpage when it was up

and running and if she was happy she would confirm our business merger in writing.

She shook our hands after I had presented her with our paperwork and said she hoped that we would enjoy the rest of our holiday. If she had any questions she knew where to find us.

Chapter 28

When Lena closed the door behind us, Amanda slapped me across the arm, "How could you?" I grabbed her hand and we ran back to our room, we hugged and jumped around, when we calmed down I opened my case and took out a business card and passed it to Amanda, she looked at the card but didn't spot the main wording, she looked at me and said "how?" I studied her face and said "Read the card again", she studied the card closer " oh my god" she looked at me with her mouth open, "is this for real?" I nodded "This is all yours my love, I have had the premises fitted out while we are here. Debs is working on a web page with a designer, the toys are being delivered in two days time the same with the catalogues. All we have to do is sort everything out when we get back. There is one thing that I have left for you to sort out and that is flights and other venues for this type of holiday. Of course it may mean that we have to sample the destinations ourselves."

From day one the business was a complete success, we posted brochures all over the world and with that came orders for sex toys and everything that went with that side of the business. Amanda and Debs never stopped working on the computers, Debs had a younger sister aged 17, she was employed to pack and lable the parcels, her name was Emma, she was fit and had a shaved fanny. You may think how do I know that? Well, I will tell you. It was quite funny really and I haven't told Amanda or Debs what I know. When I had the building fitted out I had some security cameras fitted, for my own piece of mind. As I said Emma is fit and there is no harm in looking, some evenings she would work quite late and lock up before she left, on this particular evening I was watching her working and dancing to the radio, she had a selection of toys on the table and she was checking them of against her paperwork she held a thick wrapped vibrator in her left hand while she wrote with her right hand.

She was double checking the paperwork and tapping the vibrator on her chin, she realised what she was doing and burst out laughing, and dropped it on the floor, she bent down to pick it up and it had burst out of the packaging, she looked at it closely and finding out it had no batteries fitted, she opened a pack of batteries and fitted the required number into the rubber cock. She switched it on and stood and looked at it, she tried it against her hand first, then her cheek, she then held it against her nipple.

She liked that a lot, she looked around the warehouse and placed the vibrator onto the table. She then checked all of the doors to make sure that they were locked and went back to the table picked the vibrator up and pushed it down her top. Debs looked down her top for a couple of minutes as she moved it around her tits then placed the vibrator back on the table and pulled her top over her head and dropped it onto the table. She undid her bra and placed the bra onto her top then stood facing the camera as she rubbed the vibrator all around her tits, she parted her legs and rubbed the vibrator against her fanny through her jeans with her right hand while her left hand fondled her tits.

She put the cock down again as she undid her jeans and took them off, she had on a white pair of pants and pushed them down her legs to take them off. Debs climbed onto the table and sat down opened her legs, again facing the camera, her fanny was as bald as the day she was born! She began by rubbing the cock up and down her slit, pressing harder and harder, she made herself cum, and from the look of it her, her orgasm was quite strong. After she had calmed down a little bit she lifted the cock to her mouth and lubricated it all over then pushed that thick cock deep inside her fanny. I sat and watched her slowly fuck herself, she must have been at it for fifteen minutes.

I can tell you that she came twice but it may have been more times. She finished up by pushing that cock all the way in and used her hips to make herself cum again. Finished she sat on the table and licked the cock clean. Then she surprised me, she dressed and put the cock into her bag, but don't fret, she then took a ten pound note from her purse and put the note into petty cash, she even put it down as a cash sale.

Chapter 29

Seven months on and I have recouped my investment, and I have taken all the girls out for lunch, mainly to discuss any new idea's, Amanda puts forward that we need another woman to man the computers and phones. There has been a mix up in the office this week, the problem was sorted out but it should never have happened. I want to introduce a small change and thinking about it, we should have done it at the outset, rather than just anybody answering the phones. One person is needed to take the job on and each call will be recorded on a pad and the action to be taken will be noted.

We agreed that the new woman would take that job on and it would be her responsibility. On the way home I told Amanda that any profits from now on would be hers, and from now on all the decisions would also be hers. I told her that I would be there for her and I would still come in everyday and do my bit. Back at my flat we were sitting on the settee with a glass of wine, leaning against each other when I said I had a surprise for her. She looked at me "Another?" I said "Yes, but you must never say anything, promise me." She promised so I picked up the remote and pressed play. I played her the disc of Emma in the storeroom, Amanda loved it and made me play the bit where she fucked herself again, sex that night was special, we seemed to have endless energy. Amanda insisted on sitting on the coffee table facing me and fucking herself with the biggest vibrator that we own, as Emma had done.

On my way back from the sandwich shop the next morning I passed a well known travel agency. I stopped to have a look in the window, sitting just inside at one of the computer terminals was a young blonde girl in tears, she held a tissue to her nose as she sobbed. Without thinking I walked in and sat in front of the girl, her name badge said Flick. She tried to pull herself together and be proffesional, I asked "What's the problem Flick?" she didn't answer me and just looked over her shoulder at the smirking manager, who's name tag said Simon. "

Has he been touching you?" she looked at me shocked and burst out crying, I winked at her and stood up, I walked up to Simon smiling, and asked " have you been touching my sister?" the smile disappeared as I kneed him in the balls, he sank down to his knees and groaned, I sat back down in front of Flick " can you get head office on the phone?" she nodded and picked the phone up and pressed a button and passed me the phone.

I told her to get her bag and coat, I spoke to the personnel manager and told him what I had done and unless they paid Flick 6 months severance pay, we would take them to court and I assured him that with my London lawyers we are guaranteed to win. The man that I was speaking asked to speak to Simon. I put my arm around Flick and walked out of the shop with her" thank you" she said "But what am I going to do now?" I stopped her and said "You can come and work with me." I smiled at her and took her back and introduced her to Amanda, she agreed with me and we gave her a job, and she turned out to be very reliable, she was a little bit shocked when she went out into the ware house and saw some of the stock.

My mobile rang and I was surprised when Lena said hello, it appears that she was in London and staying at the Park Royal hotel and would it be possible for me to go up to London to see her as she wanted to discuss further business with me. I told Amanda and asked if she wanted to go as the business was now hers, she declined saying that she always felt intimidated by Lena. So I took an overnight bag and drove up to town, I arrived at the hotel about 6.30 and a tanned Lena stood to greet me, I noticed that she looked me up and down, and watched my braless tits as they bounced freely, we air kissed and she had my bag taken up to her room. We sat in reception and had a large glass of red wine while we waited for our table.

Lena told me how happy she was with what we did for her and how much easier her life is now, in fact she told me that her and her husband were opening two new women only hotels, 1 in Thailand and a second in California and she wanted to know if we could handle the extra business. I assured her that the extra work would not be a problem. She smiled at me and touched me on the leg "oh and thank you for my little parcel, I've had a little look inside but I haven't [how can I say] sampled them yet, I was wondering if you might see your way to demonstrating them, on me of coarse" I smiled and said " but Lena I have a strong relationship with Amanda " she smiled back and said " and I am a married woman, and I don't want to lose that, so it will be between us, you and me" I smiled and wondered if I could get out if this, but I couldn't see how. We ate a first class meal and I tried to get Lena drunk, thinking that maybe that would be a way out, but no, she simply said "Red wine just makes me ever so horny" with that she rested her hand on my leg.

We left the restaurant and headed for the stairs, I followed her to her room, she closed the door behind us and walked nervously to the window and turned to face me " I have to tell you the truth Sarah, I have never been with a woman and until we opened the nudist hotel I had never thought about it, but seeing all of those fit female bodies and all of those naked fannies, well I take a walk every day just to look at the women, even when my husband I make love I often think of you and the large black cock that you sent me. You with it strapped around your waist and ramming me from behind, like now I get so wet just thinking about it." She walked over to me and felt my tits through my thin dress, she looked into my eyes " make love to me Sarah" I took an inner breath and turned her around and unzipped her dress and let it fall to the floor, I unclipped her bra and that followed the dress, I reached around and took both firm tits in my hands, Lena leaned back into me as I fondled her tits.

I lowered my left hand and pushed it into her pants to her naked wet fanny, she opened her legs as I rubbed my finger along her slit, she began to moan, I could feel the moan as it rumbled inside her, I pushed two fingers inside her fanny and frigged her, in seconds she soaked my fingers, I kept my fingers moving for a little while and when I pulled them out I pushed them into her mouth, as a sort of punishment. She turned around and stripped me naked, she stood back and studied my body " I just knew that you would be perfect" she took my hand and took me to bed, I thought that I may as well try and enjoy it so I laid her on her back and spread her wide, I placed a pillow under her bottom and licked her fanny from end to end several times, I put my tongue deep inside her and tasted her cum.

Lena was a vocal lover, she made a lot of growling noises, I pushed two fingers into her and began to frig her as I pushed my lips over her clit and sucked for all I was worth, I think that it was the longest orgasm that I had ever seen, when I finally pulled away from her she lay trembling where I left her. I got of the bed and went to the parcel that I had sent her, I slipped on the large black rubber cock and used some sensitive fanny lube, I got back onto the bed and pulled her up, her eyes went to that big thick cock and she didn't seem so confident anymore, I moved her around onto her hands and knees, she looked back at the swinging cock as I spread her legs, I pushed the head of the cock inside her fanny and realised that she had never had anything so big inside her before, I pushed forward and she groaned out loud as she was being stretched for the first time, I gripped her left hip as I pulled back half way, I slipped my right hand down to my fanny to find that I wasn't even wet, I began to fuck her, every time I reached full depth she would grunt, I fucked her hard, I rode her faster through her orgasms. After she had cum three times I pulled out and turned her over pulling her to the edge of the bed. Lifting her legs high and pushing them up towards her chest, I pushed the rubber cock back into her tortured body and fucked her until she went slightly limp.

When I pulled out and she immediately curled up into a ball. I covered her with the bed clothes and went for a shower, returning from the shower Lena had not moved a muscle, the only difference was that now she snored gently. I dressed and left, as I drove back to Brighton I had a lot of thinking to do, do I tell Amanda what I was more or less forced to do, or do I keep it to myself? If I am honest I didn't know. My phone vibrated with a message, it was Lena – "Sarah where are you?" I know that I am a selfish cow but I want to make love to you, if you have left the hotel I hope that we meet again soon. Lena. I deleted the message and thought "not if I see you coming first."

I phoned Amanda and told her what Lena had said and that she would need to expand the business, I then told her that I was driving up to Broadway to look at a cottage that was for sale. Amanda asked me what was wrong, I said nothing, but she knew that I was lying, it looked like I had a day to think of something, after driving almost 300 miles the only thing that I could tell her was the truth. When I arrived home I was surprised to see the lights on in my flat, when I opened the door Amanda came to meet me at the door, she threw her arms around my neck," oh Sarah, what did she do to you?"

I stood there and cried in her arms, she took my hand and led me to the settee, " tell me everything" so I told her the truth, even down to me being totally dry during the whole thing " she nodded her head " Lena rang me and told me what she had done and how she had put you in an impossible position, she said to apologise to you and if you did not want to do business with her anymore, then she would understand" I looked at the woman that I loved more than life itself. "I'm sorry Amanda, if you want to end our relationship then I understand" she shook her head and said "Don't be silly Sarah, you know that I love you, we will never speak about it again".

We went to bed and made love to each other very tenderly as if our lovemaking would make everything better, I hoped that we would survive this. We moved into new premises and took on three more female staff, things were looking very rosy for Amanda and I. I made a ridiculous offer on the bungalow in Broadway but surprisingly never heard any more about it. We received an invitation to attend the opening of 'The land of Women' hotel in California but we declined the offer. We sent flowers and best wishes for the future. Amanda had spent time on organising a women only weekend at a country retreat but she came to me with a problem. The weekend was sold out and the whole weekend would be staffed by women. The problem she had was security, she has stressed that any nudity outside of the house is at there own risk, this has been printed in big letters on the tickets, but I still think that we need some security. I told her to leave it with me and that I would think of something. The solution came to me later that day and by the evening I had the security in place at a reasonable cost. I phoned Amanda and told her that I had sorted her problem and if she wanted to see them in action, then I would pick her up at 4 pm at work.

I picked her up at 4 and we headed for East London, Twickenham RFC. I gave the guard my name and we were let through. We parked where we were told to and then we were shown to our seats by the training staff of Englands Women's Rugby team, Amanda smiled and said "You clever old thing you, but won't it be expensive to hire the whole team?" I smiled and said "that's the beauty of the whole thing, you see, they will do security at every event that we will hold, in return we will provide a week in the Caribbean for the team, each with a parcel of selected items. I am sure that if you spoke to Lena she would do you a discount for a bulk booking." She squeezed my hand "I would never have thought of that, Sarah you are clever".

The team turned up for briefing on the team coach, wearing the teams blazers and ties. Amanda was doing the briefing while guests were arriving. There were some strange looks between the rugby players and the pretty young things that would soon be walking around naked. Torches and walkey talkies were handed out. The local cadets had erected a large tent, complete with bunks and mobile toilets, all done for a small donation, this had been done for the England team to rest in. Showers and food would be taken in the hotel where the manager had taken charge of the security. I don't know if it meant anything but every one of the team volunteered to patrol the inner circle around the hotel, it must have been the thought of all those fit naked bodies on show.

Each client that was there for the weekend, on arrival to their rooms they found on their beds a parcel from Women on Women's holidays, containing a selection of toys and lubes plus all our paperwork on holidays abroad. Amanda had organised a 60s & 70s disco and we had a beauty contest for the best trimmed fanny, which was quite amusing. I must say that most of the women behaved themselves until the slow last dance. From where Amanda and I were standing, there was a lot of mound thrusting and rubbing going on.

We could see the odd hand between the odd pair of legs, the longer the slow music lasted the more gyrating of hips went on. An older woman asked Amanda if there was to be an orgy at the end of the evening? The answer to that was simple, we were going to bed, Amanda would make an announcement, at twelve midnight that the evening would be officially ended. Some women will be staying behind for adult fun and games but on no account must anyone feel obliged to stay behind.

All games would be self supervised and on no account would the games be the responsibility of organisers of the weekend. We waited until the games were about to start. There were couples making love in corners, strap on cocks and vibrators seemed to appear from nowhere, lubricants were being applied to cocks all over the room. We decided to leave them to it and have a party of our own.

The weekend was a great success, there was not a single complaint, there were no security breaches but there had been a reprimand given out as one of the coaching staff, who was on indoor security was caught naked on the pool table with a nubile 20 year old blonde with big tits. We organised rounders on the front lawn which began fine but decended into chaos when a woman player stuck the bat up her fanny and everyone stood round and cheered. There were couples laying together naked in the sunshine. Naked waitresses walked around passing out drinks and groups sat around and talked. All in all it was a nice weekend, the spa was kept busy at all hours and the staff joined in with the party as the evening went on. At one stage I think the only dressed people in the whole hotel were Amanda and I, even some of the rugby players were naked and mixing in with the guests.

Chapter 30

The company grew and grew, everything that we touched turned to gold, we were even organising private women only parties at people's homes. Sometimes these would begin with sex toy demonstrations, we used local women for these parties. To find these women we handed out a few cards at local parties and we got more names than we could use. Things were perfect until November12th 1998 when we had a visit from the local police, a complaint had been made that we were organising sex parties and promiscuity. Leading the investigation was detective ins Helen Oaks my old lover, she came into the office all business like, she cautioned us and said that a full investigation would be held. I sat opposite her and said simply, "any party or event that we have organised has been recorded on disc, all parties involved have been consenting adults which we can prove beyond doubt. All profits have been declared and taxes paid, as you should know from our time together I do not take risks and I cover all of the angles. Now, Helen. Do your colleagues know that you have had a sexual relationship with me, because I do not think that you should be allowed to handle this case. I suggest that you make this go away and quickly," she folded her note book closed, "I didn't mean to hurt you Sarah, I loved you and I have been with no-one since you" she said. "What about Simon?" I asked, she shook her head "He was the biggest mistake of my life, he promised a lot but delivered very little, he lasted 30 seconds then wiped his small cock down my skirt and went back to the party. I went home and cried, because I knew what I had lost in you, all through my own stupidity, I will pass on my report to my superiors, it will be up to them then. Goodbye Sarah". She went to leave then turned back and said "If you are ever lonely Sarah, you know where I am." I spat out the words " Don't hold your breath".

The investigation that followed did nothing but take up time, we had every angle covered, in the end we had to get lawyers involved and they don't come cheap. Our security guards were in the Caribbean and we had already received future bookings from some members of the team. Amanda and I finally decided to move in together after all this time and if after 6 months we were still together then we would get married. Now that the company ran itself Amanda could take some time off, we decided to spend some of her company money and go shopping in Las Vegas I had a plan in the back of my mind about another venue actually in Las Vegas for a women only party. We left from Heathrow for our long flight. We arrived and stayed at Ceasers Palace, we shopped for three days, took in shows and visited the sights, I had arranged to have a meeting with a Johny Leness the owner of Ceasers, again I had not told Amanda, but with one hour before the meeting I filled her in on my idea about having a weekend here at the Palace, in the ballroom, we would need to book every room in the hotel, and the main concession would have to be the security cameras. They would have to be switched off for the duration. Having told her all of this I asked her if she wanted to take control of the meeting, she said "I will if you are by my side" she took the meeting but Mr Leness wanted all of the profits and he wanted to be able to film everything, in the end we decided not to bother.

We hired a car, bought a large blanket and a picnic and drove out into the desert. We actually made our way into the mountains where it was cooler and found a spot miles from anywhere, I spread the blanket on the ground and stripped Amanda naked removing my own clothes, I took the ice cold champagne and ice from the boot and teased Amanda with ice cubes, rubbing them around her nipples, and down her stomach. I poured champagne into her belly button and sucked it out, I even poured some into her fanny and sucked that out as well, I made love to her as I had never made love to her before. When I was done I lay back in the sun and Amanda said "I'm not complaining, but what was all that about?" I looked up into the clear sky " I just wanted to show you that I love you" she rolled half way onto me and put her lips to mine," you don't have to prove that you love me, I know that you love me, and I love you with all of my heart" with that she slid her hand down to my fanny and slid her finger slowly down my slit and into my entrance. She finger fucked me all the way to a beautiful climax, she then moved around and sucked all of the warm cum from me. We stayed out there on our own for the whole day making love when the fancy took us. Finally we drove back into the city, both of us wearing the same, a thin summer dress and a pair of flip flops, we were braless and pantyless, Amanda did a very naughty thing on the way back, we were sitting in traffic and there was an huge truck by the side of us, the driver wore a stetson and dark glasses. He sat staring down at us in our open top car, and stayed by our side, as we crawled along, Amanda looked up at him and he smiled and nodded at her, she then realised that her dress had inched up, and she was showing a lot of leg, when she looked up again he made a motion with his finger and looked at her dress. She looked down at her dress which was maybe 2 inches from her naked fanny and glanced up to see him smiling. She eased her bum forward and parted her legs quite wide. The truck driver edged forward trying to see up her dress. Amanda began making signals to him and he was making signals back to her, she then surprised me by pulling her dress up and flashing her naked fanny at him. She let him get a good look and then pulled her dress back down. He had become very excited, she started pointing at him, he began fiddling in his lap, the next time he stopped and signaled that he wanted another look, so Amanda pulled her dress up to her waist and then undid her shoulder straps and flashed her tits at him. Then she reached over to my lap and pulled my dress up and showed him my naked fanny, he slammed his brakes on and stood up in his cab and flashed his hard cock. Then he began wanking, Amanda pushed two fingers into her fanny and began wanking too. She reached over and pushed two fingers into me as well. I helped matters by pulling my top down and flashing my tits, the drivers hand was now flying up and down his cock, he suddenly shot his spunk on to the hot tarmac. I made a decision and changed lanes and sped away, leaving a very happy driver far, far behind. You may think that was the end of that situation but Amanda kept her fingers inside both of us and took us both to our climaxes. When I pulled up outside Ceasers I slapped her on the arm and said "What are you like" she just giggled and said "That is the first time that I have ever made a man cum".

There was a message for us at reception, apparently Lena has phoned the office, and seeing

that we were in America why not jump on a plane
to California and come and see the new hotel, I
passed the message to Amanda, after she had read
it, I said " well you are the boss", she looked at me
while she thought about it " she has a way of
putting things, doesn't she?" I shrugged and said
"we could always say that we never received the
message" Amanda shook her head and said "We
can't really do that, can we?" the next thing we
knew we were on a plane to California, we were
met at the airport by limo, and taken to the hotel.
On first impressions the hotel looked American on
the outside, and more so on the inside, Lena met us
in reception and gave us the tour of the hotel, she
had reserved the best room in the hotel for us, all
free of charge. Champagne was in an ice bucket
waiting for us. She left us to unpack and said that
she would wait for us by the poolside. We
unpacked stripped naked and donned our dressing
gowns. We hung the gowns on the hooks provided
and walked naked to the pool, Lena drank in my
body as I walked towards her, we sipped
champagne while she told us how good business
was. Lena and her husband had plans for a total of
six hotels of the same ilk, which would be good for

us, business wise.

We had a great time in California except Lena kept trying to get me on her own. It seemed that she still wanted to fuck me, or she wanted some more of what I gave her before but Amanda was not going to let that happen. We were walking along the beach, when I noticed that they had huts out in the water similar to the ones in the Caribbean, so we decided to swim out and escape. The huts even had bottles of booze in the water, we lay in the sun enjoying the peace and quiet when Lena swam up to the hut and crawled out of the water to lay down by us. "Are we going to party, the three of us? "She said and with that she pushed her hand between Amanda's legs and pushed a finger deep into her fanny. Amanda slapped her hand away and stood up and dived into the water, I followed her and we swam to the beach and walked straight to our room and packed. We caught the first plane home. Amanda was devastated, she was deeply hurt but for business reasons she would have to get over what had happened, or sell the business. To be honest I wasn't bothered either way, I had enough money to live on for the rest of our lives, but it was Amanda's decision, and I would let her make it.

Amanda threw herself into work, her experience with Lena had upset her badly. Just for something to do rather than any other reason she decided to do a stock take. We did the stock take in one evening and found out that some stock had gone missing. Now she was angry and it gave her something different to focus her anger on. I called our friendly private investigator friend and explained the problem to him. He came back the next evening and set up some spy cameras, that were linked to our computer. We were to watch the playback each night and when we knew who it was that was stealing he would put a case together against her that we could do with as we pleased. The case would be good enough to take to the police. We watched the replay each evening but it wasn't until the fourth day that we discovered who our thief was. It was a new woman named Eve Brown, not only was she stealing but she was stealing to order because when everyone had gone home she walked around with a list, and ticked the items off as she went along the shelves. We gave the investigator the information that he wanted and he advised us to let her carry on stealing while he built his case, the only thing he wanted to know was when we saw that she had helped herself, we were to let him know. We did as we were asked. It took him two weeks to put the case together, he even had pictures of her selling the goods in a local pub and taking orders from one of our catalogues. I called a local friendly police officer namely Helen Oakes and gave her the file from the private detective and also showed her the recordings that we had of her actually stealing. Helen did a good job, they even arrested her clients for receiving stolen goods.

The court case was very interesting, Eve Brown had previous for similar theft so she received one year inside and each of her clients were fined for receiving stolen goods. We put signs up in the warehouse stating that all staff would be filmed while they are in the warehouse and any theft would end in prosecution. We claimed on the insurance for the theft and when they saw the steps that we had taken, both before and after the theft, they paid out in full, so all was well again.

Chapter 31

Helen Oakes rang me at home in the early evening and said that she needed to see me urgently, and could she call around straight away. I agreed and made sure that Amanda would be in the room when she turned up. While we waited we tried to figure out what she could possibly want. The doorbell rang and I walked across the room and let her in. She sat down next to Amanda but looked nervously at me "I have some bad news for you Sarah, I'm afraid that both of your parents are dead, their car was run off the road and they died when their car exploded in a ravine. The local police are convinced that it was them as they had only left a friends house seconds before, the other vehicle involved has not been traced. I have the contact details of their lawyer in Toronto, I am sorry for your loss" and with that she was gone. To be honest I don't know how I felt, my parents had been out of my life for so long, I had not thought of them for a long time as there had been no contact whatsoever. I looked down at the contact details of Cohen and Cohen, attorney at law: Toronto.

I spoke to the lawyer the next morning, he told me that if I did not want to attend proceedings then he can appoint people to sort everything out for me, as for the last will, he will appoint a law firm in London to have all legal papers signed, not quite knowing what to say, I asked if they were financially stable or will I need to send money to cover any costs " oh no", he said "your father was a very successful business man over here and as I understand it you are the sole beneficiary to a substantial fortune, but that is all for another day. Now your parents stated that they wanted to be buried in England, but under the circumstances, well without being to blunt, there is not much left to bury, so maybe a cremation over here would be best. I can see to all of that I know from my chats with your father that he regrets the way that they so selfishly treated you, taking that into consideration if you do not want to attend then everyone here will understand, anyway please let me know what you decide, at your convenience. Goodbye Sarah." We said our goodbyes and I hung up. I felt sad but then I wondered why, because they had never been very good parents, they couldn't wait to ship me off to this school or that school, obviously I did not fit in with their plans for their future. I talked things over with Amanda and quite rightly she told me that only I could make the decision, I decided not to go, maybe I would regret the decision, maybe I would not.

I had been doing some research on the computer about the state of rural farming, that may sound like a strange subject, but I had my reasons. I seemed to be going through a bad patch because I had a phone call from the office asking me to contact Tony Shore urgently, what could Lena's husband possibly want with me. I found his number and rang him, when he answered the phone, he didn't seem too happy, we exchanged pleasantries and then he told me that Lena had left him, and ran off with a young woman. The reason for the contact was that Lena was threatening to take him for every penny that she could so he was looking to sort of hide a fair chunk of cash and thought that maybe he could make a cash offer for our business. He understood about the women only thing and he would put his sister in there to run the whole thing. "How does that sound Sarah?" he asked. I explained about Amanda and he asked me if I could act on his behalf as he knew and trusted me, I asked him what figure he had in mind, when he told me, my heart raced, I told him that I would have a chat with Amanda and get in touch with him in a few days.

I sat Amanda down in our favourite restaurant and told her what Tony Shore had proposed. She seemed stunned at first but when the idea had settled in her head, she was desperate to know how much he was offering. I told her I would tell her in a while, I teased her by saying "you will accept, and when I tell you how much money you will have in the bank, you will wet yourself" Amanda clapped her hands together excitedly, I kept her in suspense until she was pleading and promising to do all sorts of things to me if I would only tell her. I waved her close and whispered into her ear " one and a half million quid." Amanda sat there with her mouth wide open, silently mouthing the words "oh my god." She began to nod her head and what I said next made her slap her hands over her mouth. I said "cash" she began to stamp her feet, I could see that she wasn't breathing, I had to slap her on her back to make her breath. We made love for most of the night and we decided to take the money and run, we also decided to get married. I phoned Tony Shore early the next day and gave him the good news, he was delighted and said that he would get the paperwork done as quickly as possible. The next day I told Amanda that I had a plan for our future and I would be taking the day off today to try and sort things out.

I drove deep into the Cotswolds to view Manor estate. The manor house itself has 18 bedrooms, 3 reception rooms lots of stables and other outbuildings and 140 acres of land. I viewed everything with my master plan in the back of my mind and it was perfect for what I wanted. The whole thing was on the market for £1.8 million I made a onetime only offer of £ 1.6 million saying I needed an answer that day as I was viewing another property the next day. As I sat in the grounds waiting, I made mental plans on what I needed to do to the place, to meet my needs. Their answer came 5 minutes before close of business and yes, they would accept my offer. I drove back to Brighton with the details on the Manor estate As I walked into my flat Amanda was cooking a meal for us, she greeted me with a kiss and I kissed her back "Successful day?" she asked. I nodded "Very successful, thank you, very successful for both of us actually" she looked at me and smiled, "I thought you were up to something, tell me?" I shook my head and said "Lets eat first" she dished up the spag. boll, and it was delicious. When we had finished eating I asked her "How would you like to live in the country?" She smiled and nodded so I passed her the brochure on Manor Estate, she flicked through the pages first, then looked at me and smiled. Then she went and sat on the settee, folded her legs underneath her, and read every word. She sat and thought things through for quite a while "Only if we pay half each?" she said, I smiled and said " let me tell you my plan first, then if you are still happy we will discuss paying for it." She waited for me to start. I readied myself and began "My plan is quite simple really, we will open a women only spa, where nudity is the norm, there will be all women staff and once a month we will hold women only weekends, on the same lines as what we already do but with a twist. We will have a lot of land to play with, there is a lake for boating, stables for riding and we will have ball games on the front lawns. We could also have a shop, selling expensive cosmetics and sex toys, anything we want. Amanda had become very thoughtful, "only if we have a manager to run the place" she said.

We drove up to The Manor Estate, the first thing that we came to was a For Sale sign with Sold splashed across it, we smiled at each other, as I drove on, we took our time and covered every field and every shed on the grounds, we looked in every room in the house, and made plans as we went, we spent all day at our new home. Later we drove into Broadway and stayed at the Lygon Arms Hotel. We met a local builder, John Taylor that had been recommended to us by the present estate manager. When we laid out our verbal plans and asked him if he could cope with the work, "I can if my brother and his lads are free?" he said, it was agreed that he would meet us there on the next Saturday with his brother and we could then get some jobs down on paper. Work began in earnest, the brother made a mistake when he made a pass at me, in no uncertain terms I told him to "FUCK OFF" and to get off the estate immediately. He left but left his men working which was lucky for us. Amanda had gone off to meet Tony Shore and finalise her deal, she agreed to take his sister to the warehouse and introduce her to the staff. Amanda suggested that Debs be made manager and that is what happened. Amanda drove back to the estate and searched for me. She found me down by the lake, talking to one of the workmen about building a boathouse. Amanda came down and grabbed my hand and dragged me away back to her car. "Whatever is the matter?" I asked, she looked all around and opened the boot of the car. There were two leather suitcases in it. "Go on, open them" she said, I bent down and opened the right hand case, it was full to the brim with English money, I looked at her and said " what have you done?" she opened the other case, and that was full of money too. "When he said cash, he meant cash, £ 1.5 million in cash" she said. I was stumped, "Have you got all of the paperwork signed?" I asked. She nodded. I phoned Mr Grattan my solicitor in Brighton and told him the complete story. He asked me what time I could get back to

Brighton, when I told him, he told me to go straight to my bank and he would meet me there.

The bank had been closed for three hours when we arrived, there were two security men waiting outside the bank, and as soon as we pulled up, they came and stood by the car. Mr Grattan and the bank manager came out of the bank and we all shook hands. Amanda opened the boot, the security men took a case each and carried them into the bank. The cases were placed on a table and opened. Everyone in the room just stood and stared into the cases then two women stepped forward and began emptying the cases. When the money was all stacked in neat piles, they began the task of running the cash through counting machines. We sat and watched the proceedings and after just over an hour the two women conferred and pressed lots of buttons on a large calculator, the elder woman looked at me " £ 1.5 million?" I nodded. All of the paperwork was checked by the solicitor and the bank manager, and then credited to Amanda's account. We were relieved as the money was finally pushed away on a large trolley to be locked in the banks safe.

Things were moving along nicely at Manor Estate. We had not been there for almost two weeks and as we drove along the main drive we could see lots of changes. The most striking was the new boat house and as we pulled up to have a closer look. I had to admit the workmanship was first class, there was room for 6 rowing boats, with staging between each boat, the smell of newly sawn wood hung in the air. The boathouse was perfect so I took a few pictures before we headed to the manor house. As we neared the house we looked across at the stables and the transformation was amazing, the finished article looked just like the architect's drawings. Upon seeing us John Taylor walked over to greet us, he took us around the stables and the other outbuildings to show us the finished work. The workmanship was again first class. The first thing that we noticed in the house when we entered was the new oak reception desk. What struck me the most was the noise of work going on, drilling, hammering, sawing and someone singing along to the radio. I asked John if we could go up to the roof. "Certainly" he said and led the way. Once up there I asked him if he could leave us alone for a while as I wanted to talk to Amanda privately. When we were on our own she looked at me with a glint in her eye, and said "It would have been more private at the boathouse, if you wanted sex" I laughed and slapped her arm, "I wasn't thinking anything of the sort" I said. "I'm just looking at the view".

Amanda walked by my side. "It's truly magical up here, isn't it?" she said. We stopped at a point where we could see most of the estate and I took her hand and said "that is why I think that we should use it for our guests" I went on to explain that as the roof was virtually flat we could cover the roof with artificial grass erect some sort of screen along the outside wall and make the whole roof totally private but low enough to be able to see over. We could have some outdoor closets for drinks and blankets. "What do you think?" she gripped my hand tighter. "I love the idea, the only thing is, I want us to be the first to fuck up here when it is finished." I nodded in agreement.

John Taylor promised that the whole project would be finished in six weeks, as long as we didn't think of any more jobs. Even though he didn't know what our plans were he thought that the roof idea was good and he would begin as soon as possible. My phone rang twice in succession the first call was for me to go up to London to sort out my parents will asap. The second was a call I had been waiting for. I told Amanda that I had to go and see a man by the main gates and could she choose a room for us to live in, she wanted to come with me, but I put her off as what I had planned I wanted to be a surprise. We stayed at the Lygon hotel again for the night. I was watching the woman who was the under manager, and Amanda told me off for staring at her. I assured her that I was staring at her for all of the right reasons and I asked the waitress if she could ask the woman to join us for a few minutes. I leaned close to my lover and said "Do you trust my judgement?" she nodded and looked at the woman as she walked towards us. The woman came over joined us and I asked her some questions. After a few minutes I gave her my card and asked her to ring me first thing in the morning. She frowned but said that she would. As she walked away, I touched Amanda's leg and whispered " I think that I have just found our new manager".

Her name was June Knight and when she rang I invited her to join us at the Manor house for a chat, as she only lived a few minutes away she said that she would be right over. June Knight turned out to be a no nonsense woman, she listened to all of our plans and our history in business. She seemed very interested and I had a sudden thought that turned out to be the clincher. "How do you feel about nudity, June?" I asked, she looked from me to Amanda and blushed "You don't want me to strip off here do you?" I laughed "no don't be silly, how would you like a holiday in the sun?" she smiled and said "Who wouldn't?" I arranged for her to go to the Caribbean to Tony Shore's place for a week, purely for research, naturally. While June was away, Amanda and I decided that as she was to be the new manager, and as she was local we would let her do the hiring of staff. Meanwhile we could be busy sorting out licenses and all the legal stuff. We had engaged a local female solicitor named Miss Julia Trent. Other than June, Amanda and I, Julia was the only other person that knew our plans for the Manor.

I had noticed a digger down by the lake doing, some work and there were other men there working. As I didn't know anything about this I asked John Taylor and he smiled and said "I am not at liberty to say, all I can say is that it is a surprise gift for you, and a nice gift it will be too". When I asked Amanda about it she smiled and tapped the side of her nose.

I took Amanda with me to London to see the Lawyer. We were sitting in their offices with the lawyer, his P.A. and another man who was introduced to us as Ian Judd my father's business partner. The lawyer read through the will. I was totally taken aback by not only the amount of money that my father had left me but also the amount of property and business interests. To cut things short my father had left me just under £5 million and when the lawyer began on the business interests the numbers just washed over me. At the end of the reading of the will Mr Judd stood up and walked around the room. He began by saying that my father was his best friend and had been for a long time and he would be willing to take everything off my hands for £ 8 million. He said that my father and him had agreed all of this a year ago because he had said how badly that they had treated you and you would not want to be bothered with the fine print. He put his hand out to mine and I shook it without thinking. The deal was done.

Chapter 32

When June Knight came back from her little holiday, she was full of smiles. "You could have warned me" she blushed, "and that is what you want to do here at the Manor?" she asked. "Yes" I said, "and we want you to run the whole thing, do you think you can do it?" She nodded, "I can do everything except the weather" we all laughed at that, we had a date for our opening and that was to be in eight weeks. When we arrived at the Manor the next day June Knight was sitting at the head of a long table on the front lawn, there were six women listening intently to her speak. She didn't break her stride as she nodded at us once in recognition. At that instant just listening to her told me that we had made the right decision in hiring her. Seeing that things were under control and in good hands, we had a meeting with her and told her that we had opened a business account in her name with £ 250.000 for her to draw on. We would require receipts for every penny spent and if she ran out of money or ran into any problems then she was to contact Julia Trent, as Amanda and I were going on holiday for four weeks and would be unavailable. If we did get chance then we would contact her. We were about to get into the car to leave when my secretive lover had a quiet word with June Knight. they talked for a good ten minutes and Amanda passed June a letter or a card. When she jumped into the car I looked at her and asked "What was all that about?" again she tapped the side of her nose.

We had discussed where we would go on holiday and decided to try something a little bit different and decided to hire a car and drive around New Zealand for four weeks. We toyed with the idea of hiring a camper van, but we like our facilities a little bit too much for that. So that is what we did, we completely lost ourselves for four weeks, [I did call Julia Trent, just to check on the Manor] but we had a perfect time just to spending some time alone without phones ringing and builders banging and shouting.

Chapter 33

As soon as we touched down at Heathrow and I switched my phone on, it instantly began to ring. Luckily there were no major problems. Before we had left for New Zealand we had agreed that the flat in Brighton would be sold and we would move into the Manor on our return. As requested I had left all of this in the capable hands of my lover, she had been on the phone more than me since we had returned home and I was dying to find out what she'd been up to. She put her arm around me in the car "Sarah, will you do something for me without asking the reason why?" I looked at her for a few seconds and nodded. "Can we go into town and stay at the Ritz tonight, please?" I smiled "Anything for you my love" and headed for London. We booked in at the Ritz and left our luggage to be taken to the room. We walked around Oxford street and spent an obscene amount of money on clothes and shoes then took a taxi to Harrods where my young lover wanted some time to herself as she wanted to buy me a gift. When she rang me two hours later and I met her outside she stood there empty handed. "Where's my special gift?" I asked with a broad grin on my face, she did the touching of the side of her nose again. It's nice to say that you have fucked at the Ritz, I mean how many of you readers can say that you have fucked at the Ritz, not many, to be honest when you get down to it, when you are in love like we are, a fuck at the Ritz is like a fuck in Brighton, warm wet and tasty.

As we approached the main gates to the Manor I told Amanda to cover her eyes, which she did and when we stopped I said to open them. Amanda screamed out in delight, over the main gates hung a huge sign that said :WOMEN FOR WOMEN'S SAKE: underneath it said. Women only past this point, and then in a heart in the corner were written our names as proprietors, Amanda kissed me hard on the mouth, then she got out of the car and came around to my door which she opened. "Out, I want to drive this bit" I did as she asked and she said "Your turn to cover your eyes" I covered my eyes as we drove along. She stopped and set the brake. "You can look now." I opened my eyes in amazement, standing before me by the side of the lake was a Canadian log cabin. Tears ran down my cheeks, "Our new home that blends in perfectly with its surroundings, Sarah it is just for us" she said and pulled me to her kissing me loving. The cabin was beautiful. Inside was every mod con that you could possible want. All my clothes were in one of the two built in wardrobes, Amanda's clothes were hung in the other, the bed was a four poster had been hand made from Harrods and it had a large pink bow across the pillows. Everything apart from the actual cabin had been hand made, and everything was perfect. Built out into the lake was a large porch with two rocking chairs. I pulled Amanda to me "Thank you my darling, it is perfect, you are so clever." Over the main door carved in oak it said. "Sarah and Amanda". We finally left the cabin and headed back to the Manor house, the whole place had been transformed. I stopped the car, got out and stood and stared. Everything was as we had planned. We left the car where it was and walked to the house, both pointing out new or changed features.

June Knight dressed smartly in her uniform came to meet us, she had done us proud in our absence. The finish in reception was a deep brown wood colour and you couldn't stop yourself from rubbing your hand over the shine. June took us on a grand tour, she had achieved everything that we had asked for and a lot more. She took us through the new dance hall, to the rear doors. She pushed the doors open to show me John Taylor and another man measuring the ground and knocking stakes in all over. When he saw us he waved and strolled over and asked "Welcome back, good holiday?" We told him that the holiday had been perfect but that coming back to all this was better. "You are clever John, what are you doing out here?" I asked. He indicated that we should talk to June. June took us to a table and sat us down. Laid out on the table were a set of building plans, "I asked John to look into extending this room for more sleeping quarters but obviously he would need your say so. The fact is we need more sleeping room, we have so many bookings and more coming in daily. I don't like to turn people away so early, especially when we haven't even opened yet, every one that rings has been on one of your holidays and wants to see what you are up to now." I looked at the plans deep in thought. "Let's go up on the roof" I suggested. The roof was exactly as I had requested, June had added a two telescopes, one either side like the ones that you see at the seaside. I walked around the roof looking out at the grounds, "How much more room do you think we want June?" When she told me, I stood looking out over the stables, "How smelly are horses?" I asked her. June's opinion was that it depended on how well they were looked after. I said "Can you call John and ask him to come up here please?" June called him on her phone and a few minutes later he arrived up on the roof.

I explained what i wanted and where I wanted it, he made a quick drawing and a few phone calls then turned to me and said "It will be expensive." I shrugged. "Just get it done as soon as possible." With the decision made, we looked around the rest of the Manor house. People were busy in almost every room, both men and women. Outside the main doors there were trucks and vans with drivers unloading boxes and carrying them indoors where a woman made notes of each delivery and signed receipts. A Polish woman was pushing a trolley loaded with fluffy white dressing gowns. She hung two in each room. I picked up one of the dressing gowns and showed it to Amanda, over the pocket it read "The Women's only Manor House." She smiled and took two from the trolley. "One each" she said. A man was busy putting up shelving in the room that was to be the shop. As fast as he put it up two women were filled the shelves with stock, from vibrators to perfume. Everywhere we looked tension was building, but at the forfront of everything was June knight.

The three of us stood in reception and watched as the Manor came to life, June explained everything that was happening. She pointed to a confident looking woman talking to another behind the reception desk. "That is Jenny Pyeman she is my under manager, she worked with me at the Lygon and is very good, she will take charge of all bookings and stock control. We have a new system being installed that will record every item from the shop that is sold and automatically reorders the sold stock, all drink dispensed from the bar will go through the same system. There is something else you should see. As you told me to us my initiative, see if you like this idea." We walked into the dance hall and there were a row of chairs set out, June picked up a remote, and as we all sat down as she pressed a button. A large screen folded down from the ceiling, she pressed another button and Summer Holiday starring Cliff Richards| began playing, it was fantastic. The screen it's self was a good twenty feet wide and ten feet high. "For those long cold evenings" she said and smiled. I took Amanda to one side and said "What do you think, lover?" her eyes said everything "It's beautiful. Can we go to the lake house now please?" I nodded knowingly, I turned to June "Walk with us to the car June please "I asked her. Amanda sat in the car waiting patiently, I went to the boot and opened my briefcase, I took an envelope with a £1000 in cash and passed it to June "Thank you for what you have done June, we couldn't have done all of this without you, a small bonus for your hard professional work".

Back at the lake house we fell into each

other's arms and kissed deeply, within seconds our hands were all over each other. I sighed deeply as Amanda's fingers took me to a strong climax, she then stripped me naked. I held her head as she made me cum again with her mouth. While she undressed I opened my case and took out my big black strap on, I slid it up my legs and clipped it into place. While I lubricated the cock in readiness Amanda had untied the pink bow and lay in bed waiting for me to join her. Once in bed our love making began slowly with kisses and touching until it all became too much for Amanda. She readied herself on her hands and knees and watched me as I prepared to mount her, I slid that thick cock deep into her body and made love to her slowly. I would take her to orgasm with a little extra speed, I made love to her until she was well and truly fucked then eased her onto her back and opened her legs wide. I soothed her sore fanny with my tongue, finally sucking her lips into my mouth until I exposed her tiny button and took her to another glorious climax. She lay there wide open to me as she quivered in the afterglow of perfect love making. Amanda pulled me up her body until I was kneeling over her mouth. I lowered my fanny to her mouth, my lover pleasured me for an age until she moved from under me and lay me down. She removed the strap on cock from me and strapped it to her hips then pulled me around until my bum was on the edge of the bed, she pushed my legs up to my chest and made me grunt as she entered me fully, she held my legs open as she made love to me passionately, going on and on until I was done. Amanda removed that thick cock and we took our time licking our combined juices from its rubbery length.

Sitting in our rocking chairs in our new dressing gowns, looking out over the lake, knowing that each other was naked underneath and tingling with love for each other, "It will work out wont it?" I asked Amanda, she nodded "June will make it work, she is really good isn't she?" It was my turn to nod. "I think we were lucky to find her" Amanda shook her head slowly as she looked at me "you know people Sarah, you can see honesty and worth in someone, so it wasn't luck at all." We sat there lost in our own thoughts as vehicles came and went and life carried on all around us. As darkness approached we strolled to the manor house it was all lit up and could be seen from every angle. As we neared the house we could hear machinery working, we followed the sound and found John Taylor and his men still working, there were four diggers digging trenches and a fork lift trucks unloading lorries full of bricks, cement and logs. When we spoke to John he told us. "We need to get this lot ready for the morning so we will stay here until it is ready." We walked around the house most of which was now quiet, the bedrooms were impressive and complete. We walked into the main room that housed the bar. There were rows of optics all with full bottles of wines and spirits and shelves full of bottles and glasses. Tables set out with comfy chairs all around them. Standing here now in the peace and quiet, it was hard to visualise that in less than two weeks everywhere you looked there would be women, women who are here to relax and have a good time, and to spend lots of lovely money.

We decided to go to a local wine bar for supper, the owners wife served us and she was keen to find out what we were doing at the big house. We invited her to have a glass of wine with us while we gave her the rundown on our project. When she left us she sat by the bar and I could see that she was having thoughts that she hadn't had for a very long time. As we were leaving, she pulled me to one side and asked me in a low voice," this nudity thing does that mean all of the women will be shaved?" I nodded "mostly why" she thought for a second "can I get a shave up there at the house?" I nodded and thought I had better phone June Knight. I wasn't able to contact her so waited for her to arrive at the house in the morning. When she turned up I asked her if we had a spare room, she thought about it for a second "There will be, we have the room that we are using for storage, will that do?" she asked "I think we need a beauty parlour with a curtained off section for shaves, and we will need someone to run it?" June thought about it for a few seconds. " I know just the person, I will go and see her tonight" she said, I shook my head. "Go now and get her up here as soon as possible, because if she needs any plumbing doing, we will have to get that done as quickly as possible".

Julie Whitehead arrived later that day, took

one look at the room and nodded, "that will do" she then turned to me and explained that she was about to close her shop due to lack of footfall on the streets and said "I could move all my stock into here as soon as the sinks are in, I have two girls working for me, will you want those as well?" I said "Yes, but I will want you to do the ladies lower shaves" she nodded in agreement and we discussed terms and conditions, again we called John Taylor and told him what was needed. " I will add it to the list" he walked away shaking his head. At six o'clock that evening he came running to the house "Come and see quick" we walked outside and coming up the long drive were a convoy of lorries, each one carried a Canadian log cabin. They were all identical. When the first one stopped in front of John Taylor the whole drive was full of log cabins, Amanda said "What are all these for Sarah?" I took her hand and said "This is our extra accommodation, all these will create: AMANDA'S VILLAGE: " she squeezed my hand "Oh, thank you Sarah" every man available helped to get the cabins into place, as soon as the last cabin was levelled, men were underneath the cabins connecting the utilities up, one by one the lights came on inside creating a Canadian village.

Two articulated lorries arrived early the next day, they were directed to the cabins, on the lorries was packed everything that would be needed to fit out every cabin from beds to flat screen TV's. All of the women from the house had to stop what they were doing and help with the cabins, even Amanda and I helped out. It took best part of two days to finish everything in the cabins. Julie Whitehead and her staff had got the salon ready and apart from the odd thing we were ready. A memo was then passed to each female involved with running the Manor to be in the main function room at 5 pm, from management to cleaners they were all required to be there. Row upon row of chairs were laid out and at 5 pm all of the staff were seated chatting excitedly amongst themselves. Champagne was passed to each person in the room. June, Amanda and I stood on the stage, I thanked everyone for all of their efforts and told them a bonus would be added to everyone's wage packet. Amanda went on to remind the staff that the customer was always right and if they were wrong then they were to be referred to Sarah.

 June stood up and talked about the nudity that will be the norm and it would be rude to stare. Customer care was most important and if there were any problems then we are to please bring it to the attention of one of us three. "As you all know we open for business on the 23rd and on the 21st we want to have a trial run. So the plan is that everyone does their jobs on the 21st and as you finish your duties you are welcome back into this room for a disco and free drinks, [a big cheer] there is one thing that you must all understand, and I know that it was explained to each and every one of you on application, but one of the main parts of this business will be nudity. On the 21st the choice will be down to you as an individual but on the 23rd remember that in certain areas nudity will be expected. Are we all clear about that? if nudity is a problem for you, then talk to one of us after. Now before you all leave tonight I want a word with all of the waitresses, please." Most of the staff left the room and all of the waitresses were asked to move to the front, when they were settled, June began again. " Now as waitresses you have all been issued with your uniform shorts, the reason for this is simple, take it from three people that have witnessed this at first hand, you as waitresses will no doubt be handled in one way or another, in all of the other similar hotels that we have been to the waitresses are naked and wear a see-through aprons, if any of you prefer this option then please say so. Now sex with customers, we know that we would never be able to stop this happening so please be discreet, don't forget you have all signed a waiver saying that you know what your job entails. Now this next bit is very important, there will be a certain group of women that at the end of the evening's entertainment will want to stay behind and indulge in adult games of one kind or another. You are not obliged to get involved in any way, if you want to get involved that is entirely up to you but don't come running to me crying when someone has pushed a great big rubber cock inside you, any questions?" A blonde girl raised her hand, June said "State your name and then the question pleas., "My name is Jerry. If any of you three come into this room will you be naked as well?" June nodded "As you have all seen there are areas that nudity is expected and yes we will be as naked as you, although we could wear a dickey bow tie, just to set us apart" this brought a lot of giggling. That was the only question, when asked if everyone was happy, everyone in the room nodded and clapped.

Chapter 34

The 21st has arrived, Amanda and I are standing in reception, not sure what is going to happen. The last we heard of June she was buried deep in the kitchens with the head chef. The chambermaids, cleaners and non essential staff were to be guests and they had all been given room numbers that tallied with their table numbers. The guests began to arrive which in itself was exciting, some had overnight bags and took them to their rooms.

One part that we never mentioned at the talk on purpose was a notice in every guests room suggesting that the guest wore the supplied dressing gown to the restaurant or main room as this lessened the risk of them losing any of their personal belongings. It pleased me greatly that almost everyone wore their dressing gown and when they entered either the restaurant or dance hall they hung the dressing gowns on the corresponding numbered peg as their room. The early guests were obviously at ease with their nakedness as they sat around talking or standing in little groups. Waitresses wearing see through aprons were busy taking food and drink orders. In the dance hall there were maybe fifty naked women and when a naked blonde woman who looked like a model entered the room to do the disco, there were lots of wolf whistles and cheers and as soon as she began playing music little groups entered the dance floor and began to dance.

I watched from the doorway as some of the younger women were pinching each other's nipples and a couple that had fanny hair, were having the hair pulled to hoots of laughter. The restaurant was doing brisk trade, although I did see one woman get her right breast stuck playfully with a fork. As the lights were slowly dimmed the dancing became a tiny bit more amorous in certain quarters. As more people entered the dance hall the dancers pushed closer together, some women were now dancing tit to tit and enjoying every moment.

June came and eased me to one side " there is a woman named Sue asking for you at reception," I walked out to reception to see the woman from the wine bar, she was all smiles, " I know I'm a little bit late for your invitation, but I heard about tonight and wondered if I could gate crash for a drink" said Sue, what could I say? "Come in, let me find you a dressing gown" I sorted her out, and within seconds she was naked and mingling on the dance floor, there was a loud shout and when I look over Sue had found someone she knew, she had a nice body too. At 11 pm there was a sudden influx as all the kitchen staff entered the room, there were a few high fives, a few of the women bumped boobs in welcome.

Then I saw the reception staff enter the room, the waitresses were all now naked as they carried the drinks high on trays. I watched as a couple had their bums pinched or slapped, they just smiled and carried on. I stood in the doorway with Amanda watching when a naked June came over, she rubbed her naked tits against me as she whispered into my ear. "There are a couple in the far corner getting a little bit carried away, what should I do about it?" I leaned over closely to speak into her ear because of the loud music, I looked down and her nipples were straining, they were that hard. "Leave them to it, that is what we would do with paying guests." She looked deeply into my eyes and nodded, she walked away from me but turned to see if I was watching her, when she saw that I was indeed scanning her she smiled and flicked her hair. I nudged Amanda as more couples were dancing even closer with their arms around each other, cheek to cheek, mound to mound, I took my dressing gown off and helped Amanda with hers we walked slowly around the room, the couple in the far corner were in a compromising position, the girl sat on the chair had her head back and her legs wide open, the other girl was on her knees with her face buried in between her friends legs.

We could see all the staff were now in the room and everyone of them was naked. We stood watching proceedings when Amanda turned sideways on to me and began rubbing her mound up against my thigh, I looked down into her smiling eyes, couples were now kissing quite openly and hands were everywhere. Amanda put her mouth to my ear "Is this fucking sexy or what?" she shouted, I dropped my hand down to her ass, she parted her legs and pushed her hips back. I leaned back slightly and reached under her ass and pushed a finger inside her wet fanny, she used her muscles to grip my finger and when I entered a second finger she moved her hips back and forth. I looked into her sparkling eyes as I frigged her to orgasm. She pulled my hand out put it over her shoulder and licked my fingers clean.

There was about half an hour left before the evening ended when a lot of laughter erupted from somewhere in the room. It seemed that someone had found my box of sample dildo's and strap ons that I had secreted in my office from the days when we had a stock room full in Brighton. Someone chucked a strap on at the couple in the corner. One woman picked it up and looked at it then put it on, there was a loud cheer as she lifted her partners legs and began to fuck her, maybe thirty woman stood and watched and began slow clapping.

When the woman who was being fucked held her head back and screamed out in climax the audience applauded the pair, then seemed to lose interest in them. Now everywhere that you looked in the room sexual things were happening. As I looked around the room I happened to look at the disco and the blond bombshell was nowhere to be seen, as we walked around the room, I could see her head low down behind the disco screen, a woman with long blonde hair was knelt behind her giving her a good fucking with a strap on.

Amanda and I watched proceedings for a few more seconds before I grabbed my lovers hand and led her from the room. We walked naked from the room, straight through reception and into my office. I closed the door and bent Amanda over my desk and attacked her with my mouth from behind. I made her cum and then opened my desk drawer and took out a double ender. I pushed a third of it into Amanda and as much again into myself I gripped the thick rubber in the middle and fucked us both. It would go into her then into me, I had complete control over the fuck.

If I went faster Amanda groaned out loud and if I slowed down she pushed back onto it. I controlled it so well that we came at the same time. After pulling it from our fannies we looked into each other's eyes as we licked each other's cum from that double ender. After we made our way back to the dance hall and the first thing we saw was Sue from the wine bar. She was on her back on a table and was getting a good fucking from one of the waitresses with a thick strap on. Everywhere people were having sex in one way or another.

The next day there were a lot of very quiet people at work, a few women had love bites and we had to send out for scarves to cover them, by lunch time the Manor house was getting back to normal, talking to the head chef a lot had been learnt from the day before, On the way back to reception I met the woman who was getting fucked in the corner, her name badge said Lisa, I stopped her and asked her if she was ok after last night, she blushed scarlet " you didn't see me did you ?" I nodded she put her heads in her hands and said " But I'm not that way at all" I pulled her to me and said " You were last night, you don't have to be again" she looked up into my face " The problem I have is this, I think that I really enjoyed it" I held her away from me, and said " you are young yet, you will sort out what you want, if you want to talk, you know where I am" she seemed reassured as she went on her way. Amanda had said that she wasn't feeling too good this morning. I thought it must be her period so I left her in bed. Later I tried ringing her a couple of times to no avail, when everything was sorted here, I would go and see if she was ok. June Knight appeared by my side, she smiled and said "There are a few sore heads about this morning" I nodded and said " Yes, but they are all doing their bit" she looked around "No Amanda today?" I told her that I had left her in bed, under the weather and she smiled and said " I will have you all to myself today then?" and walked off towards the kitchen, I thought to myself " I will have to put that young lady straight about a few things."

I walked quietly into the lake house to see if Amanda was ok, I opened the bedroom door to find Amanda doubled up in pain on the floor, I rushed to her and tried to lift her up, but she just moaned louder, I phoned for an Ambulance, I was told to make her as comfortable as I could. The Ambulance was on its way, I phoned June and asked her to bring the first aid nurse as quickly as possible. The nurse was there in a few minutes, and June tried to comfort me while my love could be dying for all I knew. Each groan from her tore me to pieces. The security woman on the gate directed the paramedics to us.

I have to admit that they were very professional, they gave her pain killers and connected wires and tubes to her. The Ambulance men had a quick discussion and one left and returned with a stretcher. He spoke to all three of us, " This young lady needs to be in hospital, we will take her to Cheltenham " Amanda screamed when they moved her onto the stretcher, she reached out to me as they went to take her away. I touched her hand and burst into tears, June said "I will drive " we got into her car and followed the Ambulance to Cheltenham. We had to sit in the waiting room waiting for news for an absolute age.

In the end I suggested that June go back to the Manor house in case there were any problems there but she wouldn't hear of it. She went outside and called her under manager who told her that everything was fine except that two guests had arrived from Germany a day early but they were settled into their room and seemed to be happy. An hour passed before anyone came out to see us. A nurse finally came and informed us that Amanda was being prepared for surgery, she has a ruptured appendix and was very poorly. She wants you Sarah but you can only see her for a minute, the theatre is being prepared as we speak. As soon as we get a phone call she will have to go. When I saw her tears rolled down her face, she held her hand out to me and I went to her. I wanted to speak but she put her finger to my lips and only said that she loved me before they took her away.

The wait was unbearable, June did finally go back to the Manor house. Before she went she did however pull me to her and told me to ring her day or night. She would stay at the Manor tonight and make sure everything was in order. She kissed me on the side of the mouth and left, three hours later the doctor came to see me, he had a grave look on his face as he sat down beside me. "Amanda is out of surgery but she is a very poorly young lady, we have taken her up to ICU because that is the best place for her. We found a small growth on her bladder, so we have removed that as well as the appendix.

The appendix had been burst for quite a while and she also has an infection. When you go and see her please don't be alarmed by all of the monitors and wires, they are mainly precautionary. The next 24 hours are critical" Anything else he said I did not hear. A nurse took me to ICU. Poor Amanda looked so frail surrounded by all of the machines and monitors. I could hardly see her face under a mask and tubes. I sat with her and held her hand, in all of the time I sat there she did not blink or move.

The nurse looking after her was named Kate May, a lovely northern lass. Her full attention was focused on Amanda, I don't know how long I had been sitting there but when a buzzer sounded doctors came running and I was pulled out of the way. The doctors shouted out orders and people were doing all sorts of things to my darling Amanda. I was finally taken from the ward and put in a room on my own. I cried and for the first time I prayed to God that she would be ok. A nurse came in and said that "Amanda has gone back to theatre, it seems she may have internal bleeding, we will keep you posted."

That is how they left me for hours, I would look along the corridors and see no-one, I made my way back to ICU, the bed where Amanda had been was now surrounded by curtains. As I approached Kate emerged from the curtains, in her hands she carried a blue tray that held tubes full of blood.

My darlings blood. Kate had not seen me as she was so engrossed in her work "Can I see her please?" I asked, Kate placed the tray on her table and took me to some seats, she sat by my side and held my hand " Amanda is very poorly Sarah, it is best if you don't see her at the moment, I will bleep the doctor and have him talk to you, he will be able to tell you more" I sat and waited for the doctor, the bleeping of machines and groaning of poorly people drives you mad after a while. The doctor arrived, he looked at the charts and spoke to Kate Then came and sat where Kate had. "Sarah isn't it? Amanda is very poorly, I have to warn you to prepare for the worse, if you have any contact numbers for her parents I should ring them sooner rather than later. If she is still with us in the morning she will have a chance. You can sit with her now" and with that he was gone, Kate came and took me to Amanda, she looked so frail and so helpless, I sat and held her warm hand, I thought she had squeezed my hand at one point, but I now know that it was only wishful thinking.

Kate never left her post at any time, but as the dawn began to break I could tell that she had become concerned, she spoke to a colleague and made a phone call, within minutes the doctor was back. He asked Kate to remove me as other staff turned up. More machines were brought in. The atmosphere had changed behind the curtains and after what seemed forever the doctor came and told me that Amanda was now on life support and it might be a good idea to say my goodbyes as soon as possible.

I sat with Amanda for most of the day, the doctor finally told me that there was no brain activity. Amanda was brain dead, he then asked me about harvesting her organs for donation, I nodded because I knew that she carried a donor card in her wallet, they asked about relatives and I told the truth when I said that I was all she had. They took her away at 10 am. I had said goodbye to the woman that I expected to spend the rest of my life with. I took a taxi back to the lake house, lay on the bed and cried. I locked the door and shut myself away. I looked out of the window and watched people arriving for the grand opening of the Manor house, in the late afternoon sunshine I saw two naked women walking hand in hand towards the lake, I watched then climb down into a boat and row around the lake, they stopped under a weeping willow tree and made love. Other women were walking around naked and still more cars arrived. Amanda would have been so proud. When I saw June walking towards the lake house, I opened the door and left it open, she tapped the door and walked in, she didn't have to ask she could tell that Amanda had gone.

I asked June if she could manage on her own, when she assured me that she could, I said that I was staying here until Amanda was finally gone, then I would decide what to do then, and that is what I did. I had a private cremation, where I said goodbye. I locked up the lake house and drove towards London, I stopped at the first travel agents that I saw and booked a cruise then spent the night in London and then flew out to meet the ship. I lost myself for 3 months.

Upon my return I drove through the gates of the Manor house and to the Lake house, I opened the door and all of the windows. Leaving the house wide open I walked up to the house. As I walked into reception the place was buzzing, there were women everywhere. I saw June about the same time that she saw me and she came over and hugged me "Welcome back Sarah" and she took me into the office. I asked her how things were going, "The business is fantastic, we have had lots of rebooking. We even have a wedding booked for next summer, and they have booked the whole resort for a week, the staff are all happy with their work. I had to recruit more waitresses and cleaners, but the bookings are fine and we are definitely in the black. Oh there is one thing that you may find amusing, you know Sue from the wine bar? [I nodded] well she is here most weekends, she loves coming here for a rest, ha, ha" I smiled at that. "June, will you come to the lake house later please?" she nodded "about seven ok?" she asked" perfect."

June arrived on time, with a bottle of red and a tray of hot ribs from the kitchen. We sat in the rocking chairs and enjoyed the ribs wine. I went into the house and picked up the casket with Amanda's ashes inside as Isat back down and held the casket I said " She loved this house you know June, and I think it is only fitting that she should be left here" and with that I tipped the ashes into the lake, I stood and watched the ashes spread out, June came and stood by my side and placed her arm around my waist, " you loved her didn't you Sarah ?" "Yes I loved her, and I don't think that I will ever recover from her loss" June pulled me into her arms and held me while I cried, she stroked my back as I calmed down.

I hated myself but I had a mental picture of her naked body at the disco, and her hard nipples as they dug into my skin, I took a deep breath of her scent, and for the first time since Amanda passed away I was wet down below. She kissed my neck and when I did not pull away she kissed me again and began to nibble my ear, I lifted my head from her shoulder and looked at her "do you want me to stop?" she asked, I looked down at her hard nipples and shook my head, she took my hand and took me into the bedroom, she reached behind me and unzipped my dress all the way to the top of my bottom easing the dress from my shoulders letting it drop to the floor then undid my bra and took it off.

My nipples were just as hard as hers, she lowered her mouth and sucked each nipple in turn, she undid her blouse and dropped it to the floor, her naked tits were the perfect shape. While she undid her skirt I reached up and fondled her tits as she dropped her skirt I could see she had on the smallest thong. She pushed it down her legs and stood there naked then reached forward and put her fingers into the top of my pants and pushed them down.

While she was bending over she pushed her mouth to my naked fanny. she was a practiced lover using the tip of her tongue along my slit to drive me mad. June eased my legs apart pulled my hips forward and made me cum a bucket full of female spunk. She pushed me down onto the bed and opened my legs again, she pushed two fingers deep inside me and frigged me, as I neared my orgasm she placed her lips to my clit and sucked for all she was worth.

This time when I came she lifted my legs and

pushed them forward and buried her tongue deep into my fanny and searched out my cum. June lapped at my fanny like a cat lapping up cream.

"Where are your toys, Sarah?" she asked. I told her and she took out the big black strap on cock fitted it around her hips and covered it with lubricant rubbing it all over the giant cock. She opened my legs again and pushed that cock deep inside me. June fucked me, on and on, she turned me over and fucked me some more. I finally had to tell her to stop as my fanny was so sore. She pulled the cock out and stood looking down at me "Feel better?" I nodded and reached for her, I unclipped the cock and placed it on the floor, I pulled her onto the bed and parted her legs.

I licked her slit from bottom to top, June moaned all the way, as I repeated the lick she moaned even deeper, it was obvious that she was close, so I closed my lips over her clit and sucked hard, her clit was long enough for me to flick it with the tip of my tongue, she was bent from the waist with her hands on my head watching me as I pleasured her. June came hard and long and as her grip loosened on my head, I lifted my face from her fanny and looked up into her face. She looked relieved so I pushed two fingers inside deep into her fanny and frigged her until she was close then bent the tips of my fingers up and located her ridged G spot.

I rubbed it back and forth, June went nuts, the noise that she was making was nothing like any human sound I had ever heard. When I pulled my fingers from her fanny her whole body reacted she lay there spread eagled. I picked up the strap on and clipped it around my hips, I turned her over and lifted her bottom, she spread her knees, I pushed that black cock into her and I fucked her hard, June was just as vocal while she was being fucked only now the noise all came from her throat, her head eventually dropped and I stopped but kept that cock buried deep inside her, I still gripped her hips just in case she wanted some more, but she had had enough.

We finished off with a fanny licking session, with June lying on top of me, I came first and it was a good job too as June growled like a dog as I sucked her clit. June dressed and looked in the mirror and adjusted her hair, "Where are you going?" I asked her "Up to the house to make sure everything is ok, can I come back when all is quiet?" I smiled "Just crawl into bed and wake me up".

Chapter 35

I slept restlessly for an hour or so I decided to get up and make a coffee. I stood leaning against the rail looking out over the still water of the lake, it was when I saw the reflection of a cloud in the dark still water. The cloud moved slowly over the water and as the moon appeared from behind it a voice spoke to me. "I thought you loved me" I suddenly realised what I had done, the lake house was Amanda's house and I had fucked another woman in her bed. My hand flew to my mouth in disgust, I threw some clothes into a bag, jumped into my car and left everything behind me.

I drove until I could not keep my eyes open. Finally stopping in a town that I did not know the name of. I found a hotel, checked in and slept until midday the next day. After a late breakfast I was back on the road heading north to where I didn't know. I had been on the road for hours when I saw a sign for The Lakes so I headed that way. I needed to hide myself away and this seemed the ideal place. The first town I came to I stopped and had lunch. The woman who owned the restaurant was obviously gay from the way she watched me. This was a relationship that was not wanted, a friend maybe but that would be all. I asked the woman if they did deliveries in the evenings, she smiled and said "Not usually but for you, I will deliver it personally anytime" with that she gave me a menu with her handwritten number on the top.

Three doors away there was a tiny estate agents, looking in the window I saw a five bedroom house with 62 acres of land called Willis House. I walked in and asked for the details on the house. The young woman who was serving me was called Gail. She said "We can arrange a viewing, anytime you want?" I smiled and said "How about now?" She stammered a little bit and said "I will get my coat" the drive to the house took 20 minutes. I fell in love at first sight, the house was basically a square with three steps leading up to the front door. Gail unlocked the front doors and stood to the side and let me enter, the house was fully furnished from top to bottom. When I looked out of the rear window and saw the grounds, I knew that I must buy the house. I turned to Gail and said that I would take it. She was as tall as me, with short brown hair, her eyes were a light green and she had a nice slim body with pert tits. She wasn't gay but when I looked at her tits, her nipples hardened, she blushed at her unnatural thoughts and looked down her body at her nipples. I expected her to cross her arms over her chest but she didn't, she let me look at them, and began to enjoy the thought. I'm not saying that I know women but Gail was wet definitely between her legs.

"Really, you will buy this house?" she seemed excited and clapped her hands. "Yes, I will buy the house, will a cheque do?" I offered, Gail nodded, I wrote the cheque out there and then and when I passed it to her, she looked at it, and said "That's the full asking price." "Yes, that's ok isn't it?" I asked as she stood looking at the cheque. " I can pay for my wedding now" and she grabbed me around the neck and hugged me hard, " oh thank you, thank you, this is not a joke is it?" I shook my head "No it is not a joke, you can even use the house for your wedding if you invite me?" I smiled as I said it" really, really, oh thank you thank you" she said excitedly. She then frowned " but why would you do all of this for me, you have never met me before?" I pulled her to me and hugged her" because I can, and because I like you." I said. Gail kissed me in the crook of my neck and whispered "Thank you." I drove her back to the estate agency, looked for a hotel and booked into the Crown hotel for a week. The first job for me was to e- mail June Knight and apologise for running out on her and for the way I used her. I asked her to pack all of mine and Amanda's stuff up and to ship it to Willis House.

Then told her that if she wanted she could move into the Lake house for as long as she wanted. I asked if the Manor was still doing ok and opened a bottle of wine and thought about my plans for Willis house. I made some drawings on a pad and a list of things to do and when I looked at my watch I decided that it wasn't too late. I called Gail on her mobile. "Hello?" she said " it's Sarah from Willis house,[we did some chit chat, before I asked her what I wanted] Gail, are you busy tomorrow evening?" I asked. "Not for you, what can I do for you?" she asked " Is there somewhere nice we could go for something to eat?" I asked her. "There is The Bridge, but it's very expensive." came her answer "Perfect, you book a table and I will pick you up can you tell me where?" She told me and we had a date.

I received an e-mail from June, she told me that I need not apologise, she understood completely, she even blamed herself for acting too soon and yes she would move into lake house and thanked me for the offer. She told me not to worry about the Manor house as they were fully book for a long time and there were many bookings for next year.

She asked if I had checked with the accountant because from where June stood I was doing very well out of the Manor and could l give her permission to make some small changes? Obviously I said that she could do whatever she wanted.

I picked Gail up from her council house, she had really made an effort with her dress, as I watched her walk to the car, I had bit of a twinge in my fanny, she looked that good. She surprised me when she got into the car and leaned across to kiss me on the cheek. "Hi" she said, she told me how to get to the Bridge and I must say it was very nice, the food was excellent. As we sat with our glasses of red wine I asked her about her wedding. She ran through all of the arrangements. When she told me she was going somewhere on the south coast, I had immediate plans for that.

I told her some of the story about Amanda and my plans for the Willis House, if she had any doubt about me being gay, those doubts were now gone. As we sat and chatted she said that she would make a list for me tomorrow that would give me all the names for my needs, she said "Can I ask you a favour Sarah? I told her to ask away. "Can I bring my mum to your house, she wants to have a look around to see what we need." I placed my hand onto hers [she immediately gripped my fingers] "Whatever she wants you must let me know, and I will get it for you." She rubbed her thumb over my fingers. "My mum wouldn't hear of it, but thanks all the same." I invited her and her mum to the house for a meal when I finally moved in which will be in the next few days.

I moved into the house at last and was immediately happy. I knew that this was my final move and I had achieved all I wanted to achieve. I would be even happier when all of my clothes and other stuff arrived in the container. It had all been packed in boxes and neatly packed into the container. I texted Gail and asked if she knew of a couple of strong lads that wanted to earn a few quid, She sent me an answer. "When do you want them and how many?"

I told her tomorrow evening and 4 should do it. The next evening Gail turned up with 4 lads. She introduced me to Brian her fiancée and his best man John, the other two lads were his brothers. Fair play, they worked hard and after they had carried every box up to the spare bedroom they were sweating.

I passed Brian £100 to take him and his mates out but he tried to give it back to me saying that I was doing enough for them, so I gave it to John instead. The four lads went off to the pub and Gail and I made a start on the boxes. When she came to Amanda's dresses. She said "These are beautiful" and held each one against her looking into the mirror. I moved up behind her and looked over her shoulder. "Why don't you try them on?" she looked horrified "Oh I couldn't, they are all designer dresses." I unzipped her dress down to the top of her bum.

She had on a white bra and white pants, as I pushed her dress from her shoulders she let it fall to the floor. She chose a flowered dress and I helped her into it when I pulled it up and did the zip up she looked a picture. Her bra showed, I said. "You wont' be able to wear a bra under that!" she tried pushing it down but she couldn't hide it " shall we take it off" she said as she looked into the mirror at me. I undid the back of her dress, [my legs were shaking] she waited while I undid her bra and pushed it down her arms then let me get a good look at her tits in the mirror before she pulled the dress back on. I did the zip up with shaking fingers and she smiled at herself knowing that she looked good. After we took the dress off she tried on at least a dozen dresses and each one fitted her perfectly.

As she removed the last dress that we had unpacked and we looked at each other in the mirror I said. "Why don't you take them on honeymoon with you, you will look beautiful, not that you are not beautiful in your own right." She looked back at me and said. "Do you really think that I am beautiful?" I placed my hands on her shoulder, she looked at herself in the mirror and standing there in her wet white pants she looked into my eyes and said "What's it like, you know, with a woman?" As she blushed I said. "If you don't want to do this Gail, I understand I don't want to lose your friendship." She turned around and placed her hands upon my tits and began fondling them.

My hands moved to her tits and began rolling

her small nipples. She pushed her hands under my top and reached up to my bra and pulled it down so that she could touch my naked tits. I reached up and pulled my top off and undid my bra. Gail pulled my bra off and looked at my tits, "You have nice boobs" she said and fondled them again, I put my fingers into the top of her pants and looked into her eyes "This is your last chance to pull out?" I said, she put her lips to mine and said "Take them off " in the next instance we were kissing passionately, I pushed my hands down to her bum cheeks and pulled her mound against mine, she was instantly into it.

Pushing her pants down and letting them fall to the floor, I took her hand and took her to my new bedroom Laid her onto the bed and began kissing her around her neck and ears, she immediately began purring quietly. I kissed her upper chest and moved down to her breasts. Sucking her nipples deep into my mouth then kissing all around her tits I moved down to her stomach to the top of her mound. I kissed all around her hips and thighs finally her pubic hair.

As I moved lower I felt her hold her breath, the first touch of my tongue on her fanny lips was enough to make her cum.

I took my time and pleasured her properly, I sucked her fanny lips then parted them and licked every inch of her sensitive flesh. Puckering my lips over her clit I sucked her to another climax. Her hand pulled my head harder against her fanny so I lowered my mouth to her opening and buried my tongue deep inside her. I licked everywhere possible inside her sex and enjoyed tasting her virgin womanly cum.

Lifting my mouth from her fanny I pushed two fingers into her making her gasp out loud. I frigged her slowly, Gail moaned out loud, her legs were as wide open as they could be, her hips were moving slowly up and down, as my fingers began to go faster her head came up and as she looked down at me I promised "I'm going to make you cum again." I watched her closely and as her hips began to go faster I pushed my lips back to her clit and she pushed her hips into my mouth.

Gail came hard, her orgasm lasted longer than any that she had had before. I continued sucking her clit causing her to moan more and more. When I lifted my head and looked into her face I asked. "Do you want to do some more or have you had enough?" She only said one word " More"

I stripped off naked and she saw my shaved fanny. "I've never seen a shaved fanny before" I moved closer and she rubbed her hand all over it, she looked up into my face as she rubbed her finger along my slit. I spread my thighs and pushed my hips forward so that she could get a good look then moved away from her and went into the other room. "You have had sex with your boyfriend haven't you?" I asked and she replied "Yes, why" I walked back into the bedroom with a red rubber cock strapped to my hips all lubricated and ready, it was 7 inches long and quite thick. Gail watched me walk towards the bed, I lifted her legs and pushed them up towards her chest leaving her young fanny at my mercy. The rubber cock found her entrance and I pushed forward, she groaned as she was stretched for the very first time.

I lowered my hands to below her knees to her thighs and pulled her bodily backwards to the right position then I began to fuck her. It was obvious she had never been fucked properly before. Holding her thighs I rode her steadily quickening my pace as she came, her tits were moving up and down. "Play with your tits" I said. Her hands came up and she gripped her nipples, with her eyes closed and her nipples being pulled Gail was in heaven. Eventually I slowed down and stopped then withdrew the rubber cock and asked her to turn over. Placing her into the position I wanted I immediately entered her again gripped her hips and fucked her to a standstill. She couldn't speak just waved her right hand at me.

I stopped fucking her and pulled the rubber cock out, she flopped forward and rolled onto her back and lay there panting and looking at me. "I've never had any sex like that before, that was fucking great. Can I do something to you now?" she asked. I unclipped the cock and placed it on the bed and lay down by her side. Gail leaned over me and began kissing me and fondling my breast, her left hand slipped down my body to my naked fanny. She rubbed her hand up and down my fanny lips. I desperately wanted her to make me cum, she must have sensed this as she pushed three fingers into my fanny and frigged me very fast as I soaked her fingers and she looked into my eyes and smiled then got of the bed and opened my legs. "Tell me if I do it wrong won't you?"

She lowered her mouth to my fanny and licked as I had searching out my clit. When she found it she flicked it with her tongue and slowly kissed me all around the area. As she licked and sucked she pushed a single finger inside my fanny and frigged me at the same time. When her mouth found my clit again, I held her head in place until I came again very strongly. I pushed her mouth down to my fanny so she could push her tongue into me. Moving my hips up and down against her mouth I came again on her tongue. Gail lapped up my cum until it was all gone. She finally pulled away from me and picked up the rubber cock and quickly figured out how it went on. Without any hesitation she pushed it into me and began to fuck me. A bit clumsy at first, the cock came out a couple of times but she soon found her rhythm and made a good job of fucking me after I came again and she stopped and lay beside me. We looked into each other's eyes."You can fuck me anytime you want " she said to me. "Even when you are married I smiled, her eyes sparkled, she smiled. "Even when I am married".

We sat naked on the floor and looked through the box of sex toys, she picked them up one at a time. She picked up the bunny rabbit and turned it each and every way pulling some funny faces. We looked at one another and she held it out to me and asked. "Tell me then?" I moved to my knees and pushed her down onto her back. "Bend your knees and let them flop open" she did as she was told, I lubricated it with my mouth and pushed it into her fanny, switching it onto slow speed it made her instantly lift her hips when I flicked the switch to fast and she gasped out loud. I moved it back and forth hitting her clit each time. She was more vocal now than she had been all night, her hips were going up and down all the time, and she almost screamed as she came.

When I slowed down, she cried out loud. "Don't stop, please don't stop" she came again and again. When I finally stopped, her cum had gathered on the right side of the base. I removed the bunny rabbit from her fanny and held it up to her. "Is that all mine" she asked and smiled. That was great, where can I get one from?" I told her that I would get her one. "Have you ever tasted your cum " I asked her she shook her head and made a face "Poke your tongue out" I instructed her and her eyes never left mine as she poked her tongue out, I touched her cum to the tip of her tongue, she took it into her mouth, and tasted it. "Not bad, but yours tasted better." she had a good taste of her cum and smiled.

We dressed and walked down to my car then drove down the drive with Gail resting her hand on my leg. "Are we doing some more unpacking tomorrow night?" she asked, I smiled "If you want to?" she took my hand from the steering wheel and pushed it up her dress to her naked fanny, she looked at me as I pushed a finger into her fanny. Gail moved her hand up my leg to my fanny, she was feeling me through my clothes. I stopped the car near the end of the drive and rather than get caught I turned around and drove back to the house.

As we entered the front door, I closed it and pushed her against it. We had our hands up each other's dresses and fingers in each other's fannies in seconds. We kept going until we had both cum. I couldn't help myself, I dropped to my knees and lifting her dress put my mouth to her fanny. She pushed forward so that I had total access. Using my mouth to take her to another orgasm, I stood up licking my lips and she pushed her tongue to mine. We were soon worked up again and I tried to pull away from her but she pulled me back and lifted my dress trying to take it off.

We went to an old antique chair and I sat her down lifting her left leg over the arm of the chair, "Pull your dress up" she exposed her lower body to me, pulling my dress over my head, I lifted my right leg over her left leg and pushed my fanny to hers. Rubbing it up and down over hers she knew what she had to do and within seconds we were rubbing fannies. This was the best yet for her, she came over and over crying out each time in ecstasy. I came as I watched her cum. Only stopping when my fanny was too sore.

Back in the car, on the way to her house Gail sat quietly, "I never could have guessed that I could have cum so much in one night, can we do that last one again tomorrow night?" I gripped her hand "If you trim your hair as it makes me sore, yes we can." Gail nodded and as I dropped her off and watched her walk up her path, she turned and waved before she entered the house. I drove back to the main house with a smile on my face.

Not feeling tired I spent a couple of hours on

the computer, sorting out things that I had in my head. First thing in the morning I received a phone call from a landscaper that I had e-mailed the night before. He had agreed to call round on his way to the job that he was on. Waiting in my conservatory with coffee and toast, Mr Green arrived in a green pick up truck.

I made him a coffee and he sat in the conservatory with me. I outlined what I required and he told me that a garden designer would call around after lunch but it was a huge job and would not be cheap. I assured him that money was not a problem but told him that I wanted receipts for everything and I would not stand being ripped off. The designer who when he did turn up said his name was Bo. We walked around the area I wanted to develop and told him what I had in mind. Bo took measurements and made notes for three hours taking pictures of the house and grounds. He made suggestions for the development before he left and promised me that he would get back to me in a few days.

I went shopping and waved at Gail, I bought what I needed and made some new friends. The butcher was a jolly round man, with rosy cheeks. He assured me that he could deliver any evening and yes he did know a good cleaner and cook. He gave me her number and I rang her, "Yes I could call and see her" and as it was only a short walk I bought a sandwich cake and headed off to meet the cleaning woman. Elsie was a middle aged woman, with grey hair, she was stick thin [not that I am a lesbian but she had no tits whatsoever].

We agreed that she would clean three days a week and she would cook as and when I needed her to. If it was for dinner parties her sister and Diane would help out. I walked back to the car and grabbing a sandwich on the way. After driving back to the house I showered and checked my e-mails. I had received a reply from a local artist that had been recommended to me. I had sent him the photograph that he required with his asssurance that the painting would only take 6 to 8 weeks. I was sure that Gail was on route so I rang her mother and asked if we could meet for a coffee, with the meeting arranged I waited for Gail.

I had emptied a few more packing cases and was halfway through another when Gail arrived. She got stuck in and helped me unpack a box and a half. We stopped and I opened a bottle of red wine and took two glasses from the shelf. We sat down on the carpet and drank the wine and chatted for a while. I asked her about Elsie and was assured that she was sound. I took her into the kitchen and asked her if she thought I needed a new one. She placed her arm around my waist and leaned against me, so I draped my arm over her shoulder.

After a few minutes I pulled her into me and hugged her, that led to a kiss, that led to a fondle and that led to me leading her to the bedroom. I stood there and let her undress me, when I was naked I undressed her. Gail had shaved her fanny but tonight she seemed to be a little bit bashful about her naked fanny. With no hesitation at all, we were into the fanny rubbing thing straight away. A few orgasms later Gail left the room and came back with my favourite black cock strapped to her hips, she was lubricating the cock with her right hand and told me to get onto my hands and knees. I smiled as she pushed that thick cock into me, she rode me well. She had learnt a lot from the previous night, when I indicated that I had had enough, she pulled the cock out and told me to stay where I was, she lay on the floor and turned over and crawled under me pulled me down so that she could get her mouth to my fanny. she had obviously given tonight a lot of thought and achieved her goal and bringing me to another orgasm.

As I unclipped the thick black cock from around her waist, she held my wrist and asked "Can I try that big one?" "You can try, but it is very thick" I strapped it onto my hips as Gail looked at it and swallowed. She sat back on the bed and lay back. I opened her legs and put that big knob to her entrance, I looked into her face and said" "If you want me to stop, just say so" she nodded. I pushed forward which made her arch her back and grunt, "ok?" I asked, she nodded again so I pushed forward again, she forced her legs wider to try and help. By then I had three quarters of that black cock inside her, I decided to fuck her with that much and see how we went on. I fucked her slowly at first going a little bit deeper at each stroke, with it all now inside her, "Is it all inside me?" she asked, I looked down and nodded. I gripped her hips and rode her a bit harder, she lifted her head as she came so I slowed down and looked at her.

She smiled at me "will you fuck me hard?" I must have looked concerned "Please" she said, I reached for a pillow and placed it under her bum then pulled her back towards me. I gave her the fucking of her life, when she finally told me to stop, I was panting with exertion. As soon as I pulled that cock out, she rolled onto her side and brought her legs up to her chest, she looked as if she was sobbing but there were no tears. I lay by her and held her tightly, she buried her face into my shoulder now I could feel the tears as they fell onto my naked skin.

Gail sat up and said " I have thought about this evening a lot today Sarah, and I wanted to try that big black cock more than anything, you see, I'm not sure that we can do this again as I don't want you to spoil me for my honeymoon, I have never enjoyed sex with my boyfriend like I do with you, and if we keep doing it I know that I won't want him. I will want to be with you, and that won't be right will it, I'm sorry Sarah." I took her hand and said "That's fine, whatever you want but you will still come round and help me won't you, and the wedding, I can still come can't I?" She smiled and looked down at her naked body I'm hardly in a position to deny you anything am I" she said. I pulled her to me and held her close, "Can I taste you one last time?" I asked.

Gail pulled away from me and stood up, she held her hand out to me and pulled me up and took me to the bed. She kneeled either side on my head and lowered her fanny to my mouth, she slowly moved her fanny back and forth over my mouth, her fingers were in my hair and she groaned out loud as she sank her fanny down onto my mouth. I drank her cum and licked her clean. We lay on the bed still naked "I hope I can resist you Sarah, and what if I want to really fuck you, what will you do, will we do it, I mean what you have just done to me, I don't think I could live without feeling that ever again." "Don't worry Gail, I will be strong enough for both of us" I said "But what if I don't want you to be that strong?" she said, I shrugged and that was it.

Chapter 36

Mr Green and his merry men were working on the land at the rear of my house. To me it looked like a giant mess, but I guess they knew what they were doing and Elsie the new cleaning woman worked like a woman possessed, What she had done in a morning would take me a week. I asked her if there was a laundry anywhere near "ney lass, ye don't need a laundry when old Elsie will do it for ya" she took the laundry and brought everything back, ironed and folded, and she even put it all away for me.

Gail came around most evenings, she had come on to me a couple of times but I had resisted her advances. The wedding drew ever nearer but Gail and Brian seemed to be growing apart slowly. After ten days with diggers and dumper trucks, men were all over the place banging in posts and building walls. Three days later I could see it all coming together. Mr Green asked me if I wanted them to start on the planting but I said "No, I want

to do it myself" he asked if I wanted him to order
the plants and again I said "No, I want to do it
myself. There is one other thing you can do for me
though, you can build me a fountain out front, with
a gravel drive around it." At last he smiled "I have
some pictures of fountains on the computer.

Maybe you should have three out back, if you
had one big fountain and two small ones you could
use the large one as a centre piece and run small
paths from the fountain to benches placed at the
outside of the flower beds. I'll fetch some pictures
of the fountains from the truck" I chose fountains
for the front of the house as they were the biggest
ones there. A large round bowl with the water
spouting up from the centre about six feet high. I
ordered three more fountains the same design but
smaller for the back and I ordered the plants that
were on the plans. It took two trucks to deliver
them all. The plants were dropped all along the
edges of the plot.

The area measured 500yards wide and

400yards long, it contained walls and paths, and at the far end there lay a raised bed in the shape of a half moon, that reached half way down the sides.

I spent my days planting plants as per the designers plans, I felt a great sense of achievement as at the end of the day I could look back and see the results of my labours. The garden had a gravel path that led to the biggest fountain, from the fountain there were twelve smaller paths that led to all of the benches and in the gaps between the paths brightly coloured flowers shone in the sunlight. There were flowers from all over the world, surrounding the garden and behind the benches stood tall oriental grasses. I would go to bed tired and wake up excited at the prospects of another day working outdoors.

I received a phone call from the artist, he said he was delivering the picture on Sunday. Just the thought of the picture arriving sent shivers down my spine. Gail and her mother came to see me about using the house for the wedding. We had tea and cakes on the lawn and made plans for the great day. While we were sitting at the table Gail used the toe of her shoe to rub the side of my foot and after two hours everything was settled. I then took them to see my new garden that was maybe three quarters finished. Gail and her mother offered to help me complete the planting but I was determined to finish it myself and declined their offer. I spent a full day in the garden planting flowers and shrubs.

Later I was sitting in the evening sun when the doorbell rang and when I opened the door I had the shock of my life. Standing there with a smile on her face was June Knight. "Hello stranger" she said " June how wonderful to see you, come in" we hugged and kissed each other's cheeks. When I took her through to the patio at the rear of the house, she breathed in the scent of the flowers and said "How beautiful the garden is" I smiled and fetched her a glass. "Nearly all my own work."

I poured her some wine and we sat in the evening sun taking in the last of the suns heat.

"What brings you here June, not that you are not welcome" I asked her. I felt her eyes on me "It has been a long time Sarah, I wanted so badly to see you, I have brought you the annual report as an excuse." It was my turn to look at her. "Is everything alright at the Manor June?" she smiled "The Manor is wonderful Sarah, we are fully booked for the rest of this year and for most of next year, in fact we could do with opening another hotel." I touched her hand and said. "I hope that you have given yourself a pay rise June?" she blushed "Just a small one!"

I had cooked some pasta and as we ate it, June dropped a few hints that she wanted me sexually, and as it had been a while since my two days with Gail maybe it would do us both good to let off some steam. I gave her the signal she wanted when I began running my fingers through her hair "You always had nice hair June." She turned her back to me and leaned back slightly so that I could have access to all of her hair as I ran my fingers through her hair and she was almost purring with delight. I asked her if she would like a tour of the house she smiled and said" Yes please". I showed her all around but the only thing that she seemed really interested in was my bed. She sat on the edge and said "Mm, nice and soft" we went back downstairs and June collected her overnight bag from her car. She placed it by her side as she sat on the settee so I sat down by her side. She placed her hand on my leg and moved it up and down, when I didn't object she looked at me and moved her hand higher towards my wet fanny, she slid two fingers along my slit through my jogging bottoms.

I pulled her lips to mine and our tongues began a mating dance, I reached to her right breast through her blouse. I tried to open the buttons but I was shaking like a teenager. June opened the buttons for me and pulled her bra down exposing her lovely tits. I fondled her tits and rolled the nipples, I lowered my mouth to her breasts and sucked each nipple deep into my mouth. June said ."Shall we go up?" I smiled and stood up. We walked up stairs and into my bedroom. She closed the door and removed her clothes, I stood and watched her strip naked, she then walked over to me and stripped me completely without touching me sexually. She slid into my bed and held her hand out to me. I took her hand and climbed into bed besides her. We lay looking at each other gently stroking each other. I was the impatient one, I touched her fanny first. At my touch she lifted her leg and bent it placing her left flat foot above her right knee.

I rubbed my flat hand along her hot fanny a few times then crooked the end of my fingers and slowly dragged them along her fanny lips watching her swallow deeply. She closed her eyes when I entered her fanny and pushed my two fingers deep inside and began to frig her. Her hips instantly began to move, she grabbed me around the neck and buried her face into my shoulder, her legs opened wider and held her left leg higher so I could enter deeper. She was groaning into my neck and holding her hips. She sucked her lungs full of air and held her breath. She came so much that her cum was seeping from her fanny. The squelching noise my fingers made in her fanny was loud even under the sheets.

June pushed me onto my back and her hands were all over me. She knelt over my right leg her mouth was sucking my tits and she had three finger inside my fanny frigging me as fast as she could. I had cum once and was heading for climax number two. She took me to my second climax then lowered her mouth to my fanny and took her time giving me as much pleasure as she possibly could until she gave me another orgasm. When she came up for breath she whispered "I love your fanny Sarah, it is the best tasting fanny ever." June sat on her haunches and I lifted my leg over her head to get of the bed.

I opened the wardrobe and took a plastic box out, full of vibrators and strap on cocks and showed it to her "Choose" I said. She chose my personal favourite, the thick black strap on as I stood to put it on I saw the bunny rabbit shining in the light. "Have you tried this ?" I asked, holding it up to her. She shook her head and I smiled " you are in for a treat" I rummaged in the box and found a slim vibrator some six inches long. With some extra sensitive lubricant I rubbed plenty all over that thick black cock then lifted her legs and rubbed some lubricant into and around her bum hole. I pushed the vibrator up her bum and left it there then lubricated the bunny rabbit and slid it all the way into her fanny. I looked into her worried face and asked "Ready?" she nodded somewhat nervously. I switched the one on in her bum hole it made her eyes open wide. With bunny on slow, her hips began jumping then when I switched it to fast June went nuts.

As I began using the bunny on her, she bent from the middle to see what I was doing to her. She was watching me every second and she through climax after climax. June became very vocal and threw her head back and howled. I used the bunny on her for ages. I asked her once if she wanted me to stop, she just shook her head and cried "Please don't stop." There was a build up of her cum on the base of the bunny. She suddenly had had enough and pulled my hand away and pulled the bunny from her fanny. She flopped back onto the bed and lay there panting. She tried three times to remove

the vibrator from her bum hole, in the end she left it
there, buzzing away.

Chapter 37

We took it in turns to pleasure each other until I laid on top of her and we made each other cum with our mouths. Finally we fell asleep in the early hours of the morning. I woke up to the smell of bacon cooking, June came into the bedroom carrying a tray of bacon sandwiches and coffee, we kissed briefly then got stuck into the bacon butties. She asked me how I felt this morning, I answered "Satisfied" and smiled "You?" "Very satisfied thank you." June left later that morning with a smile on her face and a promise to return soon.

I am glad that she has gone to be truthful because today is the day the painting arrives. I was feeling apprehensive and nervous about it though. The artist and another man came and prepared the bare wall ready to receive the painting which I had been assured was a true likeness. I was looking down the drive waiting patiently and thinking about the next few weeks. This week Mr Green is back to do more work, he is to build a large children's play area and also put down a path from the front of the house to the gardens at the back. I have ordered a large marquee and tables and chairs to be used first for the forth coming wedding and then for the cream teas when I open my gardens to the public. The garden society people are to inspect my garden to see if it suitable for the public before the opening. I have hired a retired gardener named Reg to look after the gardens and to expand them it as he sees fit. I also have another delivery due any day now but I will keep that to myself until it arrives.

A large white van was coming down the drive heading straight for me. I thought, "At last my darling, I will see you again and my heart beat a little faster as the men opened the rear of the van. I open the front doors, and stand to the side while they carry the large painting in. It has been arranged that I will stay away while they hang the painting and then leave. I want to be on my own when I first see the painting. The men leave with a large tip, and I walk unsteadily into the room. When I see the painting all of my breath leaves my body and tears run down my face, my darling Amanda is back. The life size painting is spectacular, the likeness is remarkable. I sit and weep for my loss, Amanda was the love of my life and now I will never forget her.

The visit from the garden society went well and the garden can open the weekend after the wedding next weekend. Later today at 4 pm I have the ladies from the women's institute coming for tea. It is a formality really as when I made the offer to the chairwoman that all profits could go to them to do with as they see fit. She jumped at the chance and said that she would go home and draw up a rota. I thought that when the garden is open, the WI can do all of the tea and cakes. I have been told that they are bringing some sample cakes with them for me to try. My phone rang and the sign -writer is at the end of the drive and he is checking that it is ok for him to come in.

He has done this on my instruction as I know that I will burst into tears when I see the sign. I tell him to carry on and erect the sign but that I will need another sign making saying the gardens were open. As the van disappears around the side, I stand where rooted to the spot looking out of the front window. I wait until the white van disappeared down the drive and is gone,.I grab a tissue and walk slowly out of the front door and to the side of the house, I turn the corner and see the sign. At the entrance to the garden a large green sign with white writing on it hangs from two chains. The sign reads " A Garden For Amanda" I drop to my knees and cry my heart out. I stay there until I can cry no more, I need a friend and call Gail and ask her to come over.

Gail sits and holds me as we sit in front of the painting of Amanda, I tell Gail the whole story of our love for each other and all of the things that we did together. I told her about the Manor hotel, I told her everything and she sat there like a true friend and listened. She had seen the sign that led to the garden and now she understood the significance of it. This woman holding me and I think loving me in her own way, begins to cry and now it is my turn to hold her. "Whatever is the matter?" I ask tenderly, she looks at me "Tell me Sarah, am I doing the right thing in getting married?" I try to reassure her by telling her that I will always be here for her, and Brian is a nice steady ma. She nods and kisses me softly on the lips "Thank you Sarah, you're such a lovely person, I think I love you but you already know that don't you?" I nodded "Yes I know, and in my own way I love you too." We held each other tightly, there would be no sex tonight as it would be wrong on both sides.

The day of the wedding arrives, the house and gardens are full of activity, people are laying out flowers and hanging ribbons, the tables in the marquee are being suitably decorated and the bedroom where they will spend their wedding night is being readied by the brides maids. I ready myself for the wedding in a white dress and a large white hat with a red rose on the side. The wedding was perfect. All went well and as the new Mr and Mrs Brian Jelfs stand on the steps to my house Gail looked beautiful in her white flowing dress. As I looked at her beauty she smiled at the camera's, I imagined her shaved fanny hidden in silk underwear. Strangely I felt a pang of jealousy. The guests all moved around the side of the house for more photos using my beautiful garden as a back drop. With all of the speeches and card reading done, the groom thanked me for the use of the house and gardens and now it was my turn to say a few words.

I began "Brian and Gail, I have not known you for very long but I have come to love you both, in recent weeks I have spoken to your families, and between us we have come up with a surprise gift for you. I have cancelled your honeymoon in Hastings and I have organised two weeks, all inclusive in California. I have arranged your Visas and you will fly out tomorrow morning." Everyone in the marquee stood and clapped. Gail came over and hugged me, she accidentally on purpose rubbed her mound against mine as she said with her mouth close to my ear "Thank you Sarah, I love you" with that she kissed my ear. Brian came over and hugged me as well. With the reception now in full swing and the disco man playing songs that I had never heard before. I stole Gail away from the gathering. I took her by the hand and led her into her wedding night bedroom, she closed the door. I turned her around and said. "You look absolutely stunning Gail" She grabbed me and kissed me for a long time when I pulled away from her she seemed disappointed. I bent and picked up a suitcase, "These are for you to take on your honeymoon, but I would like you to return them please" I said as I opened the case to reveal all of the designer dresses that belonged to Amanda.

Gail cuddled me and thanked me all over again. She put her mouth to my ear "I'm terribly wet Sarah, make me cum" I shook my head "This is your wedding day." I said, she smiled and leaned back against the door and turned the key. She lifted her wedding dress to show me her naked fanny through the wet silk thong "Make me cum Sarah please" she said this with a husky voice, I moved to her and did two things at once I pushed my lips to hers and my hand to her fanny. With my tongue down her throat I moved the thong to one side and buried my fingers deep into her wet fanny, she parted her legs and spread her knees and I finger fucked her to a long intense orgasm. She soaked my fingers and groaned. Gail looked me in the eyes and pushed me down to my knees. I licked her fanny for a long time until I exposed her little button and pursed my lips around it and sucked hard it until her legs began to shudder as she came again. Gail was shaking as I stood up, "That is the best wedding present I could have had." I reached down and put her thong back in place. She reached out for my dress but I stopped her, "Please don't it's not a good time." Getting my meaning, she moved over to the mirror and corrected her make up.

With the guests all gone and the wedding reception all done and dusted, the mess could be left until the next day, I lay in bed and think about Gail and whether she has made a mistake in getting married. I know that I could have taken her away from Brian but she has made her choice. No doubt that she will still call around and see me, as she likes the sex so much. I wonder if she is enjoying the sex now? Ah well and I turn over and try to sleep.

I wave at the car taking the bride and groom to a dream honeymoon, strangely I already miss her. To help with the clearing up Gail's mother volunteered. She stops by me" Hi Sarah, thank you for what you have done for our Gail, she is so excited about California, it will be the holiday of a life time."

I engaged an old retired gardener named Reg, he comes and goes as he wants, but give him his due, he knows his gardens. He brings his own dirty mug for tea and offered to scrub it for him, "Don't you dare, I've had that mug twenty five yers, and I ant washed it yet, gives the tea a bit of flavour, it does" he said. As we neared the grand opening for the gardening, I help Reg with the gardening and he takes great delight in telling me what to do. The women from the WI arrive on Saturday and set up their stand for the next days opening. Will people come? Who knows but I'm assured by the society that they have done all that they can, and people will come. I received a post card from Gail saying she is having a great time. She ended the card with, miss you, Gail and a row of kisses

Chapter 38

Well it is Sunday and the grand opening has arrived, I sit and watch two men putting up directional posts and the WI women are all ready, I have Gail's mum on the gate collecting the entrance fee's. it is 10 am and I look down the drive and a row of cars are queued up to pay, one by one the cars park on the grass next to each other, and visitors in small groups, walk towards the house and grounds, I have opened the downstairs of the house so that people can see the painting of Amanda, and see who the garden is dedicated to.

Visitors arrived steadily all day and the women at the Wi had to send for more cakes as they were running low, I did walk around and follow a group of older people, the comments were heart warming and made all of the hard work worth it. I walked proudly back to the house and watched people all over my grounds. It was at that point that I decided that I would develop some of the outer grounds, maybe put a lake in, or have some animals, I will talk to Mr Green and see what he can do, I watched the children on the play area, that all seemed to be good fun.

The day finally ended and everyone involved met in the Marquee and drank tea, and counted the takings, I stood and watched proceedings with interest, in the end I walked over to the Marquee and I received a small round of applause, the head of the WI presented me with a large cake and said that the takings were £729.54 and that was a record for a single days takings.

Chapter 39

I was sad to receive a letter from my Solicitor saying that Amanda's will had finally been settled and I was to receive her total estate. I decided to spend some of her money on an artificial stream around the outside of the grounds, with weeping willow trees, bridges and fish, lots of fish. Maybe I would build a bird aviary and fill it with brightly coloured birds, yes, that is what I would do.

Mr Green arrived on time, we sat in the conservatory and discussed what I wanted done. He said he would draw up the plans and price the job and he would check with the council if l needed planning permission. Later that day two of his men came and began putting up marker posts and ropes for the stream. Mr Green asked me to walk with him, as he would like to show me what he had planned. An hour later I was back in the house sitting with Amanda telling her mentally what I was doing in her name. A strange thing happened at that point, a gust of wind went around the room that even moved the curtains and ruffled my hair. To be honest the hairs went up on the back of my neck and from that day on many strange things happened. Things moved in the night, doors opened, one time all the lights were on when I got up. Call me mad but I knew it was Amanda trying to contact me.

A tanned Gail came to see me with a large bouquet of flowers as a thank you. She had bought me a gold chain with a crucifix, with Amanda stamped onto the cross bar of the cross. She sat with me and told me all about her honeymoon and about Brian and how nice he had been to her. I listened then told her all about my plans for the grounds and how the open days had been such an success.

I went on to tell her about the things that had begun happening around the house. Things being moved and doors opening, lights being turned on. "You need my uncle Bob to come here he is a spiritualist, he talks to the ones that have passed over and he is very good" I thought about it for a while. "But what if is not Amanda , what will I do then?" I asked "If you don't try, you don't know" she answered. So I agreed for uncle Bob to come. Uncle Bob stood well over 6ft tall and he was stick thin. He had a mass of thick grey hair and was slightly bowed legged. His big red nose was hooked, with thick hairs protruding from both nostrils

Bob walked into the house and took a deep breath then walked around the rooms downstairs. He stood at the foot of the stairs and gazed up them for ages then nodded and walked into the living room. He stood and looked at me and said "Gail has told me very little about you or this house but she has told me your name is Sarah and you are a single woman. There is a friendly spirit in this house, it is a female and I am picking up the name Mandy or something similar and she is here to look after you Sarah. She says she loved you more than you could ever know. She also says thank you for the garden and telling me that she tried to find you at the lake but you had gone. She says that she found you by talking to Jude or Julie someone like that. She wants you to be happy Sarah and wants you to find happiness. She's telling me about a drawing; no, it is a picture. She said that she is happy with it and telling me that a great sadness is in this room but the sadness will lead to happiness.

Now, when I talk to the painting of Amanda I feel closer to her somehow. I gave Bob 10 out of 10 because he told me things that there was no way he could have known not even Gail knows about the Lake house.

The work began on the stream and the aviary. I walked out every day to watch the workers creating my dream, Gail came to see me some nights because Brian was out with his mates. We had not even touched since her wedding day, nor had we mentioned what had happened that day.

Visitors still came to the house and were interested in the ongoing works. In the end we had to erect a notice board explaining what was being developed. What happened next changed my life, it was maybe three weeks later that I was lying in bed in the early hours of the morning when I was disturbed by the front doorbell ringing.

I lay there listening just in case I had been dreaming but when the bell rang again, I put on my dressing gown and ran down the stairs. I shouted through the door "Who is it?" a tiny voice answered "It's me Gail please let me in" I unlocked the door and pulled it open Gail ran into my arms and burst out crying, the poor thing was obviously broken hearted, I took her into the living room and sat her down "What ever has happened ?" I asked her "He's gone, he's gone" she sobbed "What do you mean he's gone, has Brian left you? " I asked. "She shook her tear stained face, he's dead, he was joy riding with his mates, they hit a tree, they were all killed, what am I going to do?" I took her up to bed and undressed her, found a nightdress for her and put her into my bed. I got in beside her and held her cold body to me. She gave the occasional sob but eventually calmed down and slept.

We woke in each other's arms and I asked her quietly what had happened. She told me that they stole a car when they were all drunk and whoever was driving lost control. They all died instantly when they hit a tree. "What am I going to do I think I may be pregnant as well," she sobbed. I pulled her tighter against me "I will take care of you my darling, don't worry".

Gail found out that she was indeed pregnant. I attended the funeral with her, it was a lovely service but a very sorry affair. Gail cried and chose that day to tell her parents that she was pregnant and that she wanted to keep the baby. Her mother hugged her tightly and told her that everything would be ok and that they would manage somehow. She looked at her mother and said "Sarah said I can live at the big house with her, she said that she will look after me and the baby. I want to go there mum." Her mother looked at Sarah and asked. "Why would you do this for her, you don't really know her" I held my hands out and said "Because I can".

Gail moved into my house and we got on very well. We decorated the nursery together and learnt to do things together. Cooking, decorating and midwifery just in case. We slept together and made love together. Life was good. The stream was finished and full of water and the bird aviary was now almost finished. I received an official looking letter and when I opened it, I found that it was from the gardening society. Amanda's garden, was up for an award for the best new garden of 2008.

A team of society members would make a surprise visit and judge the garden and the winner would be announced at their annual dinner. Myself and a guest were cordially invited. Mr Green knocked on the door and told me that the fish were arriving today about 10 am. He said "I thought you may like to see them introduced into the stream, also you will have to buy some food for them, I will get all of the details from John the fish man." The way the stream had been done was very clever, the stream circulated the outer perimeter of the grounds with two pumps placed at each side. The pumps keep the water moving which force the fish to swim against the flow which in turn keeps the fish healthy. John the fish man turned up on time. I watched the men put the fish into the stream, there were a mixture of trout and golden orfe. It was very exciting to see the men taking the fish from the tanks with big nets. They showed me every net full of silver or golden fish before they put them into the stream. John the fish man left a sack of pellets to feed the fish with then John had a chat with Mr Green. As I listened to the conversation apparently John had given Mr Green some instructions because the stream has been newly made, there would be no natural food in the water. There were certain thing that could be done to create the food. The answer was to have two piles of horse manure, one at each end and that would create the natural food that the fish needed to survive.

It was nice to walk around the stream in the evenings with a bucket full of fish pellets to see and feed the fish. I had a brainwave and asked Gail's mum if she wanted to earn a few quid. She said "Yes Please." I delivered two bags of pellets and some little tubs with lids to her. I wanted 4 ounces in each tub and the tubs would be sold to the public. Sales of the tubs must be recorded because we needed to know how much food had gone into the stream. It would be nice if the public fed the fish for us and Mr Green and his merry men built four bridges over the stream for the public to feed the fish from. These looked very impressive and natural. A lorry arrived and I watched as the lorry drove slowly around the stream and dropped off benches at different places.

With that done Mr Green and another man went to every bench and moved it to the best position before fixing the bench to the ground. Another man in a small white van arrived and looked at the bird aviary, he went inside carrying a cardboard box. Curious, I walked to the Aviary and watched the man as he hung up swings and then fixed some nest boxes to the wall. He then took some branches into the aviary and fixed them to the wall and took feeders into the aviary and filled them with food. It was all very fascinating, "Excuse me, when will the birds arrive, and what sort are we having?" I asked. He looked me up and down and said "I will bring the birds this afternoon, there will be cockatiels, finches, and love birds. I will bring the food as well." He then told me when and how to feed and water the birds. He then asked me. "I don't know if you are interested misses but I have a dozen young rabbits, and chickens, back at the shop, I can do you a deal on the lot if you want them all?" I said that I would have a word with Mr Green, and let him know. As I walked along I decided that I would plant miniature daffodils all along the main drive and maybe some other plants. I would ask Mr Green, I think he will be pleased.

I caught up with him and told him what the bird man had said. He looked at me and said, "it's alright having all these animals, but someone has to look after them all, it's fine now in the nice weather for you to do it but what about in the winter? They've still got to be cleaned out and fed. I suggest if you have the chickens and rabbits that you find yourself a young lad from the village and ask him to do it for you. A card in the post office should do it." I said to go ahead and build the pens and I would go and write a card out for the post office.

I was sitting at the table writing the card out when Gail came up behind me and put her arms around me and asked what I was doing. "You won't need that my lovely, I will get my brother James to do it for us, he loves animals, and that sort of thing. He can come over on his bike and do it. Shall I give him a ring then?" five minutes later it was all sorted and he would ride over later in the day to see us. There was a knock on the door, I opened it and a delivery man with a sheet of paper said. "I've got your shed, where do you want it putting?" I knew nothing about a shed so I directed him to Mr Green.

I walked over to the aviary and a shed had been erected at the rear of the aviary. I asked Mr Green about it "You will need somewhere to store all of the food for all the animals and fish." I nodded in agreement and left him to it. The birds arrived and looked happy in their new home. In the grass there were some tiny cute looking birds running around." What are those?" I asked.

"Miniature Guinea fowl, folk love 'em" he said. I
stood back and looked at the aviary and I was very
pleased with the results. Within a week, the
chickens and rabbits were all in large pens and the
animal area looked very good. The public loved it.
James came every day and fed everything and said
he would have done it for nothing but the money
was great because he was saving up for a new
mountain bike. Gail and I had a walk around early
one Sunday morning in the early morning dew. She
had a fair old baby bump on her now so we didn't
walk too fast.

When we arrived at the animals Gail loved it,
we separated and I went to the birds which were
favourites of mine and she went to the animals. She
called me over to one of the pens and I looked
down to see a large herd of Guinea pigs which I
didn't know we had. A beat up old truck came to a
stop by us and an obvious farmer got out of the
truck and said "Morning misses, I heard you was
putting some things in fer the little uns, so I come to
offer ya some free babby goats and lambs if yer
wants um. The little ums love 'em ya know" I said

ok without really thinking about it and agreed they would be delivered the next Sunday morning.

Another phone call to Mr Green. I told him what I wanted now, and he joked that it would be cheaper for me to employ him and his men full time. I promised him that this would be the last project. He laughed and said "We will see". True to his word the farmer turned up as he said he would. He got out of his truck and inspected the pen. Mr Green had even built the animals sleeping quarters that were full of straw. Happy with what he saw the farmer reversed his trailer up to the gate and let the baby lambs and goats loose into the pen. Gail and I walked up to the farmer and stood with him watching the animals as they settled down.

I offered to pay him but he would have none of it. "It's for the little uns. If ya wants, you could let me and the misses hav a look round, one artnun." I said that they were welcome and they could even come to the house for tea and cake if they wante. He smiled " ah, the misses would like that, hee hee, real posh like, oil let ya know misses, thank thee" he said as he left. Gail and I laughed as we walked back to the house, "Did you understand all that ?" I asked her. "That be ow thee locale talks thee noess" she replied and burst out laughing "That is how the old locals speak, that farmer Jones I bet that he has not taken his wife out in twenty years. So this will be a real treat for her, we will have to make it special for her. We could get that woman from the WI to do the sandwiches and cakes and we could hire a butler for the afternoon, that would be great fun. I will look on the internet and sort it out" I stopped on the steps of the house and looked around. I put my arm around her and said."Doesn't it look wonderful Gail?" with that the first of the days visitors arrived and Gail and I disappeared upstairs.

Gail was huge now that she had reached her full term. We had the bags packed and ready and the car full of petrol and parked by the front door. All through her pregnancy Gail had had some weird cravings, the worst being pickled onions and pickled eggs. The eggs gave her terribly smelly wind and now she craved Jaffa cakes. She had had a few twinges and was walking around a lot, rubbing her back. As she was leaning over the back of the settee and I was rubbing her back, she turned to me and said. "I think you had better take me now." I put everything into the car and when I went back into the living room, she was standing in a pool of water. "My waters have broken" I cleaned her up and helped her to the car. When we arrived at the hospital, Gail was doing her breathing exercises and moaning. The next few hours were a blur. Finally I now held a baby girl in my arms, she was perfect and beautiful. Gail lay on the bed exhausted, but happy. She said "I wish Brian were here to see her."

She phoned her parents who said they would be right over and then phoned Brian's parents who also said that they would come straight away. I said I would go back to the house and leave her to her family but would come back later.

I leaned over and kissed her "Well done you."

I said, she stared me in the eyes and asked "I want to call her Amanda Sarah, is that ok?" I smiled and tears ran freely down my face "Thank you darling" and left her and baby Amanda to get some rest before her family arrived.

Chapter 40

As I arrived at the gates, a woman I had never
seen before said "Are you the misses of the house?"
I said. "Yes and who are you?" she replied "I'm
Gail's aunty, I've taken over for the afternoon
while they go and see the baby but the inspectors
are here, a mini bus full of them. I let 'em in for
nothing is that alright?" I nodded and said thank
you for everything then caught up with the
inspectors as they walked around the stream. Some
were feeding the fish and smiling as they walked so
I introduced myself and asked if they had any
questions.

The man in charge said that they would find
me later "In the Wi tent?" I smiled. "He nodded
"That would be perfect." I watched them from the
steps of the house, the judges stood on one of the
bridges and fed the fish and some of the others were
pointing down into the water in excitement. They
stroked the lambs and goats and stood for an age at
the aviary. The judges finally headed towards the

WI marquee. They all stopped and looked at my house then stood talking in a little circle. When they arrived at the marquee they sat down to an afternoon tea put on by the WI. It was perfect and all the judges were excited by the delicacies in front of them. As they were about to mount their mini bus each judge shook my hand and smiled. The man in charge took me to one side and said. "You will be coming to the presentation dinner won't you?" I said that I would do my best to attend and he held my arm above the elbow and whispered "I'm not allowed to say anything, but if I were you I would write a thank you speech." He then tapped the side of his nose and smiled. I waved as they left and each one of the judges waved back happily.

Gail and Amanda have arrived home, her parents have followed the car and are excited. I spend the day making tea and coffee and dishing out WI bought cake. It was like this for three weeks, after that the novelty wore off a little bit and we were left to it, with the occasional visit from the parents. They were happy to baby sit whenever we wanted them to so we had been able to go out for meals a few times. Tonight it was the presentation night, a black tie event giving us a chance to show off our designer dresses. The evening was boring, the food was ok, but the speeches, well I could have slept through them all. Gail had to nudge me when it came to the award for the best new garden. We held hands under the table as the judge told every one of the two hundred guests there about the most remarkable new garden he has ever seen.

[He dropped me a big hint,] when he said. "I can't wait until the spring next year when all of the Daffodils and Tulips come up along the stream, it will look truly remarkable." He named me as the winner of the best new garden. I was presented with the trophy and made my thank you speech. The judge said that it was a truly a remarkable garden and he hoped that he had given me a way to improve the garden for the spring. He said he couldn't wait to return.

Gail sat me down one evening around Christmas time and said "My uncle bob was right wasn't he, Amanda is watching over us. I know that Amanda is looking over us I have seen her moving things in a nice way, and when I was feeding the baby Amanda this morning I sensed her watching over me. So I spoke to her quietly and told her that I loved you and I would take care of you" I hugged her to me and said "Thank you darling". I spent the next few days planting bulbs, hundreds of them. I also planted a lot of bushes to attract butterflies around the boundary fences. The bushes were Buddliea The Butterfly Bush and had long purple blue blooms that the butterflies loved. Visitor numbers increased due to the Garden for Amanda wining the prize and late in November we introduced a walkey talkey system.

I had found it very useful only this morning, Gail's mum's voice from the front gate, came over the air waves "There is a Mr Jones and his wife here for a visit and he said that he was a guest and he didn't have to pay, it that right?" I had to think at first who Mr Jones was, then it all came back to me. I answered that he was indeed a guest and if they would like to come to the house for afternoon tea they would be most welcome?" A message came back they would like that, so I contacted the WI marquee and ordered afternoon tea and asked if one of them could wait table for a very special guest.

Afternoon tea with the Jones was an experience that I will remember for a long time. The WI lady did a good job. TheJones put on their airs and graces and Mr Jones kept looking from me to Gail. He asked a question that suprised me when he said " I thought you two was lezzies, so how come you got a babby?" His wife slapped him across the head! I looked at Gail and answered "Yes we are lovers, Gail was married for a short while and she became pregnant by her husband who unfortunately has died" The Joneses both nodded in unison.

Then he spoke again "we never had kids, it just never happened for us, [he chuckled to himself] we tried hard enough" his wife slapped him playfully, and chuckled herself, "Did you know that we be your neighbours?" I shook my head "No I didn't know that, which side are you?" I asked. "All down that left side as you comes in." he replied. He told us all about his farm then stood up and said."We've have had a lovely afternoon misses, thank you kindly," We got up and said that we had enjoyed it as well, although old Mrs Jones hardly spoke at all. We thanked her for coming and said that they were welcome anytime. We said our goodbyes and the old couple spent the afternoon walking slowly around the garden and then the grounds.

Christmas came and went, I had Mr Green busy again building new tea rooms to keep the WI ladies warm. These was taking shape nicely and little Amanda was gaining weight and chuckling away. Gail and I were back to fucking each other senseless after the long break because of baby Amanda. The bulbs had all come up and the results were beautiful, everywhere we looked spring had arrived. I received a letter from June asking if she could come up and I had to tell her I was now living with someone. She was very disappointed and asked if I would like to visit her at some point, saying "I can be very discreet." Again I decided to decline the offer. Life was perfect, the Manor was doing very well thank you and the money was rolling in. The properties in Brighton were still making me money. I tried to think of other projects to do but could not think of any but was sure I would. We had a strange episode in the middle of the night on June30th we were woken when the curtains began flapping and billowing out. Gail ran to the baby's nursery to find baby Amanda was having trouble breathing. We called the hospital and told them we were on our way. Gail sat and cried as the doctors examined Amanda, I held her tightly as we looked on. Amanda cried out when the nurse took some blood from her tiny foot. It turned out that she had an infection and she was put on antibiotics. She was fine again in a few days. When we returned home we knew that Amanda's spirit was waiting for us as it was her that had alerted us to baby Amanda's plight.

I received a letter from a Mr Lennis who was acting on behalf of the late Mr Jones and I had been invited to the reading of his last will and testament.

The letter gave me the date and time of the reading. I told Gail about the letter, and she said "Maybe he has left you some more animals." We made our way to the reading and Mr Lennis said "I will skip all the legal bumf and get down to the gist of the will. Mrs Jones died in a nursing home, just after Christmas and Mr Jones passed away shortly after, of a broken heart, in the will he says to thank you, for your kindness to him and his wife. They came to me the day after the tea and changed their will, it seems that they have left everything to you, the farm and everything on it, plus £734.007 which is in his bank account. He also left you this letter." Mr Lennis stood up and left the room while we read the letter. iI read-

Dear Sarah

I hope I have not burdened you by leaving you all we own. We were so happy to see what you have done for the children at your home and by leaving our farm and funds, we hoped that you would continue your work by coming our way. There has always been planning for lakes on our

We couldn't believe it, what were we going to do with all that land? Gail and I had the plans for the farm so we decided to have a walk over and have a look. When we walked through the gate that led to the farm we made our way towards a barn and there was a white car parked outside it. As we got closer and we were walking along the side of a small wall we could see into the barn. A tall blonde man with long hair was standing naked and on her knees in front of him was a very young naked dark haired girl. Her head was moving back and forth as her mouth went up and down his long thick cock. He moved his hands from his hips and began fucking her mouth, his huge cock seemed to be going a long way down her throat. The girl gagged and pulled her mouth from his cock. He pulled her up and turned her round then bent her over some bales of hay. He moved up behind her and pushed his cock all the way into her fanny, the girl cried out as he roughly entered her body. He gripped her hips and began fucking her. He was a selfish lover, he was almost raping her, maybe it was how she wanted him to fuck her but I doubt it very much. He came inside her, making her scream as he pushed against her.

He pulled her back, she genuinely wasn't happy. I almost went over there. He pulled out of her and left her crying in the position he had put her in. The man sat on a bail and lit a cigarette. She didn't moved for a long time and he finished his smoke and got dressed. When she did not move he shouted " c\mon you fucking slag, get your clothes on, I want to get back to the pub." The girl walked towards him and he pushed her away, towards her clothes. We could see that she was young by her body development. She sobbed as she dressed but all he did was shout at her. "Hurry up or I will leave you here." She began crying again as she pulled her jeans on. He pushed her over and walked towards the car, got in and drove away leaving her sitting there crying.

As we walked over to the girl she tried to stand but couldn't make it. I told Gail to stay with her while I fetched the car. I ran as far as I could and then walked as fast as I could until I got the stitch. I finally got to the car and drove around to the young girl. Gail was sat holding her talking quietly to her. This is Ann" she said as we got her into the car and took her to our house. We took her to a spare bedroom and put her to bed. I asked if she was on the pill and she shook her head, I asked her how old she was. 13, was all she said, "Who was that man?" I asked her "My mum's boyfriend, you won't tell her will you?" she cried. "Has he done this to you before?" she nodded and I said. "Right leave that bastard to me, first I will get you the morning after pill, then I will make a phone call." I came back from the town with the pills and some sanitary towels and made sure that she took the pill.

Then I phoned Helen Oakes in Brighton and told her what we had witnessed and asked her what we needed to do about it. She told us to sit tight and she would get back to us as soon as she could.

Chapter 41

The doorbell rang about an hour later, I opened the door and two women were standing there "Are you Sarah?" one asked, I nodded, she then said "Police, can we come in please?" I stood to the side and let them pass, the taller woman spoke,." I am inspector Annis and this is sergeant Emelia Exon we will be handling this case. can you tell us what you saw please?" Amanda and I told then exactly what we had seen, and Gail showed her the recording that she had made with her phone. They interviewed us separately.

The doorbell rang again and as I went to stand up I was told to stay where I was. One of the police women answered the door. It was a police doctor and a woman from forensics. "Where is this Ann now?" the inspector asked me, I took them to the room but asked if I could speak to her first?" The inspector nodded and whispered "Leave the door open" I crept into the room and sat by Ann, she was fast asleep. I touched her shoulder and she jumped.

"It's ok Ann, it's me Sarah, are you ok?" she
nodded. I told her "I phoned my friend and she has
sent someone to help you, they are outside. Can I
bring them in?" She nodded but looked terrified.
The two police women walked into the room, and
the inspector sat on the bed. She asked Ann to tell
her everything that had happened from the
beginning. Ann told a terrifyingly sad story and to
me there was no doubt she was telling the truth. She
let the forensic woman take her swabs and she took
the sanitary towel Ann had been wearing.
Everything went into plastic bags and were sealed
up. I was asked if Ann could stay at my house
while the investigation was underway.

A few days later a fat woman came to the
door banging on it with her fist, I opened the door
and looked down at her. "Yes?" I asked, she tried to
push past me but I stood my ground. "You got that
lying slag of a daughter of mine here, the fucking
little cow. I will ring her lying fucking neck" she
growled. I calmly said "Yes Ann is here and here
she will stay, there is no way that she will come
back to you, a woman who doesn't even believe her

own daughter "She is lying, Ted wouldn't touch her she is only a kid" she said.

I said to her "What if I told you we have your precious boyfriend with his big cock up your daughter, and ever thing he said and did has been recorded. Just like now every word you have said has been recorded." "You mean she is telling the truth." She asked and I said. "Yes every word is the truth, now fuck off." and slammed the door in her face. Ann sat quietly and watched the TV. I tried to talk to her but she would rather talk to Gail and help with the baby, so I left it at that. The inspector came around a few times, it seemed to me she thought that we were all lying.

On the way out I stopped her "Can I have a word please inspector?" I picked up a bucket of fish pellets and walked to the stream with her. We sat on a bench and fed the fish "You do believe us don't you inspector?" I asked, she lowered her head "I have dealt with these young girls before, things go too far and they cry rape." "And you think that is what has happened here?" when she shrugged, I said " Right then I want you to leave here at once, I will use every penny of my millions to punish this man, I will have every top lawyer in London up here, and I will make sure that you are off the force within a week, now you can fuck off as well!" She went to speak, but I turned from her, took my phone from my pocket and phoned Helen.

The next afternoon a chauffer driven car came up the drive. We watched as the chauffer got out of the car and opened the door for a man dressed in a smart uniform. I opened the door before he could knock, " ah" [he said] are you Sarah Briany?" I nodded "May I come in please Sarah, my name is Bromley, Chief of police Bromley?" I stood to the side and indicated that he should go into the living room Bromley entered the room to find Gail and the baby sitting there "Ah, I thought that we could talk on our own ?" he said, I shook my head "I want a witness to what you have to say" He sat down and looked from one of us to the other. "Now about this Ted Harris fellow, he has been arrested this morning, for sex with a minor, and rape. Inspector

Annis has asked me to apologise for her behaviour towards you, she now realises that she was wrong and in future she will listen more carefully when she is being given information. I can only apologise for her actions" He said all this with his nose in the air. I said "And you are happy with that are you? As you may know I have some powerful friends in high, very high places and I want that bloody woman punished for calling me, Ann and Gail liars.

Not only were we witnesses, but we had video and verbal evidence as well. We have recorded what you have said and will consult a well known newspaper man to ask him his advice on how to proceed with all the evidence that we have." The Chief put his hands up. "There will be no need for all that now Sarah. Let me think about it, I will contact you before end of business today, will that do?" Bromley stood up ready to leave then looked at me and said "I would hate to get on the wrong side of you Sarah" and left. Gail smiled at me "You bossy cow" we both laughed out loud. I did hear from him later and the bloody woman has been demoted back to constable and sent for retraining.

Chapter 42

The next afternoon there was a quiet knock on the door, I opened the door to find young James, Gails brother who looked after the animals and fed the fish. I asked him to come in and he sat down next to his sister and played with Amanda. I asked. "How can I help you James, is there something wrong?" He looked nervous "Me mam said that now that I have left school, I have to get a proper job and give her my keep.

So I have to leave. I'm really sorry," he said. I smiled and said "Did you like your work here James" he nodded his head "Yes, I loved it, I made friends with the sheep and goats and the birds eat out of my hand" he said excitedly. "How would you like a full time job here, at say £250 a week? I would like you to go to college I day a week to learn about gardening. Then you'll be able to help Reg and when he retires you can take over looking after the whole place. We could even get you a lad to work under you, how does that sound?"

"Really," he said," I can keep my job, £ 250 a week all for me?" He clapped his hands which woke up Amanda. We watched him ride his bike down the drive and by the way he rode we could tell that he was very excited.

Mr Green the builder came at his appointed time, under his arm he had a lot of papers regarding next doors farm. He spread his papers out on the dining table and began "I have looked at what you suggested and have done some rough drawings, after a lot of thought I decided on an Aerial view knowing that that would be best. We had the drillers on site and found the water, so we can build a lake no problem. There are three options: 1, a boating lake. 2, a fishing lake. 3, a nature reserve.

The house is basically sound and could be converted to whatever you like and the woods would make a perfect adventure playground. We could put ropes throughout the trees, and there's room for a caravan park or a site for static caravans. If you want the place for children then I suggest a boating lake with the adventure playground. You could then introduce archery, and an assault coarse, the choice is yours, either way you will have to employ people." After he had said all this and sat down. I asked him to leave the plans and told him I would get back to him in a few days. Gail and I studied the plans with Ann and asked her opinion on every point. I didn't need to make any more money, so we decided on a boating come fishing lake, a rope experience adventure wood, and an assault course.

We would build long wooden acommodation with showers, bunks and cooking facilities. there could be lots of other activities added as we thought of them. It would be called Teddy's Farm. The house would be converted to offices with sweet shops, fishing tackle shops and tuition available to run the business from. Teddy's would be mainly for groups of school children. We would leave it up to Mr Green to see to the planning permission and meanwhile I would find someone suitable to run the place. Who had passed the relevant police checks.

I woke up in the middle of the night not feeling too good, I had a stabbing pain in the base of my stomach. When I pushed onto the pain it seemed to disappear, so I tried to ignore it. The next day became very interesting when social services arrived about Ann, there were lots of questions and accusations.

They left saying that they would return. Baby Amanda took her first step on the same day and that seemed to take our mind off things a little. I had found an ex soldier that was interested in running Teddy's. He thought that he could recruit a couple of other ex soldiers and told me that he would sound them out and let me know. As the day went on my pain came and went, again I ignored it. Gail asked me what was wrong? "Oh nothing, must be my period" I said but I knew that it wasn't, I would give it a few more days, before I went to the doctors. Then things became very busy, what with Teddy's, the social services and poor old Reg not feeling too good. On top of all that, Gail caught

Ann with our box of vibrators. She was sitting on the floor, surrounded by strap-ons and vibrators. It took Gail an hour to explain things to her, and according to Gail it put her off touching them ever again.

Mr Green began complaining that he was spending too much time in the planning office, trying to sort out Teddy's. He had a date for starting the lake and had taken advice from the appropriate people. Work would begin in under a week, or as soon as the machinery was on site. The lake had been marked out and readied, Baby Amanda was fascinated by all of the diggers and lorries as we stood and watched proceedings as work began. A yellow car pulled up by the field and four army chaps got out, the chap that I had met before John Thompson, had brought his mates to have a look at the layout and see if they could come up with new ideas. I asked them to call at the house for a beer afterwards. I had forgotten about the pain, it was more of a dull ache now. The army descended on us and drank all of the beer that I had. They had come up with some interesting ideas and were going away to write them up.

I asked John if I found him a secretary could
he run the whole venture. I said that he could
convert the top of the farm house as his home and
office and with that he seemed very keen. I
informed him that I would want not expect to make
any money back from my investment for three
years. My investment would come after the monies
Teddy had left had been used up. Gail showed me
the web page for Teddy's Place and I must say it
was very impressive considering it wasn't fully
completed yet. Gail asked me if I was ok as I
looked very pale and she said that I was walking a
bit strange, I laughed it off, but knew that I would
have to go to the doctors soon.

A strange thing happened that I can't explain,
as dusk was setting in on June the twenty first. I
was sitting in my rocking chair with a glass of wine
looking at my flower garden. The evening breeze
swept like waves across the flowers bringing a
mixture of scents towards me. I stood and began

walking towards the flower garden. I followed the path until I reached the farthest point from the house and sat on a bench looking down at the house. I swear someone sat beside me. I looked to the side and it was if someone blew into my face. I knew that it was Amanda trying to contact me.

I opened my hand and could have sworn that she gently placed her hand into mine. I sat there until dark and a voice came into my head and said "Come to me, my darling" I waited there until the stars began to shine then walked back to the house and found Gail leaning against the door frame. "Who was that you were sat with?" I replied that I was on my own, Gail smiled and said. "It looked like someone from here." I didn't sleep much that night and took it as a sign. I made an appointment at my solicitors for that day.

Chapter 43

As I undressed for bed that night I looked at my naked body in the full length mirror. I was shocked at what I saw I looked gaunt. I knew that I had not been eating properly but even so I looked too thin and drawn. I had been putting off going to the doctors but decided I should go. I called him made an appointment to see him. I caught a train down to London then a cab to Harley street. My Doctor Tina Symms examined me and took some blood for testing. She then sent me for x\rays, and I was to wait for the results. Tina called me back into her office and told me that she had to consult a colleague. As I sat and waited two men went into the office and stayed for over an hour. At last I was called back in and Tina told me that I had to go to theatre that day and the theatre was being prepared as we speak.

When I opened my eyes Gail was sitting holding my hand, she rubbed the back of my hand with her thumb and a single tear ran down her cheek. She said "Welcome back you." I only managed a weak smile. The surgeon came to see me, examined my wound and looked at my charts. He left the room without a word. Tina came into the room and she looked grave as she took my hand. "it's bad news Sarah, maybe if you had come to me sooner, we could have done something, but." and she lowered her head "How long have I got?" I asked, she shook her head "Weeks" she said quietly, Gail burst into tears and put her head to my hand. I reached for the hand of Tina and said "I want to go home as soon as possible." Within a week I was discharged and sitting in my rocking chair looking at my garden. Gail asked. "What's going to happen to me, Sarah, what about Amanda?" I took her hand "You will stay here, this all yours now, yours and Amanda's and everything that goes with it. You are now a very wealthy woman" I reassured her, "But I can't do what you do Sarah I wouldn't know where to begin " I smiled at her " Then I will get you some help".

I called June Knight and asked her to come as soon as possible, she arrived later that day and when she saw me she burst into tears. She sat down and I told her about my illness and prognosis. I took her hand and said "I have taken care of you June, I have left you the Manor but in return I want you to do something for me. I want you to look after Gail and Amanda There are a lot of things going on at our farm next door and I want you to finish what I have started. There is more than enough money put aside to finish the job and the solicitors will be here later so we can go through everything together." I seemed to have fallen asleep, for when I woke up June, Gail, Ann and the solicitors were sitting around the table talking quietly. I joined them and it took nearly three hours to get things down roughly on paper.

I looked out of the doors to the gardens and saw Amanda with her hand held out towards me. I know that I said "Soon my darling." and everyone sat looking at me. I smiled around the table and lowered my head. When it came to the time for bed I asked to be left looking out at the gardens. Gail had switched all of the outside lights on so that I could see properly. I saw Amanda sitting on a bench waiting for me. Gail came down in the middle of the night and sat with me holding my hand. As she stroked it she spoke quietly "Oh, Sarah, I know that I could never take the place of Amanda but I loved you enough for both of us, and I know that she is waiting for you. I can see her on the bench watching us now.

Promise me that you won't be too far away from us. Go now my darling, go to the one you love and be happy for always. Don't fight it anymore, go to her, look, she is coming for you." I could now clearly see my darling Amanda, I reached out and took her hand and she led me, hand in hand down the garden through the flowers, to eternal peace and happiness.

Epilogue

Baby Amanda is now 5 years old and is a pretty little thing. At Amanda's garden there have been a few changes, Teddies farm is a total success and we have spent many hours watching the children playing in the tree tops and on the boating lake. As for the house they have employed three young men from Pershore college of Agriculture to help Reg who had stopped coming to us. Gail had gone to his house to see him and to find out what was wrong. "My old legs won't turn the peddles no more, I miss your garden and young Amanda" Gail offered to send a car for him but he wouldn't have any of it. Gail thought about it and had one of those electric bikes delivered to Reg.

Bright and early the next morning Reg came up the drive on his new electric bike with a smile on his face and as he rode past the house towards the three gardeners, he held his legs out from the peddles and shouted "Wheeeeeeeeee." He never said thank you but Gail received a "Good morning misses" and that was a first, in all of the years Reg had been working here, that was the first time he has wished anyone good morning. Gail took his greeting as a thank you. Jenny Pyeman, who was June Knight's under manager, was now living at the Willis house and running everything very efficiently.

She was happy with her lot. While she was sitting with Gail in the rocking chairs on a late summer evening, looking out over the garden that was full of brightly coloured flowers. Behind the benches tall grasses swayed in the gentle late summer breeze and the scents that swirled around the garden attacked their senses. Jenny said. "You know Gail, I miss the nudity and the sex at the Manor, take now, I feel as randy as fuck, and I am so wet." five minutes later Jenny began a relationship with Gail that was to last a lifetime. At the age of 29 Jenny had donor insemination and became pregnant. She gave birth to a baby boy and named him Thomas Shaun Pyeman.

Little Amanda would walk to the furthest bench and sit there for hours, no- one could be seen but it was obvious that she was deep in conversation. It had to be Sarah and Amanda but when asked about it, all she said was "Just my friends." We at the house did on occasion feel the presence of the two deceased women but it was little Amanda who connected with them the most. The most evident time Sarah showed herself was when we were making plans for the three new gardeners and a small garden centre. Gail suggested caravans on the same site that the gardeners could live in. Every time the word caravan was mentioned the plans lifted up on the side of the site where the gardeners were to be. Sarah calmed down when Jenny changed it to Canadian log cabins.

Jenny and Gail and the two children lived happily at the Willis house, the money that they made from different ventures all went back into the local community. A private school was opened by Gail called Amanda's School not a mile away from Amanda's garden. Little Amanda and Thomas received a brilliant education at the school, and as they grew older, they learned how to look after Willis house in the future.